SHORT BREAD

◀ ◀ ▶ ▶

The dwarf examined his cigarette, then crushed it out in a soapstone ashtray. "So now you would like to make money?"

"It would be a change."

"When a war ends," the dwarf said slowly, "there are a number of ways for the enterprising to make money. The most obvious, of course, is to deal in scarce goods — the black market. Another is to provide certain services for the rich who have managed to remain rich even though they themselves were, in effect, casualties of the war. This I propose to do. Does it interest you?"

"I don't know what you're talking about."

"No, I really didn't expect you to."

"But it's a way to make money?"

"Yes."

"Is it legal?"

"Almost."

"Then I'm interested," Jackson said.

THE EIGHTH DWARF

ALSO BY ROSS THOMAS

Out on the Rim
Chinaman's Chance
The Fools in Town Are on Our Side
The Singapore Wink
Cast a Yellow Shadow

Published by
THE MYSTERIOUS PRESS

THE
EIGHTH DWARF

ROSS THOMAS

THE MYSTERIOUS PRESS

New York • London • Tokyo

MYSTERIOUS PRESS EDITION

This Mysterious Press Edition is published by arrangement with
Simon & Schuster, 1230 Avenue of the Americas, New York, N.Y. 10020

Mysterious Press books are published in association with
Warner Books, Inc.
666 Fifth Avenue
New York, N.Y. 10103

A Warner Communications Company

Printed in the United States of America

First Mysterious Press Printing: December, 1988

10 9 8 7 6 5 4 3 2

FOR
JANE JENNINGS WEGENER

THE EIGHTH DWARF

1 During the war Minor Jackson had served with the Office of Strategic Services, in Europe mostly, although some four months before the fighting there was done they had flown him out to Burma. He hadn't liked Burma much, or its jungles, or what he'd had to do in them, but now that the war was quite finished, as was the OSS, Jackson had almost decided to go back to Europe, because he suspected that one way or another he might be able to make some money there. Perhaps a lot of it.

Whether Jackson went back to Europe in that early autumn of 1946 would depend in large measure on what the dwarf had managed to arrange. Jackson was waiting for him now in the Green Gables cocktail lounge on La

Cienega, just down from Santa Monica Boulevard; and as usual, the dwarf was late.

Jackson, at thirty-two—in fact, almost thirty-three—had taught himself how to wait during the war, which, he had been mildly surprised to learn, was almost 90 percent waiting. And even though the dwarf was nearly forty-five minutes late, Jackson sat patiently without fidgeting, not quite slouched down into the deep chair at the low table. He had sipped his beer slowly to make it last, and it still was not quite half gone. For entertainment there had been the bitter argument at the next table to listen to.

The argument had been going on in furious whispers for nearly as long as Jackson had been waiting. It was between a young couple, and at first it had been about money—or rather, the lack of it—and the woman's careless handling of what little there was. But now she had launched a vicious, devastatingly intimate counterattack, choosing as her weapon the man's sexual inadequacy.

Because Jackson was a normally curious person, actually a bit more so than most, he shifted slightly in his chair—a casual move that he hoped would afford a quick, undetected glance at the victim.

The young man sat with his head bowed, his lips bitten, listening to his damnation, which must have been made more awful by the caressing whisper that delivered it. He was also quite pale, although when the woman's attack first began he might have blushed pink or even scarlet. He looks like a blusher, Jackson thought.

The woman seemed to be about the same age as the man, and although far less than beautiful, she was more than pretty. However, Jackson had not expected her to be quite so observant. She detected his scrutiny almost immediately and broke off her whispered denunciation to glare at him and demand, "What're you looking at, Pop?"

Jackson shrugged. "I just wanted to see where he was bleeding."

If it hadn't been for the "Pop," he might have smiled or grinned when he said it. Jackson's hair was gray—in fact, almost white—and although he had thought about it often enough, a kind of reverse pride or vanity had prevented him from dyeing it. Sometimes when asked, usually by women, he would claim that it had turned that way overnight during the war while he was on some romantically mysterious mission for the OSS. Actually, it had started turning gray when he was twenty-three.

After Jackson's crack, the young man rose abruptly. In doing so he accidentally knocked over his beer, which flooded the table and even slopped over onto his club sandwich. Some color had crept back into the young man's cheeks. His lips started working as he stood there. They trembled a little at first, but finally he got it out.

"You're a real bad rotten bitch, aren't you, Diane."

Since it certainly was no question, the young man didn't wait for an answer. Instead, he turned and hurried around the tables to the three carpeted steps that led down to the cocktail lounge's foyer.

The woman stared after him for a moment or two, her own lips working as though she were still silently rehearsing some undelivered lines. Then she looked down at the table with its two uneaten sandwiches and the spilt beer. She seemed to study the mess carefully, as though she might want to paint it someday from memory. Finally, she looked up at Jackson. He saw that her rage had gone, perhaps drained away into some secret hiding place for possible reuse. She also wore a new expression, one of slightly puzzled dishonesty.

"Who's going to pay for all this shit?" she said.

Jackson shook his head. "One wonders."

She stood up quickly and almost darted around the tables to the three steps.

"Hey, Johnny!" she called. "Wait up!"

But Johnny was long gone. She started down the three steps, in a hurry, looking for Johnny and not at all at where she was going. On the last step she knocked over Nicolae Ploscaru, the dwarf.

The dwarf didn't have far to go, but still he went down

11

hard and landed on his butt. The woman glanced down at him; said, "Aw, shit," by way of apology; and hurried out the door after the vanished Johnny.

Nobody offered to help the dwarf up. He didn't seem to expect it. He rose slowly, with considerable dignity, and thoughtfully brushed off his hands. After that he shook his big head in mild disgust and again started up the three steps, climbing them one at a time because of his short, slightly bowed legs.

Ploscaru made his way through the tables to where Jackson sat. "I'm late," the dwarf said, and hoisted himself up and back into one of the deep chairs with a combined hop and wriggle that seemed practiced.

"I'm used to it," Jackson said.

"I don't drive," the dwarf said, as though revealing some long-hidden secret. "If you don't drive in this town, you should depend on being late. When I was in New York I took the subway and was almost never late. I wonder why they don't have subways here."

The dwarf had a noticeable Romanian accent, probably because he had learned his English fairly late in life, long after the French that he spoke with virtually no foreign accent at all and his almost equally flawless German. During the early part of the war, in 1940 and '41, Ploscaru had worked for British intelligence in Bucharest—or rather, for two English spies who were posing as correspondents for a couple of London dailies. One of the spies, Ploscaru had once told Jackson, had been rather competent, but the other one, constantly aflutter about a play of his that was being produced in London at the time, had turned out to be pretty much of a bust.

When the Germans finally moved into Romania in the spring of 1942, the dwarf had fled to Turkey. From there he had managed to get to Greece and somehow from Greece to Cairo, where he sometimes claimed to have spent the rest of the war. Although Ploscaru would never admit it, Jackson suspected that the dwarf had somehow had himself smuggled into the United States, possibly by the Army Air Corps. At any rate, the dwarf always spoke warmly of the Air Corps, in spite of what it had done to Ploesti.

"You want a drink?" Jackson said.

"Did you see her knock me down? She didn't even stop."

"She didn't pay for her lunch, either."

The dwarf nodded glumly, as if he had expected something like that. The big head that he nodded was almost handsome except for a trifle too much chin. "A martini," he finally replied to Jackson's aging question. "I think I'll have a martini."

"Still the barbarian."

"Yes," the dwarf said. "Quite."

Jackson signaled for a waiter, who came over and stood hands on hips, a bleak look on his face, as he surveyed the lunch that the young couple had neither eaten nor paid for. The waiter was young and gossipy and a bit effeminate. He gave Jackson a knowing look.

"Well, I could certainly tell when they came in, couldn't you?" he said.

"No," Jackson said, "I couldn't."

"Well, I certainly could. Didn't you notice how close together her eyes were? That's the sure sign of a deadbeat—well, almost, anyway. You want another beer?"

"And a martini for my friend here."

"Extra dry?" the waiter said to Ploscaru.

"Extra dry," the dwarf said.

After the drinks were served, Jackson waited while Ploscaru took the first swallow of his martini, shuddered, and lit one of the Old Gold cigarettes he favored.

"Well?" Jackson said.

Before replying, Ploscaru took another swallow of his drink, a larger one. This time there was no shudder. Instead, he sighed and, not quite looking at Jackson, said, "The call came through at eleven this morning. A little after eleven."

"From where?"

"Tijuana."

"They both came up?"

"The daughter did. The old man stayed in Ensenada. He doesn't speak English, you know. The daughter does, after a fashion. They would like a meeting."

"Did you talk about money?"

The dwarf looked at Jackson then. He had green eyes which seemed clever, or perhaps it was just their glitter.

"We talked about money," Ploscaru said, "and she seemed to think that our price was too high; but then, she's a Jew." The dwarf shrugged, expressing his mild contempt for any Jew who would be foolish enough to believe that she could out-haggle a full-blooded son of Romania.

"So we negotiated," Ploscaru continued. "In English, of course, although German would have been preferable, but the war hasn't been over quite that long. It's very difficult to negotiate over the phone, especially with someone who's speaking an unfamiliar language and speaking it badly. One misses the—uh—nuances."

"So what did you come up with?" Jackson said.

"A thousand for you; five hundred for me."

"That's slicing it a bit thin, isn't it?"

Ploscaru pursed his lips in disagreement. "My dear chap, to strike any bargain that requires two separate payments, you should *appear* to resist with your last breath all attempts to reduce the initial payment. But then, when your arguments are exhausted, you should give in grudgingly and then hurry on to the second payment. This one you can inflate, if you are clever and persistent, because your fellow negotiator knows that if you fail in your task, he will never have to pay." The dwarf took another swallow of his martini, licked his lips, and said, "I really should have been a diplomat."

"How much?" Jackson said. "The second payment?"

"Ten thousand for you and five for me. To be paid in Switzerland."

"If we find him."

"Yes. Of course."

Jackson thought it over. It was more than he had expected, almost two thousand dollars more. The dwarf had done well, far better than Jackson himself could have done. He decided to pay the dwarf a small compliment—a tiny one, really, because anything larger would have gone to Ploscaru's head and made him insufferable for the rest of the afternoon.

"Not bad," Jackson said.

"Quite brilliant actually." Whenever the dwarf paid himself a compliment his British overtones deepened, possibly because the two spies he had worked for in Bucharest had seldom given him a decent word and he now liked his praise, even that which came from his own lips, to be wrapped in a British accent.

"I'll still have to sell my car, though," Jackson said.

"What a pity," Ploscaru said, not bothering to disguise his sarcasm.

"The meeting," Jackson said. "When do they want it?"

"The day after tomorrow at their hotel in Ensenada. They've insisted on a couple of code phrases for identification—really dreadfully silly stuff; but I'll give you all that tomorrow."

"What do you want to do this afternoon?"

"Let's drive down to the beach and drink beer and look at women."

"All right," Jackson said.

2 They had shipped Captain Minor Jackson back to the States aboard a hospital ship in mid-1945 because of an acute case of infectious hepatitis he had caught in the jungles of Burma where he, along with a couple of enlisted hard cases and a dozen or so even tougher Kachin tribesmen, had harassed the Japanese behind their own lines. Jackson's small unit had been part of a freewheeling OSS outfit called Detachment 101. The reason it was called Detachment 101 was that the OSS felt the name would make it sound as if there might be a few other similar detachments around, although, of course, there weren't.

Jackson had spent the day and night of the Japanese surrender aboard the hospital ship in Seattle harbor watching the fireworks and listening to the sounds of the celebration. The next day in the hospital at Fort Lewis the Red Cross had told him that he could make a free long-distance call home.

This posed a small problem, because Jackson's parents had been divorced for nearly twenty years and he wasn't at all sure where either of them might be. However, he was quite positive that his mother wouldn't be in Palm Beach—not in August, anyway.

He finally had placed a call to his father's law firm in New York, only to be told by a secretary, who might have been new in her job, that Mr. Jackson was in an important conference and was taking absolutely no calls.

Later, Jackson wrote his father a postcard. Two weeks went by before a letter arrived from his father congratulating Jackson on having survived the war (which seemed to have surprised his father, although not unpleasantly) and urging him to get out of the Army and settle down to something "productive and sensible." Sensible had been underlined. A few days later he received a telegram from his mother in Newport, Rhode Island, welcoming him home and hoping that they could get together sometime soon because she had "oodles" to tell him. Jackson translated oodles into meaning a new husband (her fourth) and didn't bother to answer.

Instead, when the Army asked where his hometown was so that he could be transferred to a hospital nearby to recuperate from his jaundice, Jackson had lied and said San Francisco. When he arrived at the Army's Letterman General there, Jackson weighed one hundred twelve pounds, which the doctors felt was a bit light for his six-foot-two frame. It took them more than six months to fatten him up and get his icterus index back down to normal, but when they did, Jackson was discharged on February 19, 1946, from both the Army and the hospital as well as from the OSS—which, anyway, had gone out of business on September 20, 1945.

Jackson's accumulated back pay, separation allowances, and not inconsiderable poker winnings amounted to nearly $4,000. He promptly spent $1,750 of it to purchase an overpriced but snappy 1941 yellow Plymouth convertible. He also managed to find and buy six white shirts (still scarce in early 1946), a rather good tweed jacket, some slacks, and a gray worsted suit.

Thus mounted and attired, Jackson had lingered on in San Francisco for nearly six months, largely because of the charms of a redheaded Army nurse. But then the nurse, convinced that Jackson was no marriage prospect, had accepted a posting to an Army hospital in Rome. So Jackson, his plans still purposely vague, had driven south in early September, heading for Los Angeles, the first stop on his roundabout return to Europe.

Three principal reasons took Jackson to Los Angeles. The first was that he had never been there. The second was a woman who lived in Pacific Palisades and who had once gone to bed with him in Washington years before and who might again, provided she remembered him. The third reason was that during the war Jackson had made friends with a more or less famous actor who had also served in the OSS. For a while Jackson and the actor, who also was something of a sailor, had run guns and supplies across the Adriatic from Bari in Italy to Tito's partisans in Yugoslavia. The actor had made Jackson swear to look him up should Jackson ever be in Los Angeles or, more precisely, in Beverly Hills.

As it turned out, the woman Jackson had known in Washington had just got married and didn't think it would be too smart if they started seeing each other again—at least, not yet. "Give me a couple of months," she had said.

The actor, however, had seemed delighted when Jackson called. He even urged Jackson to stay with him, but when Jackson politely demurred, the actor gave him some halfway-useful advice about where to find a room or apartment in the midst of the housing shortage that still gripped Los Angeles. He then insisted that Jackson come to a cocktail party that same evening. It was at the actor's party, by the pool, that Jackson met the dwarf.

A quartet of drunks—two writers, a director, and an agent—had just thrown the dwarf into the pool and were making bets about how long it would take him to drown. The writers were giving odds that it would take at least fifteen minutes. The dwarf had never learned to swim, and it was only the violent splashing of his immensely powerful arms that kept him afloat. Jackson might not have interfered had not the two writers tried to sweeten the odds by stamping on the dwarf's hands whenever he managed to gasp and splash his way to the edge of the pool.

Jackson went up to one of the writers and tapped him on the shoulder. "I think you ought to let him out," Jackson said.

The writer turned. "Who're you?"

"Nobody."

"Go away, nobody," the writer said; he placed a large, curiously hairless hand against Jackson's chest, and shoved him backward.

The writer was a big man, almost huge, and it was a hard shove. Jackson stumbled back for a step or two. Then he sighed, shifted his drink to his right hand, went in fast, and slammed a left fist into the writer's stomach. The writer doubled over, gagging, and Jackson, amazed at his own temerity but enjoying it, gave the writer a slight push which toppled him over into the pool.

The other three drunks skirted nervously around Jackson and hurried to their friend's aid, although before fishing him out, the director and the agent tried to get bets down on how long it would take the writer to drown.

Jackson knelt by the edge of the pool, grasped the dwarf's thick wrist, and hauled him up onto the cement. Ploscaru sat wet and gasping, his stubby, bowed legs stuck out in front of him, his big head down on his chest as he leaned back on his powerful arms and hands. Finally, he looked up at Jackson, who, for the first time, saw the almost hot glitter in the dwarf's green eyes.

"Who're you?" Ploscaru said.

"As I told the man, nobody."

"You have a name."

"Jackson. Minor Jackson."

"Thank you, Minor Jackson," the dwarf said gravely. "I am in your debt."

"Not really."

"What do you do?"

"Nothing."

"You are rich, then?"

"No."

"But you would like to be?"

"Maybe."

"You were in the war, of course."

"Yes."

"What did you do—in the war?"

"I was sort of a spy."

Still staring up at Jackson, the dwarf nodded slowly several times. "I can make you rich."

"Sure."

"You don't believe me."

"I didn't say that."

The dwarf rose and thoughtfully dusted off his still-damp palms. It was a gesture that he often used whenever he was trying to decide about something. It was also a gesture that Jackson would come to know well.

"Drowning is thirsty business," Ploscaru said. "Let's go get some drink and talk about making you rich."

"Why not?" Jackson said.

They didn't have their drink at the actor's. Instead, they left without saying goodbye to their host, got into Jackson's Plymouth, and drove to the dwarf's place.

On the way, Jackson learned for a fact that the dwarf's name was Nicolae Ploscaru. He also learned, although these facts were totally uncheckable, that Ploscaru was the youngest son of a minor Romanian nobleman (possibly a count); that there were vast but, of course, long-lost estates in both Bessarabia and Transylvania; that until the war, Bucharest had boasted the most beautiful women in Europe, most of whom the dwarf had slept with; and finally, that before escaping to Turkey, the dwarf, when not spying for the British, had slain four, or possibly five, SS officers with his own hands.

"I strangled them with these," the dwarf said holding up the twin instruments of death for possible inspection. "The last one, a colonel—rather a nice chap, actually—I finished off in a Turkish bath not too far from the Palace Athénée. You know the Palace Athénée, of course."

"No."

"It's a hotel; quite a fine one. When you get to Bucharest, you should make it a point to stay there."

"Okay," Jackson said, "I will."

"And be sure to mention my name."

"Yes," said Jackson, not quite smiling, "I'll do that too."

The dwarf's place was a house with a view high up in the Hollywood hills. It was built of redwood and glass and stone, and it obviously didn't belong to the dwarf. For one thing, the furnishings were too feminine, and for another, nearly everything that could take it had a large, elaborate intertwined double W either engraved or woven or branded into its surface.

Jackson stood in the living room and looked around. "Nice place," he said. "Who's WW?"

"Winona Wilson," the dwarf said, trying very hard to keep his w's from sounding like v's and almost succeeding. "She's a friend of mine."

"And what does Winona do?"

"Mostly, she tries to get money from her rich mother up in Santa Barbara."

"I wish her luck."

21

"I want to get some dry clothes on," the dwarf said. "Can you make a martini?"

"Sure."

Ploscaru gestured toward a long barlike affair that separated the living room from the kitchen. "It's all over there," he said, turned, and was gone.

By the time the dwarf came back, the drinks were mixed and Jackson was sitting on one of the high stools at the bar looking down across the slightly sunken living room and through the glass to the faraway lights of Hollywood and Los Angeles which were just beginning to come on in the early-September evening.

Ploscaru was wearing a long (long on him, anyway) green silk dressing gown that obviously had been tailored. Peeping out from underneath the skirt of the dressing gown were a pair of red Turkish slippers whose toes turned up and back and ended in small silver bells that jingled not unpleasantly when he moved.

Jackson handed the dwarf his drink and said, "What do you do, friend—I mean, really?"

Ploscaru smiled, revealing large white teeth that seemed almost square. He then took the first swallow of his martini, shuddered as he nearly always did, and lit one of his Old Golds. "I live off women," he said.

"Sounds pleasant."

The dwarf shrugged. "Not altogether. But some women find me attractive—despite everything." He made a curiously sad gesture that was almost an apology for his three-foot-seven-inch height. It was to be one of only two times that Jackson would ever hear the dwarf make any reference to it.

Ploscaru glanced about for some place to sit and decided on the long cream-colored couch with its many bright pillows, all with WW woven into them. He settled back into it like a child, with much wriggling. Then he began his questions.

He wanted to know how long Jackson had been in Los

Angeles. Two days. Where had he been before that? In San Francisco. When had he got out of the service? In February. What had he done since then? Very little. Where had he gone to school? The University of Virginia. What had he studied? Liberal Arts. Was that a subject? Not really. What had Jackson done before the war?

For a time Jackson was silent. "I'm trying to remember," he said finally. "I got out of school in '36. Then I went to Europe for a year, bumming around. After that I was with an advertising agency in New York, but that only lasted six months. Then I went to work for a yacht dealer on commission, but I didn't sell any, so that didn't last either. After that I wrote a very bad play, which nobody would produce, and then—well, then there was one winter that I skied, and a summer that I sailed, and a fall that I played polo. And finally, in '40, I went into the Army. I was twenty-six."

"Have you ever been poor?" Ploscaru said.

"I've been broke."

"There's a difference."

"Yes," Jackson said. "There is."

"Your family is wealthy." It wasn't a question.

"My old man is still trying to get that way, which is probably why he married my mother, who always was rich and probably always will be as long as she keeps marrying rich husbands. The rich tend to do that, don't they?—marry each other."

"To preserve the species," Ploscaru said with a shrug as though the answer were as obvious as preordination. He then frowned, which made his thick black hair move down toward his eyes. "Most Americans don't, but do you speak any languages?"

"French and German and enough Italian to get by."

"Where did you learn your languages?"

"At a school in Switzerland. When I was thirteen my parents got divorced and I turned rotten. They packed me off to this school for three years, which was really more like a boys' prison. Rich boys, of course. You either learned or else."

Ploscaru examined his cigarette and then crushed it out in a soapstone ashtray. "So now you would like to make money?"

"It would be a change."

"When a war ends," the dwarf said slowly, "there are a number of ways for the enterprising to make money. The most obvious, of course, is to deal in scarce goods—the black market. Another is to provide certain services for the rich who managed to remain rich even though they themselves were, in effect, casualties of the war. This I propose to do. Does it interest you?"

"I don't know what you're talking about."

"No, I really didn't expect you to."

"But it's a way to make money?"

"Yes."

"Is it legal?"

"Almost."

"Then I'm interested," Jackson said.

3 There was a gas war going on in Long Beach, and Jackson pulled the Plymouth into a station with a big sign out front that boasted of gasoline for 21.9 cents a gallon. Catty-corner across the street, the man at the Texaco station, a grim look on his face, was taking down his own sign and putting up a new one that would match his competitor's price.

The top was lowered on the convertible, and music was coming from its radio. The music was Jimmy Dorsey's version of "Green Eyes," and the dwarf sang along while the attendant filled up the tank. The dwarf liked to sing.

That was one of the several things Jackson had learned about Ploscaru since their meeting at the actor's pool three weeks before. A week after that, Jackson had accepted the dwarf's invitation to move in and share the house in the Hollywood hills that belonged to Winona Wilson—who, it seemed, would be staying on in Santa Barbara indefinitely as she struggled to get money out of her rich mother.

It was during those same three weeks that Ploscaru had carried on his often mysterious negotiations with the people in Mexico—negotiations that Jackson would be concluding later that day in Ensenada. And it was also during those same three weeks that Jackson had discovered that the dwarf knew an incredible number of people—incredible, at least, in Jackson's estimation. Most of them, it turned out, were women who ran the dwarf's errands, chauffeured him around, and took him—and Jackson—to parties. At the parties Ploscaru would often sing and play the piano, if there was one. Sometimes the songs would be sad Romanian ones, and if the dwarf had had enough to drink, he would sing with tears streaming down his face. Then the women would cuddle and try to console him, and while all that was going on the dwarf would sometimes wink at Jackson.

But more often than not, the dwarf would sing popular American songs. He seemed to know the words to all of them, and he sang in a true, deep baritone. His piano playing, while enthusiastic, wasn't really very good.

Jackson came to realize that most men resented the dwarf. They resented his singing, his size, his charm—and most of all, they resented his success with women, which small knots of them would often discuss in prurient whispers at the endless succession of parties. Ploscaru seemed to enjoy the resentment; but then, the dwarf, Jackson had learned, doted on almost any kind of attention.

With the tank now full, Jackson followed the coast highway south toward San Diego. It was still early morning, and the dwarf sang most of the way to Laguna Beach, where they stopped at a hotel for coffee.

After the waitress had poured him a refill, Ploscaru

said, "Are you sure you remember the code phrases?"

"I'm sure."

"What are they?"

"Well, for one thing, they're silly."

"In spite of that, what are they?"

"I'm supposed to call her on the house phone and tell her my name and then, like a fool, I say, '*Wenn der Schwan singt lu, lu, lu, lu.*' Jesus."

"And what does she reply?"

"Well, if she can stop giggling, she's supposed to come back with, '*Mach' ich meine Augen zu, Augen zu, Augen zu.*' "

The dwarf had smiled.

After the coffee they continued down the coast, stopped for lunch at La Jolla, and then drove on into San Diego, where Jackson dropped Ploscaru off at the zoo.

"Why don't you go to a picture instead of hanging around here all afternoon?"

The dwarf shook his head. "There'll be children here. Children and animals and I get along famously, you know."

"I didn't, but I do now. I'm going to try to get back here before midnight. Maybe when you get through with the kids and the animals you can locate us some bourbon. Not gin. Bourbon. I can't take any more gin."

"Very well," the dwarf said, "bourbon."

A half hour later, Jackson was across the border checkpoint, through Tijuana, and driving south along the narrow, much-patched coastal road into Baja California. There was a lot of scenery and not much else to look at between Tijuana and Ensenada. Occasionally there would be a cluster of fishing shacks, a substantial house or two, and the odd tourist court, but mostly it was blue sea, steep bluffs, fine beaches, and on the left, dry, mulberry-colored mountains.

Jackson made the sixty-five-mile trip in a little less than two hours and pulled up at the entrance of the sprawling, mission-inspired Hotel Riviera del Pacífico, which had been built facing the bay back in the twenties by a gambling syndicate that Jack Dempsey had fronted for.

It was a little after five when Jackson entered the spacious lobby, found the house phones, picked one up, and asked the operator for Suite 232. The call was answered by a woman with a low voice who said only "Hello," but even from that Jackson could detect the pronounced German accent.

"This is Minor Jackson."

The woman said nothing. Jackson sighed and recited the prearranged phrase in German about the swan singing lu, lu, lu, lu. Very seriously the woman replied in German that it made her eyes close. Then in English she said, "Please come up, Mr. Jackson."

Jackson went up the stairs to the second floor, found 232, and knocked. The woman who opened the door was younger than the dwarf had led him to expect. Ploscaru had said that she was a spinster, and to Jackson that meant a maiden lady in her late thirties or forties. But Ploscaru's English, sifted as it was through several languages, occasionally lost some of its exactness.

She was, however, certainly no spinster. Jackson guessed her to be somewhere between twenty-five and twenty-nine, and on the whole, he found her almost beautiful, but if not quite that, at least striking. Her face was oval in shape and light olive in complexion. She wore no makeup, not even a touch of lipstick on her full-lipped mouth, which was smiling slightly now.

"Please come in, Mr. Jackson," she said. "You are just in time for tea."

It sounded like a phrase that had been learned early from someone with a British accent and hoarded carefully for later use. Jackson nodded, returned her small smile, and followed her into the suite's sitting room, where a tea service rested on a table.

"Please sit down," she said. "My father will join us presently."

"Thank you, Miss Oppenheimer," Jackson said, and picked out a comfortable-looking beige chair near the window. The Oppenheimer woman decided on a straight chair near the tea service. She sat down slowly, keeping her ankles and knees together, and was not at all concerned about what to do with her hands. She folded them into her lap, after first smoothing her dress down over her knees, and smiled again at Jackson as though waiting for him to say something observant about the weather.

Jackson said nothing. Before the silence became strained, the woman said, "You had a pleasant journey?"

"Very pleasant. Very . . . scenic."

"And Mr. Ploscaru, he is well?"

"Very well."

"We have never met, you know."

"You and Mr. Ploscaru?"

"Yes."

"I didn't know that."

"We have only talked on the telephone. And corresponded, of course. How old a man is he?"

"Thirty-seven, thirty-eight, somewhere around there."

"So young?"

"Yes."

"On the telephone he sounds so much more older. No, that is not right. I mean—"

"Mature?" Jackson supplied.

She nodded gratefully. "He could not come himself, of course."

"No."

"The trouble with his papers."

"Yes."

"They are very important these days, proper papers. Passports. Visas."

"Yes."

"He is a large man, Mr. Ploscaru? From his voice he somehow sounds quite large."

"No, not too large."

She again nodded gratefully at the information. "Well, I am sure you will be able to handle everything most satisfactorily."

"Thank you."

Jackson had never prided himself on his small talk. He was wondering how long it would continue, and whether he might risk lighting a cigarette, when the blind man came in. He came in almost briskly from the bedroom, carrying a long white cane that he didn't really seem to need. He moved into the center of the room and stopped, facing the window.

"Let's see, you are near the tea, Leah," the blind man said in German.

"Yes, and Mr. Jackson is in the beige chair," she said.

The blind man nodded, turned slightly in Jackson's direction, took two confident steps forward, and held out his hand. Jackson, already up, accepted the handshake as the blind man said in German, "Welcome to Ensenada, Herr Jackson; I understand you speak German."

"I try."

The blind man turned and paused as if deciding which chair to select. He moved confidently toward a wing-backed leather one; gave it a cursory, almost careless tap with his cane; and settling into it, said, "Well, we'll speak English. Leah and I need the practice. You've already met my daughter, of course."

"Yes."

"We had quite a nice chat about Mr. Ploscaru," she said.

The blind man nodded. "Damned clever chap, that Romanian. Haven't met him, of course, but we've talked on the telephone. Known him long, Mr. Jackson?"

"No, not terribly long."

The blind man nodded again and turned his head slightly so that he seemed almost to be looking at his daughter, but not quite: he was a trifle off, although no more than a few degrees. "Think we might have the tea now, Leah?"

"Of course," Leah Oppenheimer said, and shifted around in her chair toward the tea service, which Jackson, for some reason, assumed was sterling.

Afternoon tea was apparently a studied and much-enjoyed ritual in the Oppenheimer household. It was certainly elaborate enough. There were four kinds of delicate, crustless sandwiches, two kinds of cake, and a variety of cookies.

While the daughter performed the tea ritual, Jackson scrutinized the father, Franz Oppenheimer, the man who the dwarf had said spoke no English. Either Ploscaru had lied or Oppenheimer had deceived the dwarf. Jackson bet on the dwarf. For if Ploscaru was not a congenital liar, he was certainly a practicing one who regarded lying as an art form, although perhaps only a minor one.

Franz Oppenheimer was at least sixty, Jackson decided, as the daughter served tea, first to her guest and then to her father. He was also a well-preserved sixty—stocky, but not fat, carrying perhaps ten or twelve too many pounds on a sturdy five-ten-or-eleven frame. Jackson concluded that it might be a good idea if the Oppenheimers were to cut out their afternoon tea.

Over his sightless eyes the blind man wore a pair of round steel-rimmed glasses with opaque, purplish-black lenses. He had gone bald, at least on top, and his scalp formed a wide, shiny pink path through the twin hedgerows of the thick, white, carefully trimmed hair that still sprouted on both sides of his head.

Even with the dark glasses, it was a smart man's face, Jackson thought. To begin with, there was all that high forehead. Then there were a pair of bushy almost white eyebrows that arced up above the glasses which rested on the good-sized nose. The nose thrust out and then down toward a wide mouth with thin, dubious lips. The chin was heavy, well-shaved, and determined, perhaps even stubborn.

Oppenheimer ate two of the small sandwiches quickly, sipped some tea, and then patted his lips with a white

31

linen napkin. There had been no fumbling in his movements, only a slight, almost undetectable hesitancy when he replaced his cup on the small table beside his chair.

With his head turned almost, but not quite, toward Jackson, Oppenheimer said, "We are, of course, Jews, Mr. Jackson, Leah and I. But we are also still Germans—in spite of everything. We intend to return to Germany eventually. It is a matter of deep conviction and pride. Foolish pride, I'm sure that most would say."

He paused as if waiting for Jackson to comment.

In search of something neutral, Jackson said, "Where did you live in Germany?"

"In Frankfurt. Do you know it?"

"I was there for a short time once. In '37."

The blind man nodded slowly. "That's when we left, my family and I—in '37. We put off leaving until almost too late, didn't we?" He turned his head in his daughter's direction.

"Almost," she said. "Not quite, but almost."

"We went to Switzerland first—Leah, my son, and I. My son was twenty-three then. He's thirty-two now. About your age, if I'm correct."

"Yes," Jackson said, "you are."

Oppenheimer smiled slightly. "I thought so. I've become quite good at matching voices up with ages. I'm seldom off more than a year or two. Well, the Swiss welcomed us. In fact, they were most cordial. Correct, of course, but cordial—although that cordiality depended largely on the tidy sum that I'd had the foresight to transfer in a roundabout way from Frankfurt to Vienna to Zurich. The Swiss, like everyone else, are really not too fond of Jews, although they usually have the good sense not to let it interfere with business."

Oppenheimer paused, looked in his daughter's general direction, smiled, switched to German, and said, "Leah, dear, I think it's time for my cigar."

"Yes, of course," she said, rose, and crossed the room

to where a box of cigars rested on a table. She took one out—long, fat, and almost black; clipped off one end with a pair of nail scissors; put it in her mouth; and carefully lit it.

"Would you care for one, Mr. Jackson?" Oppenheimer said as his daughter handed him the cigar.

"No, thanks, I'll stick to my cigarettes."

"Damned nuisance, really. One of the few things I haven't been able to learn how to do for myself properly —light a cigar. Hard on Leah, too. Keeps her from wearing lipstick."

"I don't mind," she said, resuming her seat by the tea table.

"I always like a woman who powders and paints. What about you, Mr. Jackson?"

"Sure," Jackson said, and lit a cigarette.

Oppenheimer puffed on his cigar for several moments and then said, "Miss the smoke, too—the sight of it. Ah, well. Where was I? In Switzerland. We stayed there until 1940. Until Paris fell. Then we went to England—London. At least, Leah and I went. Some people call me an inventor, but I'm not really. I'm more of a—a *Kesselflicker*."

"Tinker," Jackson said.

"That's right, tinker. I take other people's inventions and improve on them. Patch them up. I had an idea for a cheap way for the British to interfere with enemy radar. Well, they almost clapped me in jail. I wasn't even supposed to know about radar. But eventually they used my idea anyway. Long strips of foil. Someone else got the credit, though. I didn't mind, I had other ideas. A long-lasting electric-torch battery. I gave them that. Then an idea for a metal-less zipper. They didn't seem to think that zippers had anything to do with the war effort. I should've tried that one on the Americans. That's where I made my money originally, you know: in zippers. Damned near the zipper king of Germany. Didn't invent it, more's the pity, but I improved on it. But no matter. Then, toward the end of the war, I developed cataracts, and that's why I'm here."

"Why Mexico?" Jackson said.

"There's an eye surgeon in Mexico City who's supposed to be the best in the world. I don't know whether he really is or not, but he's a German Jew like me, and I feel comfortable with him. He's going to operate next month, and that's why I wanted to get this business about finding my son settled."

"What makes you think he's still alive?" Jackson said.

The blind man shrugged. "Because nobody's come up with any proof that he's dead. If he's not dead, then he's alive."

"He stayed on in Switzerland when you went to England."

"Yes."

"And then went back into Germany."

"Yes."

"He went underground?"

"Yes."

"Was he a member of any particular group?"

"I don't know. My son is a Communist. Or thought he was, anyway. He almost went to Spain in '36, but I persuaded him not to, although I couldn't persuade him to go to Britain with us."

"When was the last time you heard from him?"

"Directly?"

"Yes."

"There were a few letters in 1940. Two in '41 and then nothing. And then, about a year ago, we heard that somebody had heard that he had been seen in Berlin just before the end of the war. It was no more than that: just hearsay, rumor. But we started writing letters—to the Americans and the British." He made a small gesture with his cigar. "Nothing. Finally, we heard about Ploscaru from someone who'd known someone in Cairo who'd used him for something similar to this during the war. We

34

made inquiries and found that Ploscaru was in Los Angeles. So we came here from Mexico City and started negotiations—which brings us up to date. Ploscaru tells us that you were an American spy during the war."

"Something like that," Jackson said.

"With the Office of Secret Services."

"Strategic Services."

"Oh, is that what they called it?"

"Yes."

"Well, what do you think, Mr. Jackson: do you think you can find my son?"

Jackson lit another cigarette, his second, before answering. "Maybe. If he's alive and if he wants to be found and if he hasn't gone East."

"Yes, that's a distinct possibility, I suppose."

"No," Leah said. "It's not. He wouldn't go East."

Jackson looked at her. "Why?"

"Kurt didn't trust the Russians," she said. "He despised them."

"I thought you said he was a Communist."

"A most peculiar type of Communist, my son," Oppenheimer said, and added dryly, "but then, my son is most peculiar in many matters. Some of his peculiarities we've written down in a kind of dossier that we've put together for you. There are some pictures—a bit old by now, I should think. Kurt must have changed considerably."

Oppenheimer nodded at his daughter, who crossed to the table where the cigar box lay, opened a drawer, and brought out a thick envelope, which she handed to Jackson.

"Does he have it yet?" Oppenheimer asked.

"Yes."

"Your fee is in there too, Mr. Jackson: fifteen hundred dollars. Correct?"

"Yes."

"I must apologize for those rather silly code phrases that I insisted upon, but we've learned that there are a number of confidence tricksters about down here—Americans mostly. Wouldn't want the money to fall into the wrong hands, would we?"

"No."

"Probably made you feel a bit silly, though, all that lu, lu, lu-ing."

"A bit."

Jackson by now had discovered that the blind man spoke two kinds of English. One was an almost breezy form of chatter which had only a light accent. Oppenheimer employed it, perhaps unconsciously, when engaging in his rather heavy-handed persiflage, which was something like a salesman's banter. But when the blind man wanted to make a point or find out something, the accent grew heavier as he hammered out his nouns and verbs into a more formal structure.

His accent was quite heavy when he asked Jackson, "When do you think you might arrive in Germany?"

"In about a month," Jackson said. "I'll be going to Washington first. There're some people there who might be helpful. After that, if I can't get a seat on a plane, I'll take the first boat I can get out of New York."

"My daughter will be leaving for Frankfurt immediately after my operation, which will be two weeks from now. That means that she'll arrive in Germany at about the same time that you do. The address where she'll be staying is in the envelope we gave you. I suggest that you get in touch with her. I'm sure that she can be most helpful."

Jackson stared at the remote, solemn-faced woman who sat motionless in the straight-backed chair with her eyes lowered.

"Yes," he said, trying to keep the surprise out of his voice, "I'm sure that she can be."

4 It had grown dark by the time that Jackson tipped the Mexican attendant a quarter for bringing the Plymouth around. He got in behind the wheel and fooled with the radio, trying to find something besides the strident, slightly off-key mariachi band that the attendant had tuned in. Jackson had just about settled for a San Diego station when the man came out of the shadows, got quickly into the car, slammed the door shut, and said, "Let's take a little spin."

The man's accent came from somewhere in England; probably London, Jackson thought. As he turned to look at him, Jackson let his left hand slide from his lap down between the seat and the door to where the tire iron was. After he found it, he said, "Where to?"

"Anywhere," the man said, and motioned a little with

something that poked at the cloth of his jacket's right pocket.

"You know what I've got in my left hand?" Jackson said.

"What?"

"Got me a tire iron. So if that isn't a gun in your pocket, you'd better watch your kneecap."

The man smiled and took his hand from his pocket. It was empty. "No gun," he said. "Let's take a spin and talk about that rotten little dwarf."

"All right," Jackson said. He released the tire iron, making sure that it clattered against something, and started the engine. He drove to the end of the drive and turned right into the street. When he came to the first street lamp, he pulled over and parked under it.

"The spin ends here," Jackson said. "Now tell me about him, the rotten little dwarf."

The man looked up at the street lamp and then at Jackson. He was about Jackson's age, perhaps four or even five years older. He wore a jacket that was a salt-and-pepper tweed, wrinkled flannel trousers, a white shirt, and a dark tie. He had a thin face that just escaped being gaunt. His brown hair could have used a trim, but the mustache that he wore under his sharp nose seemed well cared for. There was too much bone to his chin.

"We found him in Cairo," the man said.

"Ploscaru."

The man nodded and smiled again. "Old Nick."

"During the war."

"That's right. We signed him on."

"Who signed him on?"

"My old firm."

"And who are you?"

"Baker-Bates. Gilbert Baker-Bates."

"Hyphenated."

"That's right," Baker-Bates said, and slipped his left hand into his jacket pocket. It came out with a package

38

of cigarettes. Lucky Strikes. He offered them to Jackson, who refused with a shake of his head. Baker-Bates lit one for himself with a wartime Zippo lighter that was olive drab in color.

"It must be a burden, that hyphen," Jackson said.

"I don't notice it much anymore."

"What was the old firm in Cairo—SOE?"

"Not bloody likely."

"The other one?"

Baker-Bates nodded and blew some smoke out.

"What'd you want with the dwarf?"

Baker-Bates waited until a car went by. The car was a 1938 Ford standard coupé with a blown muffler. Two men were in it, Mexicans. Baker-Bates stared at them as they drew abreast of the Plymouth, slowed, and then sped off.

"He did some odd jobs for us once in Bucharest. When I found him in Cairo he was starving, living off some Gyppo bint that he'd lined up. Well, we took him on again; gave him a bath; ran him through the odd course in Alex —cipher stuff mostly; and then dropped him and a fist man back into Romania with twenty bloody thousand in gold."

"Dollars?"

"Pounds, lad, pounds. Gold sovereigns, although, thank God, they were yours and not ours."

"Mine?"

"OSS. We put it together; they paid for it. Your chaps wanted two things: first of all, information on how good a job of work your bombs had done on the Ploesti refineries, and secondly, how the Romanians were keeping your pilots that they'd shot down. We'd take anything else that the dwarf could skim off and send back. Plus any mischief he could create. That's what the gold was for."

"You dropped him in by parachute, huh?"

"Right."

"That must have been a sight."

Baker-Bates shrugged indifferently.

"So he went in with about a hundred thousand dollars in gold."

Baker-Bates blew out some smoke. "About that."

"I'd say you made one damn-fool mistake."

"Well, as they say, if ever you need a real thief, you should cut him down from the gallows or hire a Romanian. We hired two."

"The fist man was also Romanian?"

"Right."

"And you never heard from them again."

"Oh, we heard from them, all right," Baker-Bates said. "Once. A five-word message: 'Ploscaru dead. Police closing in.'"

Jackson leaned back in the leather seat, looked up at the street lamp, and chuckled. The chuckle went on until it turned into a laugh.

"What's so funny?"

"I think Nick's already spent your money."

"That doesn't worry us. We wrote the rotten little bastard off long ago. He's ancient history. Besides, it wasn't really our money, was it?" As if to answer his own question, Baker-Bates flipped his cigarette out into the darkness. "You two, you and the dwarf, you don't interest us much. You're spear carriers. It's the chum at stage center that we're really interested in."

Jackson stared at the thin Englishman for several moments. "Kurt Oppenheimer," he said finally.

"That's the lad. Kurt Oppenheimer, the zipper king's son."

Jackson nodded. "And you're going to tell me about him."

Baker-Bates seemed to think about it. He glanced at his watch and said, "Your treat?"

"Sure," Jackson said. "My treat."

The bar that they found was only a few blocks from the hotel. It was a small, hole-in-the-wall kind of place, a bit dank, a bit smelly, and its few customers were sad Mexicans who seemed to have even sadder problems which they discussed in low tones. Both Jackson and Baker-Bates ordered beers and drank them out of the bottle.

"The first thing I should tell you is this," Baker-Bates said after a long swallow. "We don't want Oppenheimer in Palestine."

"Why?"

"He had a bad war, very bad, but it developed his talents."

"What kind of talents?"

"Remember Canaris?"

"The Abwehr admiral."

Baker-Bates nodded. "They say that Canaris had him once in late '43, but let him go. They say that he fascinated Canaris, that they had long talks."

"About what?"

"The morality of political assassination. Canaris was a jellyfish, you know. They'd have done for Hitler early on if Canaris had ever been able to make up his mind. But Canaris had him and that's a fact, although some still say that Canaris didn't let him go, that he escaped."

"Oppenheimer."

"Oppenheimer." Baker-Bates held up a thumb and forefinger that were less than an inch apart. "Some say that he was that close to Himmler once. That close, they say, though it's probably cock. And there're even some who'll say that he did in Bormann there at the end, but that's cock too—although there's no doubt about the SS Major General in Cologne and that Gauleiter down near Munich and maybe two dozen others."

"So you're looking for him?"

"That's right; we are."

"What're you going to do if you find him—put him up for an OBE?"

"The war's over, chum, long over."

"One year," Jackson said. "One year and twenty-seven days."

"Oppenheimer hasn't heard. Or if he's heard, he hasn't paid any attention."

"How many?"

"Since V-E Day?"

Jackson nodded.

"At least nine, perhaps ten, perhaps more. Mostly minor bods and sods, nobody very important, but still, we'd've liked to have got our own hands on them. It's almost as though he were going around tidying up for us—to save us the bother, so to speak."

"And now you're afraid he might turn his talents to Palestine."

Baker-Bates took another swallow of his beer. You know what's going on there, don't you?"

"The Empire's in trouble," Jackson said. "When the League of Nations handed you the mandate for Palestine back in—when, 1920?"

"Officially, it was '23."

"Okay, '23. That was when you promised the Jews a national homeland. That was in one breath. But in the next you swore to the Arabs that the Jews wouldn't create any problem. But then Hitler started in on the Jews, and those who could get out decided to take you up on your promise. The Arabs didn't much like it."

"I was there," Baker-Bates said.

"Where?"

"In Palestine during the troubles. I went out with Orde Wingate in '36 in the Fifth Division. In '38 I helped him organize the Jews into special night squads. He spoke it —you know, Arabic. But he turned into a bloody Zionist. He also proved that Jews make damn fine soldiers. Or terrorists. You were in Burma; you ever know him there?"

"Wingate?" Jackson said, not bothering to ask how Baker-Bates knew about Burma.

"Mmm."

"He was before my time."

Baker-Bates nodded—rather gloomily, Jackson thought. "Some of those chaps that Wingate and I trained are probably in the Irgun now—or the Stern Gang," Baker-Bates said, his tone as gloomy as his nod.

"Group," Jackson said automatically.

"What?"

"Stern Group. They don't like to be called gang."

"Now, that's too bloody bad, isn't it? You know what they're doing, don't you—your precious Irgun Svai Leumi and your Stern Gang?"

"They're blowing up your hotels and killing your soldiers."

"Last July, the King David Hotel. Ninety-one killed; forty-five wounded."

"So I read."

"But that's not all. There's a rumor."

"What kind of rumor?"

"That the Irgun's recruiting in Europe. That they're looking for killers, good ones. That they don't even have to be Jewish—if they're good enough." Baker-Bates paused and then went on. "As I said, that's rumor. But this isn't. This is fact; they're looking for Oppenheimer."

Jackson finished his beer. "Do his father and sister know?"

"I might have mentioned it to them."

"What did they say?"

"We only had our one little chat. That was earlier this month, and then they turned mysterious on me. It took only a few quids' worth of pesos to find out why. A certain telephone operator on the hotel switchboard is frightfully underpaid. But that's how I got on to you and that rotten little dwarf. I ran a check on you. You're rather harmless. But he's bad company, you know—very bad."

"Probably."

"Not to be trusted."

"No."

"Actually, the little bastard's a menace."

"But he's good at it, isn't he?"

"At what?" Baker-Bates said.

"At finding people. If you weren't afraid that he might

43

turn up Oppenheimer before you do, then you wouldn't be romancing me."

Baker-Bates sighed. "And I thought I was just being rather nice."

"You are. You're paying for the beer."

Again, Baker-Bates nodded slowly as he stared at Jackson. "You haven't been in Germany since the war, have you?"

"No."

"It's a little murky there now. A bit unsettled. You might even say it's a bit like Palestine. No one's sure what's going to happen, what with the Russians and all. Some feel it could go one way, some another. But if the Oppenheimer heir decides to take out the wrong chap, it could send up the balloon. So that's why we're looking for him —that and the fact that we damned well don't want him in Palestine either. But we and the Irgun aren't the only ones looking for him, of course. So are your people. But even more interesting, so are the Bolshies."

"Why's that so interesting?"

This time when Baker-Bates smiled, he showed some teeth. They were slightly gray.

"Why? Because, dear boy, they probably want to hire him."

With that he rose, started toward the door, paused, and turned back. "You might tell the rotten little dwarf that. It just might scare him off."

"It won't scare him," Jackson said.

"No, but tell him anyway."

"All right," Jackson said. "I will."

Leah Oppenheimer entered the dark hotel sitting room and switched on a lamp. Her father, still seated in the same chair, smiled. "It's grown quite dark, hasn't it?"

"Yes. Is there anything I can get you?"

"Perhaps another cigar."

She again went over to the box, took one out, and lit it for him. He took several puffs and smiled again in what he thought was his daughter's direction. He was only slightly off.

"I've been sitting here thinking," he said.

"About Kurt?"

"Yes, about him. But mostly about being German. I'm rather an anachronism, you know, although our Zionist friends think I'm worse than that. They think I'm somewhere between a fool and a traitor."

"We've been over all this before, Father."

"Yes, we have, haven't we? But young Mr. Jackson started me thinking again. I will always be a Jew, of course. And I will always be a German. I'm too old to change, even if I wished to. One does not shed one's nationality like a suit of old clothes. But you and Kurt are young. There is no reason why either of you should follow my example."

"You know my feelings."

"Do I really?" he asked, and puffed on his cigar again. "Well, I suppose I do. But we don't know Kurt's, do we?"

"He was never a Zionist."

Oppenheimer's mouth twisted itself into a wry smile. "No; his peculiar politics precluded that. But no matter. Our responsibility is to find him before the authorities do. Do you really think he's quite mad?"

Leah Oppenheimer replied with a shrug, but then realized that her father couldn't see it. "I don't know," she said. "We've been over it so many times, I no longer know what to think."

"If the British or American authorities find him before Jackson and Ploscaru do, they will simply lock him away. If they don't hang him."

Concern seemed almost to ripple over Leah Oppenheimer's face. "They couldn't," she said. "He's—well, he's ill."

"Is he?"

"He must be."

"Nevertheless, we have to consider it as a possibility. Therefore, we must have a contingent plan should Ploscaru and Jackson fail. And that is what I've been thinking about. If you will bring me my wallet, I will give you the address of those you must reach."

Leah Oppenheimer rose. "The ones in Cologne?"

"Yes," her father said. "The ones in Cologne."

It was shortly before midnight when Jackson arrived back in San Diego at the El Cortez Hotel, where the dwarf had booked them adjoining rooms. He got his key from the desk, learned that the bar was still open, and went in for a nightcap.

The bar was called the Shore Leave Room, and it was deserted save for the bartender and two Navy lieutenants who were with a pair of coy blondes who didn't seem to be their wives. Jackson ordered a bourbon and water and carried it to a far table. After sampling his drink, he took from his inside breast pocket the envelope that Leah Oppenheimer had given him. The envelope was sealed, and Jackson slit it open raggedly with a pencil.

He took the money out first and counted it on his knee beneath the table. It was all there. He counted out ten $100 bills, folded them once, and stuffed them into his pants pocket. He put the remaining $500 back into the envelope, after removing four photographs and two folded sheets of paper.

The photographs seemed to have been taken with a box camera. One of them showed a young man, possibly twenty-two, seated astride a bicycle. From the height of the bicycle, Jackson judged him to be about six feet tall. His sleeves were rolled up above the elbows, his shirt was open at the throat, and he wore shorts that might have been leather. On his feet were heavy shoes with thick white socks. The young man looked fit and lean and possibly tanned. His mouth was open as though he were saying something jocular, and there was a half-humorous expression on his face. Jackson turned the photograph over. On the back was written, "Kurt, Darmstadt, 1936."

The other photographs seemed to have been taken later,

although there were no dates. In all of them Kurt Oppenheimer wore a white shirt, a tie, and a coat. In only one of them was he smiling, and Jackson thought that the smile seemed forced. Jackson also thought that Kurt Oppenheimer looked very much like his sister, although he had his father's thin, wide mouth. Jackson studied the photographs carefully, but made no attempt to memorize them. He tried to detect signs of brutality, or animal cunning, or even dedication, but all that the photographs revealed was a pleasant-faced young man, almost handsome, with light-colored, not quite blond hair, who looked quick and clever, but not especially happy.

Jackson put the photographs back into the envelope and unfolded the two sheets of paper. Both were covered with jagged, Germanic script written in dark blue ink. The heading was "My Brother, Kurt Oppenheimer." The body of the two pages, like the heading, was written in German and began, "On the first of August, 1914, the day the terrible war began, my brother, Kurt Oppenheimer, was born in Frankfurt."

The essay, for that was how Jackson came to think of it, went on to describe an uneventful, not particularly religious childhood composed mostly of school, sports, stamp collecting, and vacations in Italy, France, and Scotland. A paragraph was devoted to the death of the mother "in that sad spring of 1926 when Kurt was 11 and I was 7." Their mother's death, Leah Oppenheimer wrote, "was a deeply felt loss that somehow drew our small family even closer together."

Leah Oppenheimer went on to recount how her brother had been graduated from a *Gymnasium* in Frankfurt, "where he was a brilliant student, though given to many high-spirited pranks." From the *Gymnasium* he had gone on to attend the university at Bonn, "where he developed his deep interest in politics." Jackson interpreted that to mean he had joined the Communist Party, sometime around 1933, when he was 19. From what Jackson had heard, the university at Bonn had been a rather stodgy place at that time, not much given to radical politics, although it had developed a nicely virulent case of anti-Semitism, which may have explained why Kurt Oppenheimer had wanted to chuck everything in 1936 and head for Spain and the Loyalist cause.

The elder Oppenheimer, according to his daughter, had had his hands full trying to convince his son that Spain wasn't such a good idea. "The impossible political situation that had developed in our own country was my father's telling argument," she wrote. "Kurt agreed to return to Bonn to continue his studies, at least while Father dealt with his increasingly difficult business problems, which he solved in late 1936." Jackson wondered if the zipper king had managed to get a good price for his business.

It was in early 1937 that Kurt Oppenheimer had left Bonn for the last time. Whether he had earned his degree his sister didn't say. But it was then, she wrote, "that the three of us departed Frankfurt, in the dead of night, almost stealthily, forsaking our many friends, and journeyed to Switzerland." For the next three years her brother had grown "increasingly unhappy, restless, and even bitter, especially in 1939 when Von Ribbentrop signed the evil pact with Russia. Although retaining his fierce ideals, Kurt grew ever more critical of the Soviet leaders while retaining, of course, his steadfast opposition to the Hitler regime."

Jackson was growing impatient both with Leah Oppenheimer's florid prose and with her brother's quirky politics. He scanned the rest of the letter quickly. There wasn't much. After the war had started in 1939, her brother had joined an organization that smuggled Jews into Switzerland. He had made a number of trips back into Germany which his sister described as being "fraught with peril, although my brother withstood these dangerous journeys with cool resolve and quiet bravery."

Jackson sighed and read on. In 1940, just before Paris

fell, Father Oppenheimer had decided to get to England while the getting was good. Between father and son there had been what Leah Oppenheimer described as a "terse debate," but which Jackson interpreted as a shouting match. Father and daughter had packed off to London, leaving elder brother behind—a sad parting, Leah Oppenheimer wrote, where "the tears flowed unashamedly." And that was the last they had heard from elder brother, except for a few letters that were, she said, "understandably guarded in content, but nevertheless brimming with confidence." After that, Leah's portrait of her brother ended abruptly except for a half page listing the names of Kurt Oppenheimer's friends and acquaintances in Germany and their last known addresses.

Jackson sighed again, folded the two pages, and put them back into the envelope. It hadn't been much of a dossier. Rather, it had been a younger sister's romantic notions of her idealized brother. Jackson felt that she might just as well have been writing about the Scarlet Pimpernel. Well, perhaps she was. He only wished that she hadn't developed such a wretched style.

He finished his drink, put the envelope away in his pocket, and headed for the elevator. On the fifth floor, he found room 514, opened it with a key, went in, moved over to the door that joined the two rooms, and tried it. It was unlocked. He opened it. A night-light was burning. In the large double bed was the dwarf, fast asleep. Next to the dwarf lay a brunette of about thirty who might have been rather pretty except for her smeared lipstick. She was also asleep and snoring, although not enough to complain about. Neither the dwarf nor the brunette seemed to have any clothes on.

Jackson went over to the bed and bent down until his mouth was only a few inches from the dwarf's left ear. What came out of Jackson's mouth came out half shout, half roar:

"Baker-Bates wants his money back!"

5 The dwarf, barefoot and fuming, but wearing his rich green dressing gown, stalked into Jackson's room with a glare in his eyes and a scowl on his face. "You damned near frightened Dorothy to death," he snapped.

"Poor Dorothy."

"You didn't have to yell in my ear. It made her cry. I can't stand it when they cry."

"What was her last name—Dorothy's?"

"I don't remember."

"Is she gone?"

"She's gone. What's this about Baker-Bates? I don't know any Baker-Bates."

"Sure you do, Nick. Gilbert Baker-Bates. A British chappie. He dropped you and your fist man back into Romania with a hundred thousand bucks in gold."

"He lied. It wasn't anywhere near that much. More like fifty."

"Still a tidy sum."

The scowl left Ploscaru's face. In its place spread some lines of what Jackson took to be apprehension or even fear. "He wants the money back?"

"Not really. They've written you off, Nick. You're old hat. Ancient history."

"Did he say that?"

"His very words."

The dwarf relaxed, and the lines of apprehension—or fear—left his face, which reassumed its normal look of benevolent cunning. He studied Jackson for a moment. Then without a word he turned and, not stalking this time, went back into his own room. When he returned, he was carrying two glasses and a bottle. "Bourbon," he said. "Bonded stuff. Green label. See?" He held up a bottle of Old Forester. Jackson realized that it was more than a bottle of bourbon. It was a peace offering, a mollifying gift that would help to smooth over some of the lies the dwarf had told him.

Ploscaru used a carafe of water to mix two drinks and handed one to Jackson, who was sitting in an armchair. The dwarf hopped up onto the bed and wriggled back. "How'd he get on to you—Baker-Bates?" Ploscaru tried to make it a casual question and almost succeeded.

"He wants the assassin."

"Assassin? What assassin?"

"What assassin? Why, the one that slipped your mind, Nick. The one you forgot to mention. The one you described as being just a lost boy strayed from home whose kinfolk would pay us a little money to see if we could get him back. Kurt Oppenheimer. That assassin."

"I know nothing of it. Nothing."

"Come off it, Nick."

The dwarf shrugged. "I may have heard some wild rumor. Idle gossip, perhaps. But—phht." He shrugged again—an eloquent Balkan shrug that dismissed the notion. "How was your meeting with the Oppenheimers?"

Jackson took the envelope from his pocket and tossed it to Ploscaru, who caught it with one hand. "Your cut's in there," Jackson said, "along with Leah Oppenheimer's schoolgirl version of her brother, the brave underground hero. Read it and I'll tell you how our meeting went."

"Tell me now," the dwarf said, counting the money. "I can read and listen at the same time. I have that kind of mind."

As a matter of fact, he did. By the time Jackson had described his meeting with the Oppenheimers, Ploscaru had read Leah Oppenheimer's essay twice, counted the money three times, and made a careful study of the four snapshots.

"And Baker-Bates?"

"He picked me up outside the hotel. We went to a bar and had a drink and talked about you. He doesn't like you."

"No," Ploscaru murmured, "I suppose he doesn't."

"He called you names."

Ploscaru nodded sadly. "Yes, he probably would. How did he look, poor chap—a trifle seedy?"

Jackson stared at him. "A little."

"A bit down on his luck?"

"He paid for the drinks."

"Still claiming to be with the old firm?"

"He implied as much."

Ploscaru sighed—a long, breathy sigh full of sorrowful commiseration. "He's not, you know. They cashiered him back in—let's see—early '44, I believe it was."

"Why—because of you?"

The dwarf smiled unpleasantly. "Not really. It was a number of things—although I may have been the last

52

straw. He must be free-lancing now, poor old dear. He's seen the Oppenheimers, of course."

"Once."

The dwarf nodded thoughtfully. "They wouldn't talk to him," he said, more to himself than to Jackson. "His bona fides are all wrong." Ploscaru brightened. "What else did he tell you?"

"He told me about all the people Kurt Oppenheimer supposedly killed during the war—and afterwards."

Ploscaru sipped his drink. "Probably mentioned the SS major general and the Bavarian Gauleiter."

"I thought you didn't know anything about it."

"I told you I'd heard rumors—most of them a bit fanciful. What else did he say?"

"That the British don't want him in Palestine. Oppenheimer."

The dwarf seemed to turn that information over in his mind for several moments, sorting it out, estimating its worth, probing its validity. He nodded then, a number of times, as though satisfied, and said, "An interesting point. Very interesting. It could lead to all kinds of speculation."

"Yes, it could, couldn't it?"

Ploscaru made his eyebrows go up to form a silent question.

"I mean," Jackson said, "that there's a possibility that we're not being paid by a retired zipper king, but by the Zionists."

"I should make it a point never to underestimate you, Minor. Sometimes you're most refreshing. Would that bother you, if it were true—the Zionist thing?"

Jackson raised his glass in a small, indifferent toast. "Up the Israelites."

The dwarf smiled happily. "We're very much alike in many ways, aren't we?"

"I'm taller," Jackson said.

"Yes, I suppose that's true." The dwarf gazed up at the

ceiling. "You know what's really going on out there, don't you?"

"Where?"

"In the Middle East."

"A power struggle."

"Exactly. Between Russia and Britain."

"That's not exactly new."

Ploscaru nodded. "No, but there is a new government in Britain."

"But not one that's dedicated to the liquidation of the British Empire."

"No, of course not. So Britain has got to keep some kind of physical grip on the Middle East. Russia's still nibbling away at Turkey and Iran, and Britain's either going to pull out or be kicked out of Egypt and Iraq."

"So that leaves Palestine."

"And Trans-Jordan, but Palestine mostly. Palestine is key. So if Britain is going to keep on being a world power, which means keeping the Russians out of the Mideast, then it must have a base. Palestine will do quite nicely, especially if the Jews and the Arabs are at each other's throats. It would be easier to control. It always has been —except for one thing."

"The Jews have started knocking off the British."

"Exactly," the dwarf said. "A rather interesting situation, don't you think? But to get back to poor old Baker-Bates. What else did he say?"

"He said that both the Americans and the British are after Oppenheimer."

"The French?"

"He didn't say."

"Probably not. The French are so practical."

"But the ones who want him most of all are the Russians."

"Well, now. Did he say why?"

"He said it's because they want to hire him. He also said to tell you that."

"Yes," Ploscaru said as, without thinking, he clasped the glass between his knees so that he could slowly dust his hands off. "Yes, I'm very glad that you did."

Two days later, at six o'clock in the morning of the day that he and the dwarf were to leave for Washington, Jackson finally met Winona Wilson. There had been a farewell party somewhere the night before, and Jackson awoke with a mild hangover and the slightly blurred vision of a tall blond woman of about twenty-six who stood looking down at him, her hands on her hips.

Jackson blinked his eyes rapidly to clear his vision and said, "Good morning."

"Somebody's been sleeping in my bed," she said. "I think that's what I'm supposed to say, according to the book."

"I think I've read that one."

"Your name's not Goldilocks, though, is it?" she said. "No, not with that hair. I actually used to know a Goldilocks, although he spelled it with an x. Old Sam Goldilox over in Pasadena."

"You must be Winona Wilson," Jackson said. "How's your mother, Winona?"

"Stingy. Tightfisted. Parsimonious. Who're you, a friend of Nick's?"

"Uh-huh. One Minor Jackson. Where is he, Nick?"

She nodded toward the bedroom door. "Asleep. I've just made a quick tour—counting the spoons, stuff like that. You've kept it very neat. I'm surprised."

"We had a maid in yesterday."

"When're you leaving?"

"What time is it now?"

She looked at her watch. "Six. A little after."

"Christ. About nine. Okay?"

"No rush," she said, and sat down on the edge of the bed and started unbuttoning her blouse. When she had it off, she turned toward him and said, "When I first saw you

55

lying there, I thought you were about sixty. The hair."

"It's gray."

"I know," she said as she removed her skirt and tossed it on a chair. "I bet it turned that way overnight."

"As a matter of fact, it did," Jackson said as he watched her shed the rest of her clothes. She had unusually fine breasts and long, lean legs that some might have thought too thin, although Jackson thought they were fine. She turned and paused as though to give him a full view, and Jackson noticed that her eyes were blue. Periwinkle blue, he thought, but realized that he wasn't really quite sure whether a periwinkle was a fish or a flower or both. He resolved to look it up.

"Tell me about it," she said as she slipped underneath the covers next to him. "Tell me about how your hair turned gray overnight."

"All right," Jackson said.

It was about eight when Ploscaru wandered into the bedroom holding a saucer and a cup of coffee. He took a sip, nodded pleasantly at Jackson and Winona Wilson, said, "I see you two have met," and wandered out. Winona Wilson giggled.

Their departure from the house in the Hollywood hills was delayed nearly an hour because of the Grand Canyon, Yellowstone National Park, and New Orleans. Ploscaru wanted to visit all of them on the way to Washington. It was only after a bitter debate, with Winona Wilson siding with the dwarf, that a compromise of sorts was reached. Yellowstone was out, but both the Grand Canyon and New Orleans were in.

"It's still about a thousand miles out of the way," Jackson said grumpily as he studied the oil-company map that he had spread on the hood of the Plymouth.

"But well worth both the time and expense," Ploscaru said. He jumped up on the convertible's running board, took Winona Wilson's hand, and brushed his lips against it with a bit of a flourish. "Winona, you have, as always, been more than generous."

"Anytime, Nick," she said as she smiled, leaned over, and kissed him on the top of his head.

Jackson folded the map, stuck it in his jacket pocket, moved over to the tall blond woman, put an arm around her, and kissed her lightly on the mouth. "You're the best thing that's happened in a long time. Thanks."

She smiled. "If you're ever out here again, Slim, stop by. You can tell me more war stories."

"Sure," Jackson said. "I'll do that."

6 His papers said that he was a journeyman printer. The papers were tightly wrapped in yellow oilskin tied with stout string and were now pressed against his lean stomach by his belt. The papers also said that his name was Otto Bodden, that he had been born in Berlin thirty-nine years before, and that his political preference was the Social Democratic party, a preference which had cost him five years in the concentration camp at Belsen.

He had been a printer. That much was true. And he had been born in Berlin and grown up there. That was not only true, but also necessary, because the people around Lübeck distrusted Berliners—despised them, really—and could recognize them in a second by their gab as well as by their figuratively big noses which they were always poking into places that didn't concern them. Berliners were Prussians. Wisecracking Prussians, perhaps, but still Prussians.

As for the name, well, Otto Bodden would serve as well as any. There had been many names since he had taken his first alias thirteen years before. He tried to remember what that first one had been. It came to him after a second or two. Klaus Kalkbrenner. His lips twitched into a smile as he crouched in the trees and studied the three early-morning anglers across the canal. Young Klaus Kalkbrenner, he remembered, had been something of an idiot.

He had no watch, so he had to depend on the sun. He turned to examine it. It was already up, but not quite enough. It would be a few more minutes until the patrol came along. He turned back to continue his study of the fishermen across the canal. One of them had caught something; not a bad-sized fish; a carp perhaps, although Bodden wasn't at all sure whether carp swam in the Elbe-Trave Canal.

He adjusted the rucksack on his back which contained his one coat and the shirt and trousers he would change into once he made it across the canal. They too were all wrapped up in oilskin. No spare shoes or socks, though. That would have been overdoing it, because no refugee printer would have an extra pair of shoes. He would have sold them by now, or traded them for something to eat.

He turned for another look at the sun. Ten more minutes, he estimated. Turning back, he fished out his last cigarette. It was an American cigarette, a Camel. They had given him a pack of them in Berlin a week before, and he carefully had made them last until now. American cigarettes were another thing a refugee printer wouldn't have. He wondered what the black-market price for an American cigarette was in Lübeck: three Reichsmarks; four? It had been five in Berlin.

He took a match from one of the three left in the small

waterproof steel canister and struck it against the sole of his shoe. He lit the cigarette and pulled the smoke down into his lungs. He liked American cigarettes. He liked their names, too: Camels, Lucky Strikes, Old Golds, Chesterfields, Wings. For some reason, Wings didn't bring as good a price on the Berlin black market. He wasn't sure why. He pulled in another lungful of smoke, held it down, and then luxuriously blew it out. It was his first smoke in three days, and he could feel it—a slight, pleasant, dizzying sensation.

Someone had once told him that the Americans used treacle to cure their tobacco. He wondered if that was true. He also wondered how good his English really was. He had learned it in Belsen from a Pole. The Pole had been a very funny fellow who had claimed to have once lived in Cleveland and had assured Bodden that the English he was being taught was the American kind. The Pole had had a lot of amusing theories. One of them was that Poles made the world's best fighter pilots. That's the problem with us Poles, he had once told Bodden. All our politicians should really have been fighter pilots.

There wasn't much left to his cigarette now. A few centimeters. Regretfully, Bodden took one last puff and ground it into the dirt with his shoe. He heard them then, the patrol. One of them was whistling. That was how it was supposed to be.

Well, here goes nothing, he said to himself in English. That had been one of the Pole's favorite phrases, which he had also guaranteed to be proper American usage. In fact, it was the last thing he had ever said to Bodden that April morning in 1944 when they had led the Pole away to be shot or hanged. Hanged probably, Bodden decided. They wouldn't have wasted a bullet on a Pole. Gniadkiewicz. That had been the Pole's name, Bodden remembered. Roman Gniadkiewicz. A very funny fellow.

Bodden took a deep breath, scuttled out of the trees and across the path, and slipped into the canal with a small splash. Christ, it was cold! He heard the Russian patrol shout Halt. How the hell do you halt when you're swimming? he wondered. They were supposed to shout it three times, for the benefit of anyone who might be listening—for the British especially; but a lot of the Russians were dumb bastards, farm boys who might not be able to count that high. So Bodden took a deep breath and dived underwater just as the first rifle cracked.

When he came up, they were still shooting at him—well, almost at him. A bullet smacked into the water less than a meter away, far less, and Bodden dived under again. A show-off, he thought as he used a breaststroke to swim the last few meters. One of them had to be a show-off.

When he came up again, he saw that he had come up right where he had wanted to—not far from the three German fishermen, who stared down at him as he treaded water, blowing and sputtering.

"Well, what have we got here?" said one of the anglers, a man of about sixty.

"A very wet fish," Bodden said.

"Maybe we ought to throw him back," the old man said as he put down his pole. The other two men laughed. They were old too, Bodden saw; somewhere in their late sixties.

The first old man came over to where Bodden still treaded water. He knelt down and stretched out his hand. He was a big, still-powerful old man, who barely grunted as he hauled Bodden up and onto the bank of the canal. "There you are, Herr Fish," the old man said. "Nice and dry."

"Thanks," Bodden said. "Thanks very much."

The old man shrugged. "It was nothing," he said, and went back and picked up his pole.

Across the canal, the three Russian soldiers were yelling at Bodden. He grinned and yelled back at them in Russian.

61

"What did you tell them, Herr Fish?" asked the old man who had dragged him out of the canal.

"I told them what their mothers do with the pigs."

"You speak Russian?"

"Just enough to tell them that."

The old man nodded. "Somebody should."

Bodden looked around. There was no one in sight except the three old fishermen—and the Russians, of course, but they didn't count. He took off his shoes first. Then he removed his knapsack and his wet shirt and squeezed the water out of the shirt. The three old men looked away politely while Bodden changed into the dry clothes.

When dressed, Bodden went over and squatted down by the old man who had hauled him out of the canal. "How far into the center of town?"

"A little over six kilometers—along that path there." The old man gestured with his head.

"That fish you caught earlier—what was it?"

"You were watching?"

"From over there."

"It was a carp."

"That's what I thought it was," Bodden said. "A carp."

It took Bodden a little more than an hour and a half to reach the center of Lübeck. Before the war it had had a population of about 100,000, but German refugees from the East and displaced persons from almost everywhere had swollen that figure to nearly double its prewar size. Some of this Bodden learned when he stopped several times to ask directions. The refugees and the DP's flocked to Lübeck because it had been bombed only once, on Palm Sunday in 1942. The raid was supposed to have taken out the docks and the industrial belt, but instead it had wiped out about a third of the old city center.

"Because of Coventry, you know," one old man told Bodden. "We hit Coventry; they hit us. Retaliation."

The DP's, Bodden learned, were mostly Poles and Latvians and Estonians, and nobody liked them. Many of them were thieves—clever thieves, one man said, who "lust after bicycles." Whatever they stole often turned up on the black market which flourished in a small street that was pointed out to Bodden.

The street was called Botcherstrasse, and it seemed to contain not only the town's black market but also its brothels. Because it led from Fischergrube to Beckergrube, which was on his way, Bodden took it. He found that one could buy almost anything for a price in that one short block. There were cigarettes, of course, mostly British, as well as coffee, meat, poultry, fats, and clothing. Bodden even found a pair of shoelaces, which he quickly bought from a Pole who brandished a thick wad of notes. Bodden had looked for two months in Berlin for a pair of laces without luck. The ones that he bought after the customary bargaining seemed new, probably prewar, and he felt lucky to have found them despite their exorbitant price.

From Beckergrube it was only a short walk to the newspaper plant on Königstrasse. It was a crowded, busy street packed with pedestrians and bicycles, and Bodden had to shoulder his way to the entrance of the *Lübecker Post*. The street floor was given over to a job-printing shop, and after inquiries Bodden was sent to the director's office on the second floor.

He had to wait, of course. The *Herr Direktor* was a busy man, with many important affairs and responsibilities that commanded his time, but if Bodden would care to wait, it was just possible that he would be granted an audience, although a brief one.

The director's secretary hadn't asked him to sit while he waited, but Bodden sat anyway, in a straight-backed wooden chair. He sat for fifteen minutes, almost without moving, and then crossed his legs. The secretary was a stern-faced woman of about forty, skinny almost to the point of emaciation, who pounded away industriously on an old typewriter. The telephone rang four times while Bodden waited the first fifteen minutes; five times while he waited the second fifteen.

Three minutes later, he was shown into the presence of the director, Dieter Rapke, who, Bodden thought, was too young for the self-important air that he gave himself. At forty-two, Rapke looked like a man whom the war and its aftermath had cheated out of middle-aged plumpness. He had a round head that by now should have been growing some double chins, but wasn't. It gave him a curiously unfinished look. When times get better, Bodden thought, that one will eat.

Rapke peered up at the man who stood before his littered desk. He didn't ask the man to sit down. It didn't occur to him. After a moment he took off his rimless glasses, polished them with a handkerchief, and put them back on.

"So," Rapke said, "you are a printer."

"Yes," Bodden said, "and a good one."

"From Berlin."

"From Berlin."

"There is no work for a printer in Berlin?"

"There is always work for a printer in Berlin provided there are paper and ink and type—and provided he doesn't care what he prints. I care."

"So you came West."

"Yes."

"When?"

"This morning."

"Across the canal?"

"Yes."

"You experienced no difficulty."

Bodden shrugged. "I got wet. And they shot at me."

"Your papers." Rapke held out his hand.

Bodden took out the oilskin pouch, untied the string, and handed his papers over. Rapke studied them methodically. At the third document, he looked up at Bodden again. "So. You were in a camp."

"Belsen."

"How long?"

"From 1940 on."

Rapke went back to his study of the papers. "It must have been hard."

"It was no holiday."

"You look fit enough now."

"I've had a lot of outdoor exercise recently."

"Doing what?"

"Clearing rubble. There is a lot of it in Berlin. I helped clean some of it up. Before that I worked as a printer for the Russians. But I decided I'd rather clean up rubble."

Rapke started making notes of some of the information contained in Bodden's papers. "We have nothing here," he said as he wrote. "Nothing permanent, that is. Only temporary. One of our employees, a printer, was attacked by a band of DP's two days ago. Poles probably. They stole his bicycle. And broke his leg. He's an old man, so I'm not sure when he will return. But if you're interested, you can have his job until he does."

"I'm interested," Bodden said.

"Very well," Rapke said, handing back the papers. "You will report to work at seven tomorrow morning. I have some of your particulars here, but you should give the rest to my secretary, Frau Glimm. And be sure to register with the police."

"Yes, I will," Bodden said. "Thank you, Herr Rapke."

Rapke didn't look up from the notes he was still making. Instead, he said, "Please close the door on your way out."

When Bodden had gone, Rapke reached for the telephone and placed the trunk call himself. It was to a large country house located some fifteen kilometers north and west of Lübeck. A male voice with a British accent answered the phone on the second ring.

"Colonel Whitlock's office; Sergeant Lewis speaking."

Summoning up what little English he had, Rapke said, "Here is Herr Rapke. I wish with Colonel Whitlock to speak."

"One moment, please," Sergeant Lewis said.

The Colonel came on speaking an idiomatic, though strongly accented, German, and Rapke let his breath out. Rapke found speaking English a trying business, one which he did so badly that it made him sweat. He was so grateful to be speaking German that he forgot the elaborate conversational niceties he usually employed when talking to the Colonel.

"He came," Rapke said. "Early this morning, just as you said."

"Calls himself Bodden, does he?" the Colonel said.

"Yes. Yes. Bodden. Otto Bodden."

"And you hired him, of course."

"Yes, yes, just as you instructed."

"Good work, Rapke. Perhaps he will even turn out to be a competent printer."

"Yes, that is to be devoutly wished. Now, is there anything else that I am to do?"

"Nothing," the Colonel said. "Absolutely nothing. You will treat him exactly as you would treat any other temporary employee. Is that clear?"

"Yes, naturally."

"And one more thing, Rapke."

"Yes."

"Keep your mouth shut. Is that also clear?"

"Yes," Rapke said. "Most clear."

After Rapke had hung up, the Colonel asked Sergeant Lewis to have Captain Richards come in. A few moments later Richards came in, filling his pipe, and sat down in a chair before the Colonel's desk. The Colonel watched bleakly as Richards went through the ritual of lighting his pipe. The Colonel didn't mind pipe smoking. He smoked himself, cigarettes; chain-smoked them, in fact. But all that business of filling a pipe and tamping it down and lighting it and relighting it and then knocking it all out somewhere, it really was a bloody nuisance.

"Rapke called," Colonel Whitlock said.

The Captain nodded and went on with the lighting of his pipe.

"He's across," the Colonel said.

The Captain nodded again. "Came across this morning about seven. They even shot at him. Or toward him. Three fishermen were there. They saw it."

"Rapke hired him."

"Good. Does he call himself Bodden?"

"Mm. Otto Bodden."

"I'll let Hamburg know."

"Yes, do that," the Colonel said. "And you should ask them how long we might have to keep an eye on this fellow before that major of theirs arrives. What's his name?"

"Baker-Bates. Gilbert Baker-Bates."

"Coming from America, isn't he?"

"From Mexico, sir."

"Same thing," the Colonel said.

7　If the dwarf hadn't got drunk in the French Quarter in New Orleans and stayed that way for two days, and if he hadn't insisted on visiting Monticello in Virginia, and later insisted that Jackson give him a guided tour of the University of Virginia, then they could have made it to Washington in a week instead of the eleven days that it took them. During the tour of the university, Jackson had to listen to Ploscaru lecture learnedly on Thomas Jefferson. The lecture went on so long that they were delayed another day and had to spend the night in Charlottesville.

They arrived in Washington at a little after noon the next day and managed to get two rooms at the Willard. After unpacking and sending his suit out to be pressed, Jackson went down the hall to Ploscaru's room.

The dwarf let Jackson in, went back to the bed, hopped up on it, and sat cross-legged while he examined his four passports. One was French, one was Swiss, one was Canadian, and the last was German. The dwarf tossed that one aside and picked up the one issued by Canada.

"Canadian?" Ploscaru said.

Jackson shook his head and looked around for the bourbon. He found it on the dresser. "What would a Canadian be doing in Germany?" he said as he poured himself a drink.

Ploscaru nodded, put the Canadian passport down, and picked up the Swiss one. "Swiss, I think. A Swiss would have business in Germany. A Swiss would have business anywhere."

Jackson picked up the Canadian passport, flipped through it with one hand, and tossed it back onto the bed. "If these things are so perfect, why didn't you use one of them to go down to Mexico with me?"

Without looking up from the Swiss passport, Ploscaru said, "Then I would have run into Baker-Bates, wouldn't I've?"

Jackson stared at him for a moment and then grinned. "You knew he was there, didn't you?"

The dwarf only shrugged without looking up.

"God, how you lie, Nick."

"Not really."

"You lied about Baker-Bates. You lied about Oppenheimer not speaking English. You lied about his daughter, about her being a spinster."

"She is."

"She's not even thirty."

"In Germany a woman if not married by twenty-five is a spinster. *Eine alte Jungfer.* It's the law, I think. Or was."

Jackson went over and stood by the window and looked across Fourteenth Street at the National Press Building. A man directly opposite stood at a window and scratched his head. The man's coat was off, his tie was loosened, and his shirt sleeves were rolled up. After a moment, the man quit scratching his head, turned, and sat down at a desk. Jackson wondered if he was a reporter.

Jackson turned from the window, found a chair, and sat down in it. "And then there's Kurt Oppenheimer, the boyish assassin. You lied about him too."

"Actually, I didn't."

"No?"

"No. What I did was fail to mention everything that I knew about him." Ploscaru looked over at Jackson and grinned. "You're getting wet feet, aren't you?"

"Cold feet."

"Yes, of course. Cold feet."

"No. Not exactly," Jackson said. "It's just that I haven't figured out what lies I'm going to tell the Army and the State Department."

The dwarf smiled cheerfully. "You'll think of something."

"That's what bothers me," Jackson said. "I probably will."

Ploscaru had to see the White House first, of course. After that they followed Pennsylvania Avenue down to where it jogged around the Treasury Building and had lunch at the Occidental, where the dwarf was impressed by all the photographs of dead politicians on the walls, if not by the food.

When they had finished lunch, the dwarf said that he had to see some people. Jackson didn't ask whom. If he had asked, he was fairly sure he would have been lied to again.

After the dwarf caught a cab, Jackson went back up to his hotel room and started making phone calls. It was the third call that paid off. The man whom Jackson had phoned was Robert Henry Orr, and when Jackson had first known him he had been in the OSS and everyone had called him Nanny, because it was to Nanny that everyone turned who wanted something fixed. Now Orr was in the State Department, and he didn't seem at all surprised that Jackson had called.

"Let me guess, Minor," Orr said. "You finally decided that you wanted to come home and you called poor old Nanny. How nice."

"I didn't know there was one," Jackson said. "A home."

"Not yet, but give us another year. Meantime, I could put you on to something temporary, perhaps in Japan. That would be nice. Would you like that?"

"Not much," Jackson said. "Maybe we could get together for a drink later on."

There was a silence, and then Orr said, "You've got something going on your own, haven't you, Minor? Something naughty, I'll bet."

"How about the Willard at five-thirty in the bar?"

"I'll be there," Orr said, and hung up.

Robert Henry Orr had been a beautiful child in the early twenties—so beautiful, in fact, that he had earned nearly $300,000 in photographic-modeling fees not only in New York but also in London and Paris. Most adults who had been children in the twenties could still remember that beautiful face with its long dark curls grinning out at them from a box of the cereal that then had been the chief competitor of Cream of Wheat. In fact, a large portion of adult America had grown up hating Robert Henry Orr.

But when he was thirteen, Robert Henry Orr had developed a case of acne, the nasty kind for which nothing can be done other than to let it run its course. It had left him with a splotched and pitted face, which, as soon as he was old enough, he had grown a beard to conceal.

Although the beard had disguised his ruined face, nothing could conceal his brilliant mind and his mordant wit. Living nicely on the income from the $300,000 he had earned as a child, and which his banker father had prudently invested, Robert Henry Orr became a professional student. He studied at both Harvard and Yale and at the London School of Economics. From there he went to Heidelberg and from Heidelberg to the Sorbonne. After that, he spent a year at the university at Bologna and another two years studying Oriental languages in Tokyo. He never earned a degree anywhere, but in July of 1941 he was either the sixth or seventh man hired by Colonel William J. Donovan for the Office of the Coordinator of Information, which, after a number of twists and turns, was to become the OSS.

It was in the OSS that Orr had discovered his true calling: he was a born conniver. Although he was given the title of deputy director of personnel, his real job had been to champion the OSS cause against its most implacable enemy, the Washington bureaucracy. For weapons he had used his brilliance, his by now immense girth, his bristling beard, his wicked tongue, and his encyclopedic knowledge about almost everything. He had awed Congress, intimidated the State Department, flummoxed the military, and deceived them all. Most of the strange collection of savants, con men, playboys, freebooters, patriots, socialites, fools, geniuses, college boys, and adventurers who composed the OSS had adored him and called him Nanny. Many of them had needed one.

Promptly at 5:30 Orr entered the Willard bar and strode across the room to the corner table where Jackson sat. Jackson started to rise and shake hands, but Orr waved him back into his seat. He stood, carefully tailored as always, rocking back and forth on his heels, his hands clasped comfortably across his huge belly, as he inspected Jackson for evidence of sloth and decay.

"You're older, Minor," he said, settling into a chair. "You're older and thin. Far too thin."

"Your beard's gone gray," Jackson said. "What do you want to drink?"

Orr said he wanted Scotch, and Jackson ordered two of them from a waiter. When the drinks came, Orr tasted his and said, "Did you ever get it?"

"Get what?"

"Your medal. They put you in for one, you know. A Bronze Star, I think, for something wonderful and brave that you did in Burma. What thing wonderful and brave did you do in Burma, Minor?"

"I got jaundice."

"Maybe it was for that."

"Probably."

"I'll have to look into it."

"Is that what you're still doing, looking into things?"

Orr took another swallow of his drink. "We're in hiding. That's mostly what we do all day long. Hide."

"They're after you, huh?"

"Indeed. You've heard, of course."

"I've heard."

"They split us up, you know. The War Department got Intelligence and Special Operations. Research and Analysis went to State. Nine hundred of us. You should have heard the screams from the old-line State crowd. Can you imagine Herbert Marcuse in State?"

"It's hard. Who else is left?"

"Well, a few are hanging on by their much-gnawed fingernails overseas. Let's see, Phil Horton's in France, Stracey is here, Helms is in Germany, Al Ulmer's in Austria, Angleton's in Italy, Seitz is in the Balkans, of course. And—oh, yes—Jim Kellis is in China."

"What's going to happen?"

"Give us a year and we shall rise again like the Phoenix, God and Joe Stalin willing."

"The Communist hordes, huh?"

"Exactly."

"Who's going to run it—Donovan?"

Orr shook his head. "Not a chance. I suspect that he'll be made ambassador to somewhere dreadful and unimportant. Chile or Siam—one of those places. I understand he needs the money. Now tell me, what mischief are you up to, Minor? I do so hope it's something really nasty."

Jackson shrugged. "I just want to get to Germany, and

I don't want anybody to bother me when I get there."

Orr stroked his beard and pursed his lips. "Why Germany?"

"I think I can make some money there."

"Legally?"

"Almost."

"Dare I ask doing what?"

Jackson grinned and said, "A very delicate mission of a most confidential nature for old friends."

Orr beamed. "Oh, my, you do have something naughty, don't you?"

"Maybe."

"Let's see, how shall we work it? You could go as Germany's first postwar tourist. You'd be just in time for the Oktoberfest. But I think we'd better come up with something just a tiny bit more blatant so that the Army can understand it. Let me think." Orr closed his eyes. When he opened them a few moments later he was smiling. *Next Thursday at Two.*"

"Jesus."

"Surprised?"

"Nobody knows about that."

"I do," Orr said. "But then, I know everything. It really wasn't that bad a play. I'm surprised it was never produced."

"I'm not."

"But there we have it, you see. Minor Jackson, noted playwright, war hero—I must dig up that medal—and, let's see, what else have you done?"

"Nothing."

"No matter. You have decided to turn your sensitive gaze on postwar Germany and to write, I think, a book; yes, a book about what you have seen with your own eyes. A friend of mine's in publishing in New York, and I can get a letter down from him with no problem, since it won't cost him a penny. After that, I'll simply walk it through. Let me have your passport."

Jackson took his passport out and handed it over. Orr thumbed through it idly and said, "Rather a nice likeness."

Jackson swallowed some more of his drink and, keeping his voice toneless and casual, said, "Did you ever hear of a Romanian who calls himself Nicolae Ploscaru?"

Still thumbing through the passport, Orr said, "The wicked dwarf. Where ever did you hear of him? He worked for us once, you know, in—when was it—'44, '45? He was most capable. Expensive, but capable."

"What'd he do?"

Orr tucked Jackson's passport away in an inside pocket, patted it protectively, and said, "We used him to see what he could do about our wild-blue-yonder boys. You know, the ones who were shot down over Bucharest and Ploesti. We finally sent a team of our own in just before the Russians got there. Well, the dwarf had organized things to a fare-thee-well. The fly-boys swore by him. It seems that Ploscaru knew everybody in Romania —everybody worth knowing, of course. His father had been a member of what passed for nobility in that dreadful country—a count, or perhaps a baron—and so the dwarf used his contacts to see that nothing bad happened to our lads. Some of them, in fact, were living off the fat of the land by the time our OSS team got there. The fliers gave the dwarf all the credit."

Orr put his glass up to his lips and stared at Jackson over its rim. It was a long, cool stare. When he brought the glass down, he said, "Still, he was such a wicked little man. We got into a frightful flap with the British over him. It had been one of those co-op things that never work out. I think they wanted to shoot him when it was all over, except that he couldn't be found—or the fifty thousand in gold that we'd supplied. Gold sovereigns, as I recall. He simply disappeared, but we thought it was money well spent. I'm curious. Where ever did you hear of him?"

"In a bar. In Mexico."

"So that's where he is?" Orr said. "I've sometimes wondered."

"He's not there, but somebody who'd known him was."

"Who?"

"A cashiered British type who said his name was Baker-Bates."

"*Gilbert* Baker-Bates?" Orr's tone was almost incredulous.

Jackson nodded.

"*Gilbert* Baker-Bates? The manic Major. *Cashiered!* Not likely, Minor. Why, poor old Gilbert's now the rising star in the British firmament. *Who ever* told you that he was cashiered?"

"Somebody who lies a lot," Jackson said.

8 The ruined castle, or *Schloss*, lay a mile or two out of Höchst, which made it not much more than a forty-minute drive from the center of Frankfurt. The castle had been ruined by time as well as by a couple of stray American bombs. Now no one was quite sure whom it really belonged to, although the Americans apparently had staked out their claim with a big, carefully lettered, official-looking sign that read in both English and German:

Property of U.S. Army
ABSOLUTELY NO TRESPASSING

The Germans who still lived nearby respected the sign, of course. But even had it not been there, none of them would have been likely to do much trespassing. Rumor kept them away, rumor that the castle was the sometime rendezvous of a roving band of Polish and Latvian DP's—thieves and cutthroats all, naturally, or worse. Although none of the DP's had been seen there in some time, few, if any, Germans were willing to take a chance. And besides, there was the sign.

Once or twice a day, at irregular intervals a U.S. Army jeep with a captain at its wheel could be seen driving slowly up to the castle and disappearing, sometimes for long intervals, behind its crumbling walls. The Germans who noticed the Captain and his irregular appearances approved of both as sound strategy. With luck, he might catch a Pole or two.

About the only thing that distinguished the castle as a castle, and not as just another bombed-out ruin, was the determinedly Gothic tower at its north end. It was nearly four stories high, with crenelated walls and an imposing enough turret that was only half destroyed. Much of the castle's outer walls also remained standing, although there was no longer anything left for them to protect or shield.

Had the neighboring Germans been disobedient enough to ignore the warning sign, or brave enough to risk an encounter with a Polish or Latvian desperado, they might have been surprised at the new, solid-looking wooden door that led down to the area underneath the north tower which possibly, years ago, might have been a dungeon.

And the neighboring Germans would have been more surprised had they been able to watch the American Captain use his keys on the two stout padlocks that helped chain the door shut and then follow him down the old stone steps into that dank, cavernous space which was a dungeon no longer. Now, it was apparently a warehouse for all those hard-to-come-by American items which kept the black market flourishing.

There were cigarettes, for instance. One entire wall

78

was stacked high with cases of them—not cartons, but cases. Stacked against another wall were jerry cans of gasoline—the pink, American kind which, if found in the possession of a German, automatically meant a long jail sentence. Food was stacked against a third wall. There were ten-in-one Army rations mostly, but there were also sacks of U.S. Army flour and ten or twelve cases—again not cartons, but cases—of candy bars. About half of them were Baby Ruths. The rest were a mixed lot of Hershey Bars, Oh Henrys, Mars Bars, and Powerhouses.

Against the remaining wall was where the light came from. It was a gasoline lantern that rested on an upended regulation Army footlocker. Next to the footlocker was an Army cot neatly made up. Two more lockers formed an L at the foot of the cot. On one of them was a small, two-burner gasoline stove. Not far from the footlockers was a crudely rigged pole that held six U.S. Army dress uniforms. On two of the uniforms were a captain's double bars. Two more bore the single silver bars of a first lieutenant. The remaining two uniforms boasted the gold oak leaves of a major.

After securely locking from the inside the door that led to the underground room, the man in the captain's uniform used a flashlight to guide himself down the stone steps. He lit the gasoline lantern first and then carefully hung up his tunic and placed his overseas cap on a peg. He seemed to be very neat.

He lit the small gasoline stove next, opened one of the footlockers, took out a tin of tea and some sugar and an aluminum pan. He poured water from a jerry can into the pan and placed it on the stove. He next removed a teapot and a cup and saucer from the footlocker, handling them carefully because all were Meissen. After the water was boiling he put a small handful of tea into the pot, poured in the water, lit a cigarette, and then lay down on the cot. With one arm behind his head, he smoked and stared up at the ceiling and waited for the tea to steep.

When the tea was ready, he slowly drank two cups and smoked four more cigarettes. After that, he glanced at his gold Longines wristwatch. It was 3:30—almost time to go. He rose and crossed the room to yet another footlocker which rested next to the cans of gasoline. This one was locked. He removed the padlock and opened the lid. Inside were two .45 Thompson submachine guns, three .45 automatics, and two M-1 carbines. There were also an S.&W. .38-caliber pistol and a Walther PPK automatic. He selected the Walther and shoved it into his right hip pocket.

After securing the padlock, he put the tunic with the captain's bars back on and selected a garrison cap. There were five gold overseas bars on his left sleeve, each indicating six months' service outside the continental limits of the United States. On his right breast he wore a Combat Infantryman's Badge and ribbons indicating that he had served in three battles in the European Theater and had been wounded once.

He inspected the room carefully to make sure that nothing was out of place. His eyes were a greenish blue, and they seemed to miss nothing. They looked out from a narrow face with a straight nose and thin lips that could have been either dubious or cruel or perhaps both. He was almost exactly six feet tall and slim, and his hair was that curious mixture which lies somewhere between brown and blond. It was cut short, and somewhere he had picked up a nice tan.

For the second time he checked to make sure that the gasoline stove was off. He then turned off the lamp, switched on his flashlight, patted his right hip pocket to check that the Walther was in place, and headed up the stone steps to where the jeep was parked just outside the thick wooden door.

The man who sold identities called himself Karl-Heinz Damm and, because of several judicious bribes to certain authorities, was permitted to live alone in a pleasant two-story house not six blocks from the high steel fence that the Americans had erected around the I. G. Farben complex in Frankfurt. For some reason, known only to themselves, the Americans had ignored Damm's largely undamaged neighborhood when they were requisitioning housing. Instead, they had laid claim to the rather unpleasant and definitely lower-class area that immediately surrounded the Farben complex. Damm sometimes thought that the Americans felt more comfortable there.

Damm had acquired his house in late 1945, several months after his release from Dachau, where he had spent three awful years. An engraver by trade, he had wound up in Dachau after being convicted in 1942 of counterfeiting food-ration stamps. Because of his technical skills, the camp authorities had placed him in their administrative section—a job that gave him access to the camp records. By the time the Americans arrived at Dachau he had transformed himself into Karl-Heinz Damm, a minor trade-union official with a long record of opposition to the Nazi regime. The Americans had almost immediately offered him a job, which he had declined with thanks, giving as his excuse the grave heart condition—fully documented, of course—that he had developed as a result of the rigors of the camp.

He left Bavaria and headed almost immediately for Frankfurt, carrying with him only the carefully culled records of 100 former inmates of the camp; all of them dead, but with their deaths unrecorded; all of them political opponents to one degree or another of the former regime; all of them from the eastern reaches of Germany where the Russians were; and all of them, of course, Aryan by birth. And that was how Damm had acquired his house. He had traded its former owner, a minor and yet-undetected war criminal, a new identity for it. Word had got around—quietly, of course; very quietly—and now Damm was doing an extremely profitable, but extremely

81

discreet business. He also dabbled a bit in the black market. Cigarettes mostly.

Damm was one of the few Germans in 1946 who had to watch their weight. With his newly found prosperity, he had made the mistake of gorging himself on a diet that some days had gone as high as 6,000 calories. Now he was on a self-imposed diet of 1,000 calories a day, which was just enough to keep an idle man alive and allow an active man to starve slowly. It was also just 48 calories less than the official ration in the British Zone.

At forty-three, Damm was a sleek-looking man of average height, carrying perhaps twenty-five too many pounds, which were now draped in an English tweed suit that he had acquired from a once-wealthy client, a former resident of Hamburg, whom the British were especially anxious to get their hands on. The client was now enjoying his new identity and living quietly near Saarbrücken, in the French Zone.

Damm looked at his watch, saw that it was nearly 5, and set out some glasses, water, and a bottle of Johnnie Walker Scotch. Because of his diet he permitted himself only one drink a day, and the Scotch was mostly to impress his new business associate, the American Captain who called himself Bill Schmidt. Damm didn't for one second believe that that was the Captain's real name, but the Schmidt served to explain why the American spoke such fluent German. Schmidt's German had an American accent, but it was detectable only to a good ear, which Damm prided himself on having.

At a minute or two after 5, Damm heard the jeep drive up. He looked out the window and watched Captain Bill Schmidt lift its hood and remove the distributor cap. Damm was mildly displeased to discover that the Captain thought that his jeep might be stolen in Damm's neighborhood.

When the Captain came in, they shook hands and the Captain said in German, "How goes it, K.H.?" Damm had long since resigned himself to being called by his forenames' initials, which he assumed was one of those weird American customs.

"Very well, Captain, and you?" Although less than an hour after they had first met, the Captain had started addressing Damm with the familiar *du*, Damm still clung to the formal mode of address. The Captain didn't seem to notice.

Captain Schmidt took off his hat and sailed it onto a couch. He then spied the Johnnie Walker and said, "My God, Scotch."

Damm smiled, quite pleased. "I have my several sources," he said, not seeing much use in being modest.

Damm moved over to the bottle and mixed two drinks, handing one to Schmidt. After they had toasted each other, Schmidt sprawled into an easy chair, stuck his long legs out in front of him, and said, "What have you got for me, K.H.? What have you got that's worth twelve cases of cigarettes?"

Damm waved an admonishing forefinger. "No more Kools, though, Captain. I had a very difficult time disposing of that last case. People think they are being cheated when you trade them Kools."

Schmidt shrugged. "They're not supposed to smoke them. They're currency. Smoking one is like smoking a dollar bill. Who cares what they taste like?"

"Nevertheless, no more Kools."

"All right. No more Kools. Now what have you got?"

Damm raised his eyebrows. It gave him an arch look. "Diamonds?" he said. "What would you say to diamonds?"

"I'd say that I'd have to see them first."

Damm reached into the pocket of his tweed suit and brought out a small drawstring bag made of leather. He handed it to Schmidt. The Captain put his drink down on a table and dumped the bag's contents into the palm of his hand. There were twenty-four cut diamonds, none less than a carat in size.

While Schmidt inspected each diamond carefully, Damm picked up the Captain's drink and slid a small porcelain tray under it.

"How much are you really asking, K.H.?" Schmidt said, dumping the diamonds back into the bag. Damm watched carefully to make sure that none was palmed.

"Twenty-four cases."

"You're crazy."

Damm shrugged. "I must have them."

"You know how many cigarettes there are in one case?"

"Sixty cartons to a case, two hundred cigarettes to a carton. Twelve thousand cigarettes."

"At a dollar a cigarette."

"That's retail. You and I, my dear Captain, are wholesalers."

"I'll give you ten cases."

"Twenty."

"My last offer is thirteen cases."

"And mine is seventeen," Damm said.

"All right. Fifteen."

"All Camels."

"Half Camels," the Captain said. "Half Luckies."

"Done."

"That's a hell of a bargain you just made, K.H."

"And you, my friend, have not done badly either. Currency is no longer of any use to you. You can't send it home anymore. But diamonds. Well, diamonds are probably the most portable form of wealth. You can conceal a fortune of them in a packet of cigarettes. What else could be more valuable?"

Schmidt leaned forward in his chair. In his left hand he held the bag of diamonds. He tossed them up a few inches and caught them as his right hand moved slowly back to his hip pocket.

"Well, one thing I could think of, K.H., would be a new identity."

Damm grew very still. For a few moments he didn't

breathe. He felt suddenly cold, and then the flush started. He could feel it spreading over his face. He knew the American could see it. There was a harsh sound, and he realized with some surprise that it had come from him. It had been a sigh—a long, sad, bitter one. Damm forced his mind to work. It was a quick mind, a facile one. He had used it often enough before to extricate himself from more difficult positions than this. This was nothing. He made himself smile, although he knew the smile must look ghastly.

"But not for yourself, of course."

"No, of course not," Schmidt said. "I'm quite content with being who I am."

He doesn't talk the same, Damm thought. There's no more American accent, none at all. He licked his lips. "For a friend, then?" he said. "Perhaps a relative?"

The Captain took the Walther out and pointed it at Damm. "I want the records. All of them."

"We could share, of course," Damm said quickly. "There is enough for all, and besides, I've been thinking of taking in a partner. An American partner would be perfect."

"You don't understand."

"No?"

"I want the records that you keep yourself. I want the real names and current addresses of those to whom you've furnished new identities. And their new names too, of course."

The first thing Damm thought was blackmail. It wouldn't be the first time it had occurred to him, but until now he had been content to wait until his prospective victims could attain a level of prosperity that would make it worthwhile. But perhaps the American was right. Perhaps the time for blackmail had already arrived.

"It would be perfect," he said, speaking rapidly. "I furnish the records and you make the approach. It could be quite profitable."

"I want the records now," Schmidt said. "All of them."

85

He waved the gun—a careless yet curiously threatening motion.

"Yes, of course," Damm said and rose slowly. "I keep them in the safe in the bedroom."

Schmidt watched while the kneeling man opened the small safe. Damm took out a ledgerlike book and started to close the safe. "Leave it open," Schmidt said.

"Yes, yes, I'll leave it open."

Damm handed Schmidt the ledger. They returned to the living room, where the Captain used the pistol to wave Damm into a chair. Damm watched as Schmidt went through the ledger. Schmidt looked up once and smiled. "You keep excellent records."

"I think you'll find everything in order."

"Very thorough," Schmidt said, and placed the ledger on the table by his drink.

He stared at Damm for a moment and said, "I'm not an American. You must have realized that by now."

Damm nodded vigorously. "Your accent—you don't have it anymore. I have a good ear for accents. Very good."

"My name," the Captain said, "is Kurt Oppenheimer."

"I'm very pleased to meet you," Damm said, and felt foolish.

"I'm a German and also a Jew. A German Jew. At one time I was a Communist, although I no longer think that I am."

"Look, we can still do business."

"I simply thought you would like to know," Kurt Oppenheimer said, and shot Damm twice in the heart. The force of the bullets slammed Damm deep into his chair. He felt the pain and the shock, but neither kept his mind from working. The problem now was how to get himself out of this mess. He was still working on it forty-five seconds later when he died.

Kurt Oppenheimer put the Walther back into his hip pocket. He picked up the leather sack of diamonds, hesitated a moment, then shrugged and stuffed them into another pocket. He opened the ledger and counted the names of those to whom Karl-Heinz Damm had sold new identities. There were thirty-two names. He tore half of them out of the ledger, folded them, and put them into a pocket. He would take care of these himself. The other half he would leave for the Americans, who might get around to them and, then again, might not.

He looked around the room, inspecting it quickly but carefully with his blue-green eyes which missed nothing. There were fingerprints on his glass, but the Americans were welcome to them. He moved over to the body of Damm and felt his pulse. My German thoroughness, he thought, and then quickly went out the front door, got into the jeep, and drove off.

Ten minutes later, he was standing at the bar of the American officers' club in the I. G. Farben complex.

"How's it going, Captain?" the Sergeant said as he served him his usual Scotch and water.

"Not bad, Sammy," Kurt Oppenheimer said. "How's it with you?"

9 Major Gilbert Baker-Bates had been back in Germany for nearly a week when Damm was killed. He had been in Hamburg, attending to some routine chores, when an American Counter-Intelligence Corps courier brought news of Damm's murder along with a typed list of five names and addresses.

The CIC courier was a twenty-six-year-old U.S. Army lieutenant named LaFollette Meyer who was from Milwaukee and who was in no hurry to get back there. Meyer liked his work and he liked Germany, especially its women. He watched as Major Baker-Bates read the list of names and addresses.

"It gets a little more interesting, sir, when you match them up with these," he said, and handed Baker-Bates another list, which contained the real names of five minor war criminals who were living in the British Zone.

"Well, now," Baker-Bates said. "This chap Damm, he was in the business of selling new identities?"

"Yes, sir."

"How many had he sold?"

"That's hard to say, sir. In his safe he had sixty-eight new ID's all ready to go. Then there was that ledger we found. It contained sixteen names, and about that many seemed to have been ripped out by whoever killed him."

"Whoever?"

"Well, we're not positive, sir. Not one hundred percent."

"But you're fairly sure?"

Lieutenant Meyer nodded.

Baker-Bates tapped the lists. "You've given this to the right people here at HQ?"

"Yes, sir, but we also thought that you should have a copy."

"Because of my interest in him."

"Yes, sir."

Baker-Bates read the list again. "Five living in our zone, I see. How many in yours?"

"Seven in ours and four in the French."

"Have you already collected yours?"

"Last night. We got six of them. The seventh—the one in Stuttgart—killed himself and his wife just as we were going in."

"How?"

"Well, we made the mistake of knocking first—"

"I mean how did he kill himself?"

"Oh. With a knife. He cut his throat. His wife's too. They say it was a mess."

Baker-Bates brought out a package of Lucky Strikes and offered them to Meyer, who took one. Each lighted his own cigarette. When they were going, Baker-Bates said, "How was he killed? Damm."

"Shot. Twice."

"Who heard it?"

"Nobody."

Baker-Bates's eyebrows went up. The Lieutenant noticed that there were traces of gray in them. "Nobody?"

"Well, sir, that's something else that's not quite kosher. This guy Damm lived all by himself in an eight-room house almost within spitting distance of us at the Farben building. Now, you know as well as I do that nobody in Germany's got an eight-room house all to themselves, not unless they've got the fix in somewhere, which is something else that we've got our people looking into. We don't think his name was Damm, either. He came out of Dachau clean as a whistle, but we figure that's where he probably fixed himself up with a new ID. We're checking on it."

"Where did Damm work—or did he?"

"He didn't," Meyer said. "He was in the black market, apparently in a pretty big way. He had a cellar full of stuff—cigarettes, coffee; he even had three cases of Johnnie Walker Scotch, and you know how hard that is to get. So at first we figured that's why he got killed, because of some kind of black-market deal that went sour. We figured that until we found that list of names, and then we started figuring something else."

"You say nobody heard anything?"

"No, sir."

"Did they see anything?"

"Maybe."

"Maybe?"

"Well, there's this one old woman, but her eyes aren't too good. She said she saw an American soldier go into Damm's house about seventeen hundred hours and come out about seventeen-thirty. He was driving a jeep."

"What kind of soldier—could she tell?"

"No, sir. Like I said, her eyes weren't too good, but she thought he was about six feet tall and kind of blond. That would fit, wouldn't it?"

"That would fit."

"Does he speak English?"

"Oppenheimer?"

"Yes, sir."

"Yes, he speaks English, Lieutenant. Perfect English."

"Then that would be a pretty good disguise, wouldn't it?"

Baker-Bates sighed. "Like his English, it would be perfect. How many names do you think he got?"

"Well, sir, there were sixteen left, like I said, and he seemed to've torn out half the pages that had names on 'em, so we figure that's about what he's got. Sixteen."

"And he'll start going for them one by one," Baker-Bates said, and ground his cigarette out in a cheap tin tray.

"You think he's crazy, sir—Oppenheimer?"

"Possibly. Why do you ask?"

"Well, he's doing pretty much what he did during the war. He aced out some pretty rotten ones then, from what I hear. Now he seems to be going back and picking off the ones that we missed or can't find. Well, hell, sir, I know that's not right, but I don't think it makes him crazy. I think he's just sort of—well, dedicated."

"Dedicated."

"Yes, sir."

"And you're thinking that maybe we ought to let this—uh—dedication run its course."

Meyer shook his head. "No, sir, I don't guess I really think that."

"But you wouldn't be too upset if he were to—as you say—ace out a few more? I mean some really rotten ones."

"Well, hell, Major—"

Baker-Bates interrupted with another question. "You are, I believe, Lieutenant, of the Jewish faith."

"I'm a Jew," said Meyer, the atheist.

"Are you a Zionist?"

"I'm not sure."

"But you know what's going on in Palestine."

"Yes, sir. You're determined to keep the hundred thou-

91

sand Jews that're still left in the DP camps from reaching Palestine, where you promised them they could go."

"I thought you said you weren't a Zionist. That's the Zionist line if I ever heard it."

"Yes, sir, but it's also fact."

"Well, we don't want Oppenheimer in Palestine, Lieutenant, and that's why we're going to find him. We don't want him there."

"No, sir," Lieutenant Meyer said. "I bet you don't.

Every day on his way home from work, Otto Bodden, the printer, would check the letter drop near the ruined Petrikirche in Lübeck. There had been nothing in it until now, the day after Damm's death. When he reached home and the privacy of his small room, Bodden opened the envelope, which looked as if it had already been used several times. Inside was a flimsy sheet of paper with a block of numbers written on it in pencil. Bodden sighed and began the tedious chore of decoding them. When he was done, the message read: Proceed Frankfurt. Karl-Heinz Damm killed. Shot twice. U.S. Army uniform, possibly junior officer.

Bodden memorized Damm's name, then filled his pipe with the suspect tobacco that he'd bought on the black market and used the same match to light his pipe and burn the flimsy paper. The Russian was quick, Bodden thought; that much had to be said for him. The man, what was his name—Damm—was killed in Frankfurt only yesterday. The information had to be gathered and then transmitted to Berlin, and from there it had to be re-directed to Lübeck. Very quick, very efficient.

He puffed on his pipe and thought about what he must do. There was his job at the *Lübecker Post*. Well, that was no problem. He simply would not show up. They would check, of course, with his landlady, Frau Schoet-tle. Tonight he would see her and tell her that he was leaving, that an emergency had come up and that he was returning to Berlin. He would present her with a small gift, perhaps a hundred grams or so of fat. He still had plenty of razor blades left. That had been intelligent of them, to supply him with razor blades. As a form of currency, they were almost as good as cigarettes. He wondered which of his black-market contacts he should see about the fat. Probably the tall, skinny Estonian. He seemed to be the most resourceful. The Estonian might even be able to come up with a little butter instead of lard. She would like that. He would take her to bed first, tell her he had to go back to Berlin, and then give her the butter. He would also give her his ration books. They would be no good to him in the American Zone.

Bodden enjoyed dickering with the tall, skinny Estonian. After ten minutes of it, during which time the Estonian had stretched his rubber face into expressions that ranged from grief to elation, they had struck the bargain. In exchange for five brand-new American-made Gillette razor blades, Bodden received a fourth of a kilogram of real butter plus one packet of Senior Service cigarettes. The Estonian had moaned and sworn that he was being robbed, but then his face had stretched into a wide, merry grin. Before the war the Estonian had been a lawyer, and he was, by nature, Bodden had decided, a very cheerful fellow. "This is my courtroom now," he had once told Bodden, waving an arm grandly at the narrow black-market alley. "Do you enjoy my histrionics?"

"Very much," Bodden had said.

Frau Eva Schoettle, landlady of the six-room, largely undamaged house where Bodden roomed, was a thirty-three-year-old widow whose husband had been either killed or captured at Stalingrad. Either way he was now of no use to her and her two children, and so she took in roomers, who paid their rent in potatoes or bread or eggs or vegetables or anything else that could be eaten.

Frau Schoettle had twin dreads, one of them being that a British officer would suddenly appear at her door and requisition the house. The other was that her either dead or missing husband might someday return. She had never really liked Armin Schoettle, a big, coarse, loud, humorless man who, before the war, had been a contractor. Although he had built the house and had been reasonably good to their ten-year-old son and nine-year-old daughter, he had been a dull, indifferent lover with questionable personal habits. She had not seen him in four years now, or heard from him in three, and her memory of him had grown dim, almost nebulous. Her one vivid recollection of him was his underwear. She remembered that because he had never changed it more than twice a month. And his smell. She remembered that, too.

By contrast, the printer was a skilled, inventive, even laughing lover with neat habits, and she had gone to bed with him three days after he had moved into the small back room on the third floor, the room that was almost a wardrobe. She lay beside Bodden now on the narrow bed, smoking one of his British cigarettes and thinking about what he had just told her—about his going back to Berlin the next day. She realized that she would miss him. She would miss his lovemaking, of course, but that wasn't all. She would also miss those wry little jokes that he was always making. The printer was sometimes a very funny fellow. But then, a lot of Berliners were.

She turned to him and smiled and said, "I'm going to miss you, printer."

"Will you miss me or the eggs I bring you?"

"Both."

"What else will you miss?"

"This," she said, and reached for him. "I'll miss this."

"Ah, that," he said, and reached for her cigarette. He put it out carefully in a tray. "Well, that particular item you may borrow one more time, provided, of course, that you return it in reasonably good shape."

"Reasonably?"

"Reasonably."

As he made love to her for the second time that evening, she thought fleetingly of what she would have to do next. She would have to leave him and dress and then walk three kilometers to where the British Captain was billeted. For only a moment she thought of not telling the Captain, the one who was called Richards and who always smoked a pipe. She would let the printer go his way. What business was it of theirs? But no. She would tell them. If the printer left and she didn't tell them, they would take away her house. Too bad, printer, she thought, and clutched him tightly to her.

It was raining the next morning at 6:42 when Bodden boarded the crowded train to Hamburg. It was a cold, hard rain, and Bodden had been caught in it as he had walked from his rooming house to the Bahnhof. But then, so had the other fellow, he thought with a grin, the one who had fallen in behind him just as he had slipped out of Frau Schoettle's house.

The other fellow was a medium-sized, youngish man with yellow hair that flopped down over his eyes despite the cap that he wore. He looked well fed, or reasonably so, and Bodden wondered whether he was German or English. The man with the yellow hair now stood a few meters away in the packed aisle of the train. For a few moments Bodden toyed with the idea of approaching the man and trying out some of his English that the Pole had taught him in the camp. Something like "A nice day for ducks," which, the Pole had assured him, both Americans and British said all the time. But then, so did Germans.

No, Bodden decided, with just a tinge of regret, he would ignore him—at least until Hamburg. In Hamburg he would lose the fellow with the yellow hair. He had better lose him, because *es geht um die Wurst*. The sausage depends on it. He wondered if the Americans said that too, but decided that they probably didn't.

In the large country house that was located fifteen kilometers north and west of Lübeck, Colonel Whitlock stood at the French doors of the former sitting room that was now his office and stared out at the man and the woman working in the rain.

The man and the woman were in their sixties, and they were digging in a garden that had once been a smooth expanse of carefully rolled green lawn. The lawn was now planted to potatoes. The woman and man who were digging them up were the owners of the large country house. Their name was Von Alvens, and they once had been extremely rich. Now they were extremely poor, as was virtually everyone else in Germany, and they bartered the potatoes that they didn't eat for lard or eggs or a very rare chicken. They had had four sons, all of whom had been killed in the war. The Von Alvens still lived in the big house, but in a single room in the rear that once had been occupied by a servant.

Colonel Whitlock glanced at his watch and thought, Goddamn the man. This was their third meeting in two days, and each time the Colonel had been kept waiting, sometimes for as much as fifteen minutes. The Colonel was a stickler for punctuality. It was, in fact, almost a fetish with him, and he felt his irritation grow as he stood at the French doors and stared out at the old couple digging in the rain.

But it wasn't just the man's habitual tardiness that infuriated him. Everything about Baker-Bates was wrong, Colonel Whitlock felt. Wrong accent, wrong clothes, wrong school, and yes, damn it, wrong class. He knew about Baker-Bates's record during the war and had to admit that it was good, perhaps even brilliant in spots. But lots of chaps had had brilliant records—even chaps like Baker-Bates who didn't really quite fit. But when the war was over, they'd had the good sense to say Thank you very much and go back to where they belonged.

Colonel Whitlock wondered what it really was about Baker-Bates that grated so much. Was it the man's condescension, which almost bordered on mute insolence? Or was it his quick and restless mind, which flitted about hither and yon, racing on ahead of its rivals and then waiting impatiently for them to catch up, the boredom plainly evident on its owner's face?

The fellow's clever, no doubt about it, the Colonel admitted, and because he prided himself on being a realist and, at any rate, put no real premium on cleverness, he went on to admit that Baker-Bates probably was cleverer than he himself. But that didn't account for it—not for the fellow's rapid, almost spectacular rise in the secret-intelligence business. Not in rank, to be sure, although they'd probably jump him to colonel before long. That was in the wind. You could almost smell it. The fellow almost swung that much power now as a mere major. Might as well give him the rank to go with it. It was Baker-Bates's wife, of course. An ugly little woman. The Colonel had seen pictures of her in the British press. Not because she was Mrs. Gilbert Baker-Bates, though. Scarcely that. But because she was a minister's daughter. Married her during the war. Nobody had thought then that the Socialists would win. Probably one himself, Colonel Whitlock concluded with grim satisfaction.

The telephone on his desk rang. It was Sergeant Lewis.

"Major Baker-Bates is here, sir."

"Well, send him in; send him in," the Colonel said grumpily.

"Good morning, sir," Baker-Bates said as he came in and took a chair before the Colonel's desk.

"You're late."

Baker-Bates shrugged. "Sorry. The rain, you know."

"Well, he left this morning, just as that woman said he would."

97

"But not for Berlin."

"No. He caught the Hamburg train. We put that chap of yours onto him."

"Bodden'll lose him," Baker-Bates said. "Probably in Hamburg."

To hide his irritation, the Colonel lit a cigarette, his tenth of the morning. The man's insufferable, he thought; then he blew some smoke out and said, "What makes you so sure?"

"That Bodden'll lose him?"

"Mmm."

"He has to."

"You feel he's that good?"

"Our Russian friends wouldn't have sent him unless he were."

"Well, he hasn't had all that much experience, has he? As I recall, he spent four years in a camp. Belsen, wasn't it?"

"You can learn a lot in a camp. He did. They picked them out in the camps, you know, the ones that they would use later. They got the cushy jobs. From what I've been able to find out, he was one of the star pupils. After he got out, they sent him back to Moscow. They had a year to train him there. More than a year."

"After Hamburg. You think he'll head for Frankfurt after Hamburg?"

"I'm certain of it."

"You'll be on hand there, of course."

"Yes."

"And you still think he might lead you to him—to this Oppenheimer person?"

"He might."

"What about the Americans?"

"What about them . . . sir?"

The sir had been tacked on at the end, almost thoughtlessly, and it irritated the Colonel. He mashed his half-smoked cigarette out in the tray, doing it carefully, taking his time, trying to keep his anger from becoming obvious.

"What about them?" he snapped in spite of himself.

"Well, they just might feel that you were poaching."

Baker-Bates shrugged. "If their feathers get ruffled, I think I know how to smooth them down. I've dealt with them often enough before, you know."

The man's insufferable, the Colonel thought for perhaps the fifth time that morning. But he kept his tone low and casual, almost indifferent. "To be sure. But what if this chap Bodden doesn't lead to Oppenheimer? What then?"

"Then we might have to turn to someone else who's waiting in the wings."

"Who?"

Baker-Bates smiled for the first time that morning. It was his usual gray smile, and it made its appearance in anticipation of the Colonel's reaction. "Well, sir, we might have to use the dwarf."

"*Dwarf?*" the Colonel said, spluttering the word in spite of his resolve not to. "Did you say a dwarf?"

"Yes, sir," Baker-Bates said, still smiling, "the dwarf."

10

Robert Henry Orr, the man whom the OSS had called Nanny, seldom got out to the Pentagon because he didn't like the smell of burning ambition, which, he had decided long ago, had an odor all its own.

Ambition, he thought, reeked of sweat; not the jockstrap kind, or that which came from honest toil, but the sweetish-sour kind that is the product of fear, bad nerves, poor digestion, and too much Mum. Orr prided himself on his sensitive nose, and he was sure he could detect a strong trace of ambition's pungent smell in the office of the man whom he was now waiting to see.

The office was in either the second or the third ring of the Pentagon. Orr wasn't sure because, despite his many other qualities, he had absolutely no sense of direction.

North, south, east, and west remained complete mysteries to him. He knew left from right, but because he was almost ambidextrous, he always had to pause and think about it. He had, of course, become lost in the Pentagon. He always did. Pride, however, had kept him from asking directions, and he had wandered aimlessly about, sniffing the ambition, until luck had guided him to where he wished to go.

Orr was waiting for Milo Stracey, who, Orr felt, was the coldest man he had ever known. Stracey came from somewhere in Idaho, up near the Canadian line, and Orr was almost sure that he had been machined, not born. There were no rough edges on Stracey, none, and Orr was convinced that there never had been.

"If you opened him up," somebody had once said to Orr, "you know what you'd find? Dry ice, that's what."

Stracey's qualities had been quickly sized up by the man who had run the OSS, Wild Bill Donovan, nicknamed by his World War I troops after some obscure baseball player. Donovan had been about as wild as a bridge shark with the rent due. He also had had the coldest blue eyes that Orr had ever seen until the day he met Milo Stracey. Stracey's were colder, far colder. And it was because of Stracey's well-iced emotions that Donovan had put him in charge of the Swill.

The Swill had been those occasional OSS missions doomed to failure, but nevertheless dispatched because their failure was part and parcel of some desperate ploy dreamed up by the dreamers in the building at 25th and E, Northwest. Milo Stracey had been the dispatcher; obviously enjoyed his assignment, if ever he enjoyed anything; and consequently had risen quickly in the OSS power structure. He had been much feared, much hated, much avoided, and totally despised by all but Congress, who regarded him as a take-charge, no-nonsense kind of guy who, if but given half a chance, could have straightened out all those OSS pinkos that Donovan had assembled.

Stracey strode into his office, glanced at Orr, sat down at his desk, and by way of greeting, said, "What do you want?"

Orr smiled his most benign smile. "I had a little cold, but I'm almost over it now, thank you." He took Minor Jackson's passport out of his breast pocket and tossed it onto Stracey's desk. "Remember him?"

Stracey opened the passport, glanced at it, and said, "Yeah, I remember. Why?"

Orr laced his hands across his belly, tipped his chair back, and stared up at the ceiling. "I hear you've run into a snag up on the Hill."

A bill was wending its way through Congress, which, if everything went just right, would create the first national intelligence-gathering organization. Recognizing Stracey's popularity with Congress, the War Department, with no little apprehension, had made him one of its chief lobbyists to make sure that the military didn't get left out when Congress finally got around to dividing up the intelligence pie. The quid pro quo had been succinctly spelled out to Stracey by a four-star general. "You get us our piece," the General had said, "and we'll take care of you. Maybe the number five or number six spot in the new outfit."

Stracey's reply had been equally succinct. "Number five, and I want it in writing." The General, after failing to stare Stracey down, had agreed.

To Orr's observation Stracey replied, "Snag? I don't know of any snag."

"No?"

"No."

"By my troth, Milo, you really are the most obdurate person I've ever known."

"You mean thick."

"No, not thick, although that will do."

"Okay. We've got a little problem up on the Hill. But nothing that's going to make us shit our pants. What's that got to do with him?" Again he tapped Minor Jackson's passport.

"I'm not sure, really. He wants to go to Germany."

"Let him."

"He was in Mexico recently. Guess whom he ran into down there?"

"I never guess."

"No, you don't, do you? Well, he ran into Baker-Bates. You were never very keen on him, as I recall, but what ever would Baker-Bates be doing strayed so far from home?"

A mask descended over the mask that was Milo Stracey's face. His blue eyes seemed to Orr to grow a shade lighter, which made them almost the shade of ice when the light was just right. He had a curiously colorless face —not gray, not pink, but sort of a strangely smudged white. It went with his hair, which was neither gray nor blond but gray trying to be blond, or blond trying to be gray. Orr wasn't sure. Although he knew that Stracey's age was forty, he didn't look it. Nor did he look fifty or thirty, although he could have passed for either. The monochrome man, Orr thought, and became fascinated with how little the lips that formed the line that was Stracey's mouth moved when they said, "Where in Mexico?"

"Oh, no. Oh, my, no. I never, never give anything away. Of all people, Milo, you should know that by now."

"Okay, if there's anything to it, you're in."

"All the way, of course."

Stracey stared at Orr. It was a stare that could shrivel most men, but Orr returned it with the smiling certitude of the Christian holding four aces whom Mark Twain had once observed.

"Sure, Nanny," Stracey finally said. "All the way."

"Good. Baker-Bates was in Ensenada. Now, what tinkly bell does that ring?"

"When?"

103

"Two weeks ago. About that."

Stracey picked up Minor Jackson's passport, looked inside it again, put it back down on the desk, and said, "The Oppenheimers."

"Oh, my."

Stracey tapped Jackson's passport once more with a shining fingernail, and Orr realized for the first time, with a small, pleasant shock, that the fingernail had been manicured. He filed the information away for future possible use. Still tapping Jackson's passport, Stracey said, "He's not that good; he never was."

"I always thought he was rather good—in a charming, lackadaisical way, of course."

"Not up against Kurt Oppenheimer."

"Perhaps he only wants to find him. Perhaps the father and the sister will pay him a little money to do only that."

"He's not that good either."

"He'll have some help, I believe."

"Who?"

Now it's going to become truly delicious, Orr thought. Now he'll crack, maybe even breathe in and out once or twice. "Who? Why, the dwarf, of course. You remember the dwarf. You should."

"Ploscaru," Stracey said, and something might have twitched in his face up near the right eye—or was it the left? Orr had to remember which hand was which before he could be certain. But there was only that one twitch, if that, and afterward the frost came back and covered things up.

"Ploscaru's dead," Stracey said.

"Little Nick? You must be thinking of a different Ploscaru."

"The dwarf. He's dead. He died outside of Prague in July last year. The Russians got him."

"You sent him to Prague, didn't you?"

"I sent him."

"After using him in Bucharest to find that Iron Guard

104

type and the German, the one who did such a wonderful job with the ack-ack at Ploesti. He found them when nobody else could, and as a reward you sent him to Prague. He didn't go, you know. Instead, he kept the money—all that gold, you remember—and got one of his Air Corps buddies to smuggle him back to the States—to New York. He was there for about two months and then went to Los Angeles, of all places."

"You held out on me, Nanny."

"Certainly."

"I'll remember."

"I very much hope so; otherwise, what would be the point? But back to business. Suppose Jackson and the dwarf were able to turn up the Oppenheimer lad. It would be quite a plum for you—or rather, for us; something you could whisper about Congress, make them feel important, in the know, the very kind of stuff they dote on. It would all leak, of course, and the press would run with it. More accolades, thoughtful editorials about how perhaps after all the country really does need a well-run intelligence outfit. We could have all that—unless, of course, we might find some other use for Oppenheimer's rather peculiar talents."

"Such as?"

Orr closed his eyes sleepily, opened them, and stared up at the ceiling. "How many Jewish votes are there in Congress? By that I mean how many hard-core pro-Zionist votes—the kind who devoutly believe every word that Ben Hecht writes?"

Stracey didn't have to pause to add them up. "Thirteen," he said. "Three for us, eight against, and two still up for grabs."

Still staring up at the ceiling, Orr said, "Suppose we found young Oppenheimer, managed to sneak him into Palestine, and then turned him loose to do what he does best."

"Killing people."

"Yes, killing people. The right people—at least, as far as the more fervent Zionists are concerned."

"British types."

"Yes, I suppose they would have to be British, wouldn't they?"

Stracey smiled—a chilling, almost terrible smile. "It could swing a few votes—provided we can figure out a way to claim the credit."

"I'll leave that to you, Milo."

Stracey did some rapid mental calculation. "Those hard-core Zionist votes could just put us in business."

"How nice."

The two men stared at each other for a long moment. Then Stracey again tapped Minor Jackson's passport. "We'll run him—both him and the dwarf."

"He doesn't want to be run."

"Helms is in Germany; we'll put him onto it."

Orr sighed. "Not Helms. Jackson and Helms went to school together in Switzerland—at Rolle, I believe. They despise each other."

"We're going to have to have our man in on it."

"Come up with a nobody," Orr suggested. "A smart nobody, more shepherd than chaperon."

It was an intelligent suggestion, and Stracey accepted it immediately. It was one of the reasons he had come as far as he had. And it was the primary reason that he would go as far as he did. Although Stracey's expression didn't change, Orr was almost positive that he could hear a circular file filled with names ticking over inside the other man's head.

"Okay," Stracey said after a pause. "A smart nobody. One LaFollette Meyer. A lieutenant."

"Dear me," Orr said. "What part of Wisconsin does our LaFollette hail from?"

"Milwaukee, I think," Stracey said. "Why?"

Instead of replying, Orr got up to leave. As he turned, Stracey said, "Nanny."

106

Orr turned back. "Yes."

"This conversation we just had never happened, did it?"

Orr smiled. "What conversation?"

It had taken Ploscaru only thirty-six hours to locate the right Russian, the one who was now gazing, fascinated, at the Rembrandt self-portrait that hung in the Mellon Gallery on Pennsylvania Avenue.

The Argentine had put him onto the Russian; the Argentine who, before the war, had been a playboy until he ran out of money. He had married a distant, titled cousin of Ploscaru's, who had since died. Now the Argentine moved about the world as a cultural attaché at various of his country's embassies. Actually, he was an intelligence agent of sorts and had been in Washington for more than two years and knew everybody. For setting up the contact with the Russian he had charged the dwarf only $250, since Ploscaru was really, after all, some kind of distant relative.

The Russian's name supposedly was Ikar Kokorev; he was a forty-two-year-old asthmatic who wheezed heavily as he stood transfixed before the Rembrandt.

"He had much heart, that one," the Russian said.

"I don't like it," Ploscaru said, looking around.

"You don't like *him*?"

"It's far too public."

"Every day at noon I come and spend my lunch time here. Sometimes I talk to people; sometimes I don't. The federal police are accustomed to my being here. If I should talk to a little man about the master's great heart, why should they object? You and I shall meet only this once."

"I understand you want Kurt Oppenheimer."

The Russian moved slowly to the next Rembrandt, a portrait of a prosperous middle-aged man. "The light," he said. "See how he forms the light. What rare, sad ge-

107

nius. I must go to Amsterdam before I die. I must see *The Night Watch*. I simply must. We have heard of you, M. Ploscaru," he went on in the French that they had been speaking. "We have not liked what we have heard. Most unsavory."

"How much?" Ploscaru said.

"Did I say we were buying? No. But doubtless you have some price in mind. I paint, you know. Slavish imitations, really. My mind tells my hand what to do. That is my mistake. It must come from here," he said, wheezing heavily and thumping himself on the chest. "Not the head."

"One hundred thousand dollars," Ploscaru said as they moved on to the next painting, of a youngish woman with melancholy eyes.

"This one always makes me want to weep. So sad; so very, very sad. Why is she so sad? She is married to an old man, but she has taken a young lover, and now he has gone away forever. I invent these little stories. I find them amusing. Your price is exorbitant, of course."

"It could be negotiated."

"Yes," the Russian said drily. "I would think that it could. What about delivery?"

"What about it?"

"If we were at all interested, which is most doubtful, it would have to be in Berlin or on the edge of the Zone."

Ploscaru shrugged. "Agreed."

"If you are in Frankfurt within the next two weeks, someone may get in touch with you. Then again, they may not."

"Where?"

"Wherever we might decide," the Russian said, took one last look at the portrait of the sad young woman, turned, and moved briskly away.

11 That same afternoon Minor Jackson sold the Plymouth for $1,250 cash to a Negro pimp up on 7th Street, Northwest, who thought he was moving up in the world. Despite the slight chill in the air, the pimp wore a lemon-colored lightweight suit with a cream shirt and a magenta tie. He walked around the car with the half-proud, half-wary air of all used-car purchasers.

The pimp kicked a tire. "Good rubber."

"Yes," Jackson said.

"Runs slick, too."

"It does that."

"Put the top down, be good for business," the pimp said, still selling himself on his new investment.

"I imagine."

"Give you a lift somewheres?"

"No, thanks," Jackson said. "I'll get a cab."

"Catch a streetcar right over there."

"I'll do that, then."

The pimp was anxious to be off so that he could display his new possession. "Well, I'll see you around, then."

"Sure," Jackson said.

After transferring once, Jackson got off the streetcar near the Mayflower Hotel on Connecticut Avenue. He entered its dimly lit bar, blinked his eyes against the gloom, and finally located Robert Henry Orr sitting at a table in a far corner. Jackson went over and sat down.

"Don't you have an office?" he said.

"I have a very nice office."

"Why don't we ever meet there—you ashamed of me?"

"You're not all that sensitive, Minor. No one could be. What do you want to drink?"

"Bourbon."

Orr waved a hand; a waiter materialized, took the order, and went away. Orr removed a thick manila envelope from his pocket and slid it across the table to Jackson. "Here," he said. "You're now a military dependent. We're going to fly you over—free."

Jackson opened the envelope and took out his passport. Inside it was a large purple stamp with a number of impressive-looking signatures affixed. "What's a military dependent?" he said, and put the passport away in a pocket.

"It's something like an Army wife," Orr said. "Actually, it's a brand-new classification that we dreamed up—by we I mean I, of course. You'll be living on the economy, but you'll be entitled to PX privileges. Gasoline too, should you find yourself a car. Housing—well, housing you'll have to provide for yourself. It's quite tight, you know. And we're even providing you with an aide of sorts—one Lieutenant LaFollette Meyer."

"Milwaukee or Madison?" Jackson asked as he took the mimeographed sheets which were the travel orders out of the envelope and examined them.

110

"Milwaukee, I believe, and from what I'm given to understand, a most intelligent young lad."

The drinks came, and after the waiter left, Jackson tapped the travel orders. "This is Pentagon stuff, not State."

"Yes, it is, isn't it?"

Jackson took a swallow of his drink, closed his eyes, and moved his lips silently.

"Praying?"

Jackson shook his head. "I was just running over that list of names you mentioned—the ones who're still left over from the old days. Of all those, the one who was most cozy with the top brass was always Milo Stracey. Mr. Icebox. How is Milo?"

"He sends his regards."

Jackson smiled, but it was a thin smile. "You're trying to run me, aren't you, you and Milo?"

"It should be a very nice trip, Minor. A DC-4, I think, out of New York. Awfully nice ladies, mostly—generals' and colonels' wives, I believe, plus a few male civilian junketeers."

"I won't be run."

"Of course not. We just want your leavings—more or less."

"There may not be any."

"We'll take that chance."

"I'm not promising anything."

"I understand. However, Minor, I feel duty bound to give you one tiny word of advice."

"What?"

"Beware the wicked dwarf, my boy," Orr said, and smiled, but not enough to conceal the seriousness that lay behind his admonition.

"I'll do more than that."

"What?"

"I'll also shun the bandersnatch," Jackson said.

The dwarf and two young women called Dot and Jan

were down at Union Station the next day at noon to see Jackson off for New York. Dot and Jan had put on a rather interesting exhibition for Ploscaru and Jackson the night before in the dwarf's room at the Willard, and as far as they were concerned, the party hadn't stopped. Jackson, who had a slight hangover, wished that they hadn't come and was struggling to be polite.

The dwarf had presented Jackson with a going-away present—a thin, curved, very expensive silver hip flask that contained a pint of bourbon—bonded, the dwarf had assured him. Jackson thanked Ploscaru graciously and then turned to Dot and Jan.

"I wonder if you would excuse us for a moment, ladies," Jackson said, and made himself smile. "Business."

"Sure, Minor," Dot said. She took Jan by the arm and they wandered off, trailing giggles behind them.

When they were out of hearing, Jackson looked down at Ploscaru and said, "You've got Leah Oppenheimer's address—the one where she'll be in Frankfurt."

"Yes."

"We'll meet there."

Ploscaru nodded.

"I won't ask again how you're going to get there."

"No," Ploscaru said. "Don't."

"But I've got a couple of points to make."

"I'm anxious to hear them."

"I'll bet. But point one is: don't lie to me anymore, Nick. Not ever."

Ploscaru sighed. "That will be hard. It's habit, you know. But I'll try. I really shall."

"As I told you last night, they're going to try to run me —and through me, you."

"Yes, I wasn't at all surprised by that."

"So here's my second point. I don't really trust you, Nick."

The dwarf smiled. "How wise."

"So when we get to that time or place, which I'm sure we'll get to, where you think you can make a few extra bucks simply by fucking me up, well, here's some advice. Think twice."

The dwarf, dusting off his hands, and unaware that he was doing so, stared up at Jackson thoughtfully for several moments. "Why, yes, Minor," he said slowly, "now that you mention it, I really think that I shall. Think twice, that is."

That evening around 5 in New York, Jackson called his father from the New Weston Hotel. After the father had expressed surprise about the son's being in New York, he had said, "You say you're leaving tomorrow?"

"Yes."

"Well, I suppose we could have dinner tonight."

"All right."

"The New Weston suitable? The food's not too bad there."

"Fine."

"Shall we say seven?"

"Sure. Seven."

The elder Jackson's name was S. H. P. Jackson III, and he came from a long line of distinguished but generally impoverished New England parsons. The initials stood for Steadfast Honor Preserved, and rather than attend Yale Divinity, as had generations of Jacksons before him, he had gone to Harvard Law, quickly established himself in a dull but lucrative practice, married the first rich woman who would have him, and named his only son Minor after a favorite black-sheep uncle who had sailed out of Boston for Singapore in 1903 and had never been heard from since. Father and son had addressed each other only as "you" for nearly as long as either could remember.

The elder Jackson, like his son, was tall and spare, but in recent years he had acquired a slight stoop, which, along with his also newly acquired rimless glasses, gave him a somewhat fusty, almost professorial air.

What is he now, Jackson wondered, as he shook hands

with the older man: sixty, sixty-two? He was thirty when I was born, so that would make him sixty-two, almost sixty-three.

After being shown to their table, the elder Jackson retired behind his menu, peering over it occasionally to address either comments or questions to his son.

"You're looking well," the older man told his son. "Nicely tanned, I see. California must have agreed with you."

"I spent a lot of time on the beach and bought a convertible."

Over the top of the menu Jackson could see his father's forehead wrinkle into a disapproving frown, but all he said was "Never been there, California. Is it as strange as they say?"

"I suppose."

"Knew someone from Santa Barbara once. Name was Scullard. Pleasant type, but not too sound. Shall we have a drink?"

"Sure."

"They say that in the Army?"

"What?"

"Sure instead of surely. Imprecise way to speak, I should think."

"The Army can make you a little careless."

The waiter came and left, then came again with their drinks. Minor Jackson's was bourbon; his father's, sherry. After taking a sip of his sherry, the elder Jackson said, "Have you heard from her?" Her, of course, was the former Mrs. Jackson, Minor's mother, who would always be simply her or she to the man to whom she had once been married.

"I heard from her once. She was in Rio."

"Married again, you know."

"Yes, so she said."

"I gave her your address."

"Thank you."

"Have you written her?"

"No. Not yet."

"You should, you know."

"Yes."

"A postcard would do."

"Yes."

"In that letter you got from her," the older man said, looking away. "Did she mention me?"

"I don't think she did," Jackson said, and wished that he had lied.

"No, I don't suppose she would've." He sipped his sherry again, put down the menu, and said, "Well, what's all this about your going to Europe? Something for the Government, I take it."

"No, not really."

"I was assuming that you might have found something permanent."

"Not yet."

After that there was a silence until they ordered, and then the elder Jackson talked about the weather and his law practice until the food was served. As he was cutting into his steak, the father, not looking at his son, said, "Have you thought much about settling down, raising a family?"

"Not much."

"What are you now—thirty-two, thirty-three?"

"Almost thirty-three."

"What about diplomacy? You might be cut out for that. You have your languages. If you're interested, I know some people in Washington who might be helpful."

"I don't think so."

"May I ask why?"

Jackson shrugged. "It's dull."

"Dull?"

"Yes."

The father lowered his knife and fork and stared at his son. "Everything's dull. It has to be."

"The war wasn't. It might have been boring at times, but not dull. There's a difference."

"I fail to distinguish it."

115

"Many people couldn't."

The elder Jackson took a bite of his creamed spinach, chewed it carefully, as though worried about his digestion, and said, "That work you did for Bill Donovan's organization; was that useful?"

"Some of it."

"Interesting?"

"At times."

"Perhaps you should have stayed in the Army—made a career of it."

"I stayed in six years and came out a captain. I think that demonstrates a certain lack of ambition or political acumen on my part—probably both."

"Well, I know it's a bit late for me to be playing the role of the wise father, but you're really going to have to decide on something sensible soon."

"Why?"

"*Why?*"

"Yes," Jackson said. "Why?"

The father leaned forward and spoke very carefully and slowly to make sure that he was understood. "Because for a man of your background there is really no alternative."

"There's one."

"Yes? What?"

"I could marry money," Jackson said, but when he saw the flush spread up his father's bony cheeks, he wished that he hadn't.

12 The General's wife didn't like her seat in the DC-4, and so she ordered the steward, a harried Air Corps buck sergeant, to change it for her. A squabble resulted, because the Lieutenant Colonel's wife didn't want to be moved and protested bitterly until the General's wife pulled rank, using a harsh whiskey baritone to pull it with. The Lieutenant Colonel's wife, the lowest-ranking officer's wife aboard the packed plane, turned white at some of the words that the General's wife used, but said nothing and meekly settled into her new seat.

When the squabble started, the plane was nearly an hour out of New York, heading for its first stop at Gander, Newfoundland. The whiskey baritone had awakened the man sleeping in the seat next to Jackson. He was a stocky, red-faced civilian of about forty who had been asleep when Jackson came on board and had even slept through the takeoff. Now he was awake, irritably so, and smacking his lips as though something tasted bad.

"Bitches," he said and looked at Jackson. "I had it all measured out, you know."

"What?"

"The booze. I drank just enough so that I could make it to the plane, sack out, and then not wake up till Gander. Now I got a head and a mouthful of wet sand. You Government?"

"No."

"Good. I'm Bill Swanton, INS. One of Willie Hearst's drudges." Swanton held out his hand, and Jackson shook it.

"Minor Jackson. I've seen your by-line."

"No shit?"

"No shit."

"I didn't think you were Government. With that tan, maybe an actor or a comic that the USO was sending over; but you're not an actor either, are you?"

"I'm sort of a glorified tourist, really," Jackson said, deciding to get the labeling out of the way. "A publisher in New York thought I might write him a book about postwar Germany. I don't know if I can or not. I've never written a book. But he was willing to pay me a little money to find out."

That satisfied Swanton. "There's a hell of a book to be written about it," he said. "You speak German?"

"Yes, I speak it."

"Then you got it made. Ninety-nine percent of the dopes they send over here don't speak a word."

"Where're you assigned now?" Jackson said. "Berlin?"

"Yeah, that's where the news is, because that's where they run it from, although God knows why. Berlin's a mess. But so's the whole fucking country."

"So I hear."

Swanton produced a cigarette and then made a face after he had lit it. "Jesus, that tastes awful. I'd give my left you-know-what for a drink."

The last thing that Jackson had done in New York was to buy a topcoat at Tripler's. It was a warm, fleecy lamb's-wool coat with small houndstooth checks and raglan sleeves and big, deep pockets. Because the plane was chilly, he was still wearing it. He reached into one of its pockets and brought out the flask that Ploscaru had given him.

"Here," he said. "Try this."

The smile that appeared on Swanton's face was one of pure gratitude. "By God, Brother Jackson," he said, accepting the flask, "they'll canonize you for this."

Swanton took a long drink and sighed. "That's better," he said after a moment. "Much better."

"Have another."

"No, that's enough for now."

"We'll keep it handy, then," Jackson said, took a small swallow, and placed the flask in the space between them.

Swanton settled back in his seat, took a musing pull on his cigarette, blew the smoke out, and in a philosophical tone that seemed much practiced said, "You know what one of the real problems is?"

"With Germany?"

"Yeah."

"What?"

"Them," Swanton said, and made a gesture with his cigarette that took in the entire planeload of women. "The bitches. Or rather, their husbands. You know who their husbands are?"

"Officers, it would seem."

"Yeah, well, you know which officers they are?"

"No."

"They're the contemporaries of Eisenhower, Bradley, and Mark Clark, guys like that. Except when the war

119

came along, they didn't get jumped from lieutenant colonel to four-star general. No, these were guys who'd sat around for ten, fifteen, sometimes twenty years as first lieutenants and captains. But when the war started we had to have officers, so these guys got jumped up to light colonel, or colonel, or maybe even buck general. But they weren't given a line outfit. Instead they got shipped out to Wyoming to run Camp Despair, or whatever it was called. Or maybe they rode a desk in Washington. A lot of them were Cavalry types."

Swanton took another deep pull on his cigarette, blew out the smoke, and continued. "So when the war ended, these guys had a choice. They could either go back to their permanent ranks of captain or major or whatever, or they could keep on being colonels and generals, provided they got themselves sent to Germany to take over the occupation. Well, shit, you never saw such wire-pulling. Some of them even resorted to blackmail, except I can't prove that. And so that's who you've got running the occupation—a lot of it, anyway—guys who can't see how running a destroyed town of 100,000 or so with no heat, no lights, no water, and people starving to death can be much different from running a Cavalry remount post in West Kansas, which was probably their last job."

Swanton lapsed into a brooding silence for a moment, but brightened when Jackson offered him the flask again. After a drink, Swanton lit another cigarette and said, "Remember nonfraternization?"

Jackson nodded. "It didn't work out too well."

"It didn't work because the GI's wouldn't stand for it. So Ike, the great compromiser, decided that it was okay for GI's to fraternize with children—little kids. Real little ones. But that rule didn't last long either, so now the GI's can screw anyone they want to, although there're still some kind of dumb rules about not having Germans into your home."

Swanton was silent for a moment and then asked, "You know what the burning issues are now?"

"What?"

"Denazification and Democratization." He shook his head over the awkwardness of the words. "I'm no Nazi sympathizer, but the fucking country's half starving and it's going to be another cold winter and there's not going to be any coal again and a lot of 'em haven't got any place to live, so I've decided that maybe the Russians are right."

"How?"

"Well, everybody in the American Zone had to fill out the *Fragebogen*." He looked sharply at Jackson to see if he understood the German word.

"Questionnaire."

"Yeah, questionnaire. It's a six-page job with a hundred and thirty-one questions to determine if you are now or ever were a big, medium, or little Nazi or none of the above. Some *Scheisskopf* has even decided that if you joined the Nazis after '37 or so, it's not as bad as if you joined back in '33. Well, shit that doesn't make any sense, if you think about it for half a minute. Back in '33 there was a hell of a depression in Germany. You might have joined then out of desperation more than conviction. But by '37 it wasn't so easy to join, and by then, by God, you had a pretty good idea of what being a Nazi meant. But the Russians, well, they don't give much of a shit whether anybody was a Nazi or not. What they did was, they shot a lot of them, if their records were real bad, and put the rest to work. They'd say, 'You guys used to be Nazi engineers, right? Well, you're not Nazi engineers anymore, you're Commie engineers, understand?' And, like always, the Germans would say, *'Führer befehl—wir folgen'* and go out and fix the steam plant."

Swanton shook his head again. "So that's how it stands. We're denazifying them, whatever that means, and the Russians have got 'em out fixing the gas works. As for how we're gonna make small-d democrats out of 'em, I don't know."

"You like them, don't you?" Jackson said.

"Who?"

"The Germans."

Swanton thought about it. "I like people. They interest me. I have a hard time blaming Hitler on a six-year-old kid with malnutrition and no place to sleep. No matter how you slice it, it's really not his fault. But he's going to be paying for it all his life. So that's why I had to go back to New York. They had to cut 'em out."

"What?"

"My ulcers," Swanton said.

13 Otto Bodden, the printer, stood in the cold rain across from the ruined Hauptbahnhof in Frankfurt and waited for the woman. Out in the middle of the intersection a tall policeman in a long, warm blue coat directed traffic. The policeman had a cheerful smile on his face despite the rain, and Bodden decided that the smile was there because the policeman was fed and warm and had a job that let him order other Germans around.

It was Bodden's second day in Frankfurt since his arrival from Hamburg, where he was almost sure that he had lost the yellow-haired man. Last night he had slept in the cellar of a bombed-out Gasthaus whose owner, after a fashion, still followed his innkeeping trade by renting out the cellar's corners to the homeless. The innkeeper had wanted to be paid in food, but since Bodden had none, he had accepted one of the printer's razor blades. For another blade he had provided Bodden with a bowl of potato soup and a chunk of black bread.

It had been cold, but dry, in the cellar. Now Bodden was both cold and wet, and he wished that the woman would appear, although he was not sure that she was really late because he still had no watch. A spy should have a watch, Bodden thought, and grinned in spite of the rain and the cold. The profession demands it.

Five minutes later the woman appeared, better dressed than most in a long fur coat and carrying an umbrella. She walked purposefully to the steps that led up and into the ruined train station, paused, looked at her watch with the air of someone who knows she's on time, and glanced around. In her left hand she carried the yellow book. Pinned to her coat was the red carnation.

Bodden started across the street against the traffic. The policeman yelled at him; Bodden gave him a merry grin and hurried on. When he was a few meters from the woman, he discovered that she was younger than he had first thought—not much more than twenty-five or twenty-six. And pretty, by God, he thought. Well, there was no rule that they couldn't be pretty.

The woman, despite the cold and the custom, wore nothing on her head. She had long, thick dark hair that framed a pale oval face with full lips; a small, straight nose; and enormous brown eyes. That one could use a few potatoes, Bodden thought. Their eyes get like that when they don't eat—big and dark and shiny, at least for a while, and then when the hope goes, they grow dull.

The woman clutched the fur coat to her throat and nestled her chin into it. Bodden wondered what she wore under the coat. Maybe nothing. He remembered the girls in Berlin last summer who had worn their fur coats in July. That and nothing else. They had sold every last stitch they owned, or traded it for food. But not their fur coats. They remembered the previous winter too well to part with their coats. There would be no coal this winter either, and without their coats they knew they would freeze.

Bodden stopped before the woman, made a little bow, smiled, and said, "Excuse me, Fräulein, but do you have the time? My watch has stopped."

She looked at him for a moment with her enormous eyes and then glanced down at her watch. "It is five past twelve."

"Is that midnight or noon?"

"Midnight."

The woman handed him the book with the yellow cover. Bodden thanked her, moved off, and tucked the book away underneath his coat. The woman looked around as though trying to decide which way she should go and then walked off rapidly in the opposite direction.

Across the street in the right-hand seat of the blue Adler with the CD plates, Major Gilbert Baker-Bates gave his mustache a quick brush and said in German, "The woman, I think, don't you?" to the yellow-haired man behind the wheel.

"He's too good for me," the yellow-haired man said as he started the engine.

"How long did it take him to lose you in Hamburg?"

"Twenty minutes. He knows all the old tricks and perhaps even some new ones."

"A yellow book," Baker-Bates said. "I wonder why the Reds always use a yellow book."

"In Bern they liked green ones," the yellow-haired man said.

"Both are spring colors. Perhaps that has something to do with it."

"Perhaps," said the yellow-haired man as he let the Adler crawl along the curb nearly fifty meters behind the hurrying woman in the fur coat.

"You had no trouble with him yesterday?"

"With the printer? None. He hadn't counted on our flying down. Since we knew where he was heading, it was no trouble to pick him up at the station. This time I stayed far back, though. Very far back. He slept in a cellar last night and paid with razor blades. He must have a lot of them. That's what he was using in Lübeck."

"About here, don't you think?" Baker-Bates said.

"I think so," the yellow-haired man said, and pulled the car to a stop, but left the engine running.

"You know where I'll be," Baker-Bates said as the yellow-haired man got out of the car.

"I know."

Baker-Bates slid underneath the steering wheel of the car and watched for a moment as the yellow-haired man moved off after the young woman in the fur coat. He's very good, Baker-Bates thought as he noted how the yellow-haired man kept at least five or six pedestrians between himself and the woman. The Abwehr chaps must have trained their people well, at least when they weren't soul-searching all over the place. Pity about the yellow hair, though. It was like a beacon.

Baker-Bates watched as the woman in the fur coat rounded a corner. The yellow-haired man waited until he could use a couple of pedestrians as a shield and then turned the same corner. Baker-Bates put the car into gear and realized that he was hungry. That meant either a black-market restaurant or the Americans. Baker-Bates sighed and decided on the Americans, not because they were the lesser of the two evils, but because they were cheaper.

Three minutes after he left the woman in the fur coat, Bodden ducked into the door of a closed shop and took out the yellow book, which he noted, was a volume of Heine's satiric poems. That was good. He could use a laugh. He opened the book and glanced at the slip of paper inside. The name written on the paper was the

Golden Rose, which meant either a Bierstube or a Gasthaus. There was also an address with precise directions about how to get there. She was quite thorough, he thought, the miss in the fur coat, which was fine with Bodden because he liked thorough women. You also like easygoing ones with careless ways, he told himself, and grinned. What had the Pole said the Americans called them? Bimbos. That was it. You like bimbos, printer, he thought; grinned again; took out his pipe; and decided to smoke it there in the doorway out of the rain until it was time to start for the Golden Rose.

Baker-Bates stood at the bar in the Casino, which housed the American officers' club with its two dining rooms, and studied the menu. It seemed that something called chicken-fried steak was featured that day, along with mashed potatoes and gravy, stewed tomatoes, creamed corn, and, for dessert, tapioca pudding. With raisins, so the mimeographed menu said.

The Casino was located just behind the seven-story I.G. Farben building, which was headquarters for the United States Forces, European Theater—or USFET, as it was called. After his lunch of chicken-fried steak, whatever that was, Baker-Bates had an appointment with Lt. LaFollette Meyer, whose office was in the Farben building. Meyer was to take him for a look at the house where the black-marketeer had been killed. What was his name? Damm. Karl-Heinz Damm. For a fleeting moment, Baker-Bates felt a small twinge of sympathy for the dead man—not because he had been murdered, but because he had had to bear up under a hyphenated name.

"Buy you a drink, Major?"

Baker-Bates turned toward the American voice that had made the offer. It came from a tallish, slim man with a major's oak leaves on his shoulders and eyes that were more green than blue. About thirty-three, Baker-Bates thought as he debated whether to accept the offer.

"I'm just celebrating my promotion," the American said, sensing the hesitation.

"In that case, I'll be most happy to join you. Thank you very much."

"What're you drinking?"

"Scotch and soda," Baker-Bates said. "But no ice this time, please."

"Two Scotch and sodas, Sammy," the new Major ordered from the Sergeant bartender. "And hold the ice on one."

"Two Scotch sodas and hold the ice on one," the Sergeant echoed. He mixed the drinks quickly with an expert's minimal motion and slid them across the bar. "Congratulations on your promotion, Major," Sammy said. "This one's on the house."

The new Major thanked the bartender with a thanks-a-lot and lifted his glass to Baker-Bates. "Mud in your eye, whatever that means."

"I've never quite figured that one out myself," Baker-Bates said.

"Thanks for having the drink with me," the new Major said. "I've been hanging around here in limbo for about three weeks waiting for my orders to come through, and about the only person I've gotten to know is Sammy here. Sammy listens to my problems—right, Sammy?"

"Right, Major," the Sergeant said with a good bartender's automatic indulgence.

"You're not assigned here, then?" Baker-Bates said.

"Nope. Just a casual. But my orders came through along with my promotion this morning, and tomorrow I'm off to Berlin."

"That should be interesting."

"Yeah, I think it might be. Where're you stationed?"

"Place called Lübeck, up north."

"Don't believe I know that one."

"Not too bad a place. A bit crowded now. We hit it during the raids, but not too much. Where're you from in the States?"

"Texas. Abilene, Texas."

"If you don't mind my saying so, you don't sound much like a Texan."

The new Major grinned. "Before the war I was a radio announcer. They sort of like you to talk pretty." He lapsed into a drawl and said, "But when I'm of a mind to, I can talk Texan prid near as good as anybody."

Baker-Bates smiled. "Almost incomprehensible. Not quite, but almost."

"Must sound to you like Cockney sounds to me."

"Probably."

"Well, sir," the new Major said, finishing his drink, "it's been real nice talking to you."

"Thank you very much for the drink, and congratulations again. On your promotion."

The new Major gave the bar a small slap with the palm of his hand. "Appreciate that," he said with a smile, drawling the words out in a mock-Texas accent, turned, and wandered off into the crowd of lunchtime drinkers.

At lunch, Baker-Bates discovered that chicken-fried steak wasn't quite as bad as it looked or sounded, although the gravy that came with it had the texture, the appearance, and possibly the flavor of library paste.

A German waiter came by and refilled Baker-Bates's coffee cup without asking. Baker-Bates leaned back in his chair, lit a Lucky Strike, and gazed out over the crowded dining room. They do do themselves well, he thought. The best-paid, best-fed, best-equipped amateur army in the history of the world. And already demobilized. An army totally uneasy in its role of conqueror and slipping now, almost unconsciously, into the more comfortable role of liberator. And why not? Liberators are liked, conquerors aren't, and the Americans do so want and need to be liked, even by yesterday's enemies.

The new Major, for example. Not a bad chap for an American. A bit lonely, a bit overly friendly, but pleasant enough, without being completely overbearing, as so many of them were. All the new Major had wanted was a friendly face to help him celebrate his promotion. A radio announcer. Baker-Bates tried to imagine the life of a radio announcer, whatever that was, in a place called Abilene, Texas, but failed utterly. What did he announce —the news? But one doesn't *announce* the news; one simply reads it, in a rather bored manner, as they did on the BBC. Baker-Bates sighed; finished his coffee; ground out his cigarette; watched as the German waiter swooped down on it, removed the butt, deposited it quickly in a small tin box that he took from his pocket, cleaned the ashtray, and put it back on the table.

Baker-Bates glanced at his watch and thought about his next American of the afternoon, Lt. LaFollette Meyer. Well, Lieutenant Meyer wasn't one of your overly friendly Americans. Lieutenant Meyer was a very self-contained young man, a bit cool, a bit distant, who had a brain that he didn't at all seem to mind using. Lieutenant Meyer, Baker-Bates thought with approval, was looking out for Lieutenant Meyer. He would have to tell him about the dwarf this afternoon. That should cause a tremor in all that cool composure. The dwarf, in that one respect at least, was really quite useful.

The lift in the I.G. Farben building was an open-shaft, endless-belted affair with platforms that had to be hopped onto. Baker-Bates hopped onto one and rode it up to the third floor, where he hopped off. A staff sergeant jerked a thumb over his shoulder at Lieutenant Meyer's office, and Baker-Bates went in. The Lieutenant was seated behind his desk wearing a very large, but quite humorless, smile.

"I was looking for Lieutenant Meyer," Baker-Bates said, "But I seem to have come across the Cheshire Cat."

"Meow, sir."

"You have something, I take it—something that I don't have but wish to God that I did."

"Exactly."

"But you are going to share, aren't you, Lieutenant?"

"I'm still savoring it, Major."

"That tasty, eh?"

"Scrumptious."

"This could go on all afternoon."

"A picture."

"Well, now."

"A photograph. To be more precise, a snapshot."

"Where was it?"

"We finally located someone who knew someone who knew him. And this someone who knew him had managed to hang on to a photo album. In fact, that's all he managed to hang on to, but there, on the fifth from the last page, was a photograph taken in 1936 in Darmstadt."

Lieutenant Meyer reached under the blotter on his desk and flipped a photograph over to Baker-Bates. "Meet Kurt Oppenheimer at twenty-two."

The photograph was of a young man with rolled-up sleeves, leather shorts, and heavy shoes. He sat astride a bicycle. His mouth was open as if he were about to say something jocular. He was about six feet tall and, even in the photograph, looked tanned and fit.

Baker-Bates took only one look at the photograph before he softly said, "Damn!" And then, not quite so softly, "Goddamn sonofabitch!"

For the face in the photograph, although ten years younger, was the same as that of the new American Major from Abilene, Texas, who had bought Baker-Bates a drink only an hour and thirteen minutes before.

14 The Golden Rose was located only a few blocks from the Hauptbahnhof in the old *Kneipen* district of Frankfurt, which, before the war, had consisted mostly of drinking dives and after-hours joints. Now it was largely rubble—all kinds of rubble: some waist high, some shoulder high, and some two stories high. In several blocks, paths had been cleared that were wide enough for two men to walk abreast. In others, the paths were more like one-way streets, just wide enough for a single automobile. But in many side streets there were no paths at all, and those who, for whatever their reasons, wanted to traverse these streets had to climb up and over the rubble.

The Golden Rose was the only building in its block that had been spared—partially spared, anyway. It once had been a three-story building, but now the top story was completely gone. The second story was gone too, except for a bathroom, although its walls had also vanished, leaving the tub and toilet exposed. They both looked curiously naked.

Bodden entered the Golden Rose, pushing his way through the inevitable heavy curtain. Inside, several candles had been stuck here and there to help out the weak single electric bulb that hung by a long cord from the ceiling. Under it, perhaps to catch what little heat it afforded, real or imaginary, was the proprietor, leaning on the counter that served as a bar. The proprietor was a thin man with a fire-scarred face and bitter eyes. He looked up at Bodden; muttered *"Gute' MOR-je"* in the Frankfurt accent, despite the fact that it was long past noon; and went back to the newspaper he had been reading. The paper was the American-controlled *Frankfurter Rundschau*. The bitter-eyed man didn't seem to like what it said.

Bodden said good morning back to the man and then waited for his eyes to adjust themselves to the gloom. There were several persons, mostly men, sitting alone at tables with glasses of thin beer before them. All still wore their hats, overcoats—and gloves, if they had them. The Golden Rose had no heat.

The young woman in the fur coat sat at a table by herself. There was nothing on the table, only her folded hands. Bodden walked back to where she sat, but before he could sit down she said, "Have you eaten?"

"Not since yesterday."

She rose. "Come," she said.

Bodden followed her past the proprietor and back to a curtained-off passageway. Beyond the passageway was a flight of stairs that led down to the cellar. It seemed to grow warmer as Bodden and the woman descended the stairs. Bodden also thought he could smell food. Pork, by God.

He and the woman pushed through yet another heavy

curtain and entered a whitewashed room lit by two bulbs, this time, and a number of candles. A middle-aged woman stood before a large coal cookstove stirring a pot of something that bubbled. She looked around at the young woman in the fur coat; nodded in recognition, if not in welcome; and gestured with the spoon toward one of the six tables.

All the tables were empty except for one. At it sat a heavy, well-dressed man with pink jowls. Before him was a plate filled with boiled potatoes and a thick slab of pork. The man was cramming a forkful of potatoes into his mouth. He seemed to find no pleasure in his food. That one is just feeding the furnace, Bodden thought, and realized that his own mouth was watering.

The young woman chose the table that was the farthest away from the eating man.

"We will eat first," she said.

"A fine idea, but I cannot pay."

The woman shrugged slightly and brought a hand out of the pocket of her coat. In it were two packages of Camel cigarettes.

"One packet of these will pay for the meal," she said, and slid them across the table to Bodden. "And a drink too, if you wish."

"I wish very much," Bodden said, eyeing the cigarettes.

"Smoke them, if you like," the woman said. "There are more."

He lit one just as the middle-aged woman approached. Her eyes were as bitter as the man's upstairs, and Bodden tried to guess whether she and the man were husband and wife or brother and sister. He decided on husband and wife. They sometimes grow to look alike, he thought, if they live together long enough and discover that they hate it.

"Yes," the middle-aged woman said, and sniffed noisily, as though she had a bad cold.

"Pay her first," the young woman told Bodden. He handed over the unopened cigarette package.

"We'll have two plates of what the big one back there is stuffing himself with," the young woman ordered crisply. "And buttered bread, too."

"No butter, just bread," the middle-aged woman said, and sniffed again.

The young woman shrugged. "Very well, then, two *Schnapps*. Two large ones."

The woman sniffed noisily for the third time, swallowed what she had sniffed, and went away. The *Schnapps* that she brought back turned out to be potato gin. Bodden took a big swallow of his, felt it burn its way down and spread warmly through his stomach.

"A drink, a cigarette, a meal on the way, and a pretty companion," he said. "One would almost think that we were living in a civilized world."

"If that's your idea of civilization," the young woman said, shrugging out of her fur coat and letting it drape itself over the back of her chair.

"My needs, like my tastes, have been reduced to the basics," Bodden said, and allowed his gaze to rest for a moment on the woman's breasts, which thrust at the gray material of her dress. This one, he told himself, has been eating better than I thought.

"You can't afford me, printer," she said, but there was no asperity in her tone.

"Ah, you know my trade."

"But not your name."

"Bodden."

"Bodden," she said. "Well, Herr Bodden, welcome to Frankfurt, or what's left of it. I am Eva. I don't think we need to shake hands. It would only draw attention."

Bodden smiled. "You are very careful."

"That is how I have survived; by being very careful. You were in a camp, weren't you?"

"Does it show?"

She studied him with frank curiosity. "In the eyes. They look as though they still ached. What landed you in a camp, printer—your politics?"

"My big mouth."

"You advertised your politics, then."

"Sometimes. And you?"

"I'm a Jew. Or rather, a half-Jew. A *Mischling*. I had friends during the war who kept both me and my politics hidden away out of sight. I would not have lasted in a camp. Tell me something; how did you?"

Bodden shrugged. "I played politics, the practical kind. I was a Social Democrat, but after they locked me up I saw that the Communists ate better than the Social Democrats and lived better, so I became a Communist."

"Your reasons," she said after a moment. "I like them."

"Why?"

"They are better than mine."

The woman brought the food then, two large platters of pork and potatoes. They both ate hungrily in silence. When he was finished, Bodden sighed, leaned back in his chair, and permitted himself the luxury of another American cigarette. He smoked and watched the young woman finish her meal. She eats like the fat one over there with the pink face, he thought. Without joy.

The woman who said her name was Eva finished her meal and arranged her knife and fork carefully on her plate. There were no napkins, so she took a small lace handkerchief from her purse and patted her lips with it.

"Now," she said, "we will have a nice cup of coffee and a cigarette and talk about Kurt Oppenheimer."

The middle-aged woman with the sniffles apparently had been waiting for Eva to finish her meal, for she brought two cups of coffee just as Bodden lit the young woman's cigarette.

"No milk, just sugar," the middle-aged woman said, put the two cups down with a rattle, and went away.

Bodden leaned over his cup and inhaled deeply through his nose. "Damned if it isn't real coffee."

Eva watched as he took his first sip. "What instructions did Berlin give you?"

"Simple ones. Too simple, probably. I'm to find him, to isolate him, and to wait."

"For what?"

"For further instructions."

"From whom?"

Bodden stared at her for a moment and then grinned. "From you."

Eva returned his gaze for several seconds, then dropped it, picked up her cup, and gave her full attention to it.

"You seem surprised," Bodden said. "Or maybe puzzled."

"Perhaps both," she said.

"There are deep thinkers in Berlin. Very deep. I no longer question their instructions. I did a couple of times and it seemed to hurt their feelings. For example, I came across at Lübeck, in the British Zone. Do you know Lübeck?"

"I was there once long ago."

"A pleasant-enough place. Well, I did not sneak across. No, I came across with a certain amount of fanfare. There was an old man in Lübeck, a printer like myself. Two days before I arrived, his leg was broken by some DP's. I was promptly given his job on the newspaper. It was not, I'm afraid, a coincidence that the old man's leg was broken. I paid a call on him once—took him some tobacco, in fact. He was a wise old sort—tremendously well read. A lot of printers are, you know. He even thought it was lucky for the paper that I happened to show up when I did. I didn't disabuse him of his notion. Then there was my landlady, Frau Schoettle. Her name was Eva too. Well, Frau Schoettle was equally interesting in her own way. She reported regularly on her roomers to a certain British captain. His name was Richards, I believe. It would seem, would it not, unwise for me to take a room at Frau Schoettle's? But those were my instructions from the deep thinkers in Berlin, the instructions which I no longer question."

137

There was another silence as Eva watched Bodden take several sips of his coffee.

"Berlin wanted them to know," she said. "The British."

"So it would seem. But the British not only knew I had arrived, they also knew that I was coming, and, thanks to Frau Schoettle, they knew when I left. A yellow-haired man went with me—as far as Hamburg. We somehow lost each other there."

"What are you telling me, printer?"

"I'm not sure."

She bit her lower lip—chewed it, actually—for several seconds and said, "How much did Berlin tell you about Kurt Oppenheimer?"

"Very little. He kills people. So far, it would seem that those he killed have needed killing. He killed such people during the war; and now the war is over, he is still doing it. He kills with a certain amount of dispatch and efficiency. I did not ask, but I suppose that Berlin could make use of such a man."

Eva looked down at her coffee, which was growing cold. "I knew him before the war."

"Ah."

"It begins to make sense, does it, printer?"

"A little."

"Your instructions will come from me, if they do, not because I am well trained and cunning or even clever, but because I knew the Oppenheimers before the war. The sister and I were close friends, very close. I knew him too, of course. In fact, in '36, when he was twenty-two and I was fifteen, I had a schoolgirl's thing about him. I thought him very handsome and sophisticated. He thought I was a brat, naturally. I slept with his handkerchief under my pillow for months. I stole it from him. It had his initials on it, K.O." She smiled then—a sad, winsome sort of smile that spoke of better days. The smile suddenly went away, so quickly that Bodden was almost convinced that it had never appeared. When it comes to smiling, he thought, I'm afraid this one is out of practice.

Looking not at Bodden but at her coffee cup, Eva said, "The sister. Her name is Leah." She looked up then and made her voice assume a neutral, indifferent tone. "She will arrive in Frankfurt two days from now. She will stay with me. She is coming here to find her brother."

"Ah," Bodden said.

"It begins to make even more sense, printer, doesn't it?"

"In a complicated way."

Eva reached for another cigarette. "There's more, which you may as well know. It will provide you with further evidence as to why Berlin chose me not for my beauty or brains, but because of my—well—convenience, I suppose. I have a lover."

He grinned. "And I am desolate."

"An American."

Bodden tapped the pack of Camels. "You're right: I can't afford you."

"A carefully chosen American."

"Berlin's choice or yours?"

"Mine first—and then Berlin's. They approved most heartily. We have much in common, this American of mine and I. First, there is the fact that he is a Jew—an American Jew, but a Jew nonetheless. His name is Meyer. Lieutenant LaFollette Meyer. Do you speak any English?"

"A bit."

"I call him Folly."

Bodden smiled. "But not in public."

"No, in bed. He calls me Sugar." She shrugged. "He is a nice boy. Not simple, but a bit naive. His army has given him an assignment. In fact, that is how we met. His assignment is to find Kurt Oppenheimer."

"Well, now."

"He came to question me because I had known the Oppenheimers. It seemed too good an opportunity to pass up. So after checking with Berlin, I took him as a lover."

139

"Does he talk to you about his work?"

"Incessantly. He thinks that we are to be married."

"Sometime you must tell me what he talks about."

"I will. But for now all you need to know is that he is no closer to Kurt Oppenheimer than you and I."

Bodden grunted. "Then he will get no promotion soon."

"But it is a big army, and they are not the only ones interested. So are the British, which should be no surprise to you."

"None."

"The British want to keep him out of Palestine," she said.

"Ah."

"What does 'ah' mean?"

"Perhaps that the deep thinkers in Berlin would like to see him *in* Palestine." He shrugged. "But that is not my concern, of course."

"Or mine."

They stared at each other for a very long moment—too long probably, because they recognized in each other something that would perhaps be better unrecognized. But Bodden made himself examine it, if only briefly. This one, he thought, does not have the true faith. No more than you do, printer.

"There is one more thing," Eva said.

"My simple brain aches from what it has absorbed already."

"Not so simple, I think. But there is this, and this is the last. I received a letter from Leah Oppenheimer. We have been corresponding by airmail through my Lieutenant's Army Post Office. It is quicker. In her most recent letter, Leah told me that she and her father have engaged two men to help her find her brother. One of them will be arriving in Frankfurt today. His name is Jackson. Minor Jackson."

She paused and then finished her cold coffee, apparently not realizing that it was cold. "This evening my American will be at the airport. He will meet an airplane. The man on the airplane that he will meet is Minor Jackson."

"I see," Bodden said. "I don't really, but I thought I should say something. You said the Oppenheimers have engaged two men. Who is the other one?"

"He is a Romanian called Ploscaru. I am also told that he is a dwarf."

"You said 'told.' Did she tell you that?"

"No, printer," Eva said. "Berlin told me."

15 Bodden watched as she shrugged into her fur coat and turned its collar up around her chin. Her fingers stroked the fur as though its touch and feel were somehow reassuring. This one still likes a little luxury, he thought. Well, who could blame her? Certainly not you, printer, who always found the Spartans just a bit stupid.

"You disapprove of my coat?"

He shook his head. "It looks warm."

"So is wool, but I prefer marten. I also would choose caviar over cabbage."

It was another signal of sorts, weak but unmistakable, and Bodden sent back a careful reply. "Then we have that much in common."

She nodded thoughtfully. "Perhaps even more. Who knows?" Suddenly, she was all business and crisp efficiency again. "The man upstairs, the one with the scarred face. His name is Max. He is a sympathizer of sorts and can be trusted—up to a point. But not that one." She nodded slightly toward the middle-aged woman who still stood by the coal cookstove.

"His wife?"

"Sister. Max disapproves of her black-market dealings, in principle anyway, but not enough to refuse her food. Without her, Max would starve. Like many today, they are stuck with each other. But Max will be your contact with me. You should check with him every day, and you may as well eat here, too. It's not *haute cuisine*, but it's nourishing."

"I cannot afford it."

"That packet of cigarettes you gave her will buy your meals for the next four days."

He held up the partially smoked pack of Camels. "May I keep these?"

She smiled, and Bodden noticed that it came more easily this time. "You may even smoke them, if you like, printer. Although you don't know it yet, you're rich. How does it feel?"

Bodden grinned. "Tell me more and then I'll tell you how it feels."

"I noticed you have no briefcase. It makes you look naked. Sometimes I think every German's born with a briefcase in his hand. Well, you have one now. It's upstairs with Max. In it are two thousand American cigarettes."

"You're right. I am rich. And it feels fine."

"You'll need a room and transport. Max will fix you up with a room. It won't be warm, but it'll be dry. For transport, well, the best you can hope for is a bicycle. The going rate is six hundred cigarettes or three kilos of fat."

"A stolen bicycle, of course."

"What else?"

"I'll try the DP's. The DP's and I get along—especially the Poles. I knew many in the camp. Some were very funny fellows."

"What camp were you in?"

"Belsen."

She looked away. When she spoke, still looking away, her voice was elaborately casual almost to the point of indifference. "Did you ever know a man there called Scheel? Dieter Scheel?"

Bodden realized that she was holding her breath until he answered. "A friend?"

She sighed the breath out. "My father."

"It was a big camp," he said as kindly as he could.

"Yes, I suppose it was."

"Eva Scheel. A pleasant name. Was he Jewish, your father?"

She shook her head. "My mother was. My father, like you, printer, was a Social Democrat with a big mouth. Well, no matter."

She took an envelope from the pocket of her coat and handed it to Bodden. "I will leave now. In the envelope is a report on everything that my American Lieutenant has told me about his investigation of Kurt Oppenheimer. Also about the man whom they think Oppenheimer killed."

"Damm, wasn't it?"

"Karl-Heinz Damm. It seems that he sold identities to those who had need of them."

Bodden nodded. "A most profitable profession, I would say."

"Yes. The report is rather long because my Ami Lieutenant seems to think his fiancée should be interested in his work. I suggest that you read it here and then burn it in the cookstove."

"Now that I'm rich, I'll read it over another cup of coffee."

Eva rose. "The yellow-haired man, the one you parted company with in Hamburg. Did he have a long face and wear a blue cap?"

The warmth of the room had made Bodden relax. The warmth and the food and the cigarettes and the *Schnapps*. And the woman, of course, he thought. A woman can relax you or wind you up like a clock spring. She has just wound you up again, printer.

"Was he wearing a coat?" Bodden said. "A blue coat?"

"Dyed dark blue. A Wehrmacht coat."

"Yes."

"He picked me up shortly after the train station. He is very good."

Bodden nodded slowly. "The British. They must have flown him down."

"He is not British."

"No? Did you hear him speak?"

"I had no need. I could tell from his walk. He walks like a German. Haven't you heard the saying? The British walk as if they own the earth. The Germans as if they think they should own it. And the Americans as if they don't give a damn who owns it. Shall I lose him for you, printer? He is very good, but I am better."

Bodden smiled. "You have a great deal of confidence."

She nodded. "Almost as much as you do."

"Then lose him."

"They will find us again, of course."

Bodden shrugged. "Or perhaps, when the time is ripe, we will find them."

The name of the man with the yellow hair who stood outside the Golden Rose in the rain was Heinrich von Staden, and he had been a captain in Admiral Canaris's Abwehr until the twenty-first of July, 1944, which was the day after the one-armed Colonel Count Claus von Stauffenberg had placed the black briefcase under the heavy table at the *Wolfschanze*, or Wolf's Fort, in the forest near the East Prussian town of Rastenburg. Captain von Staden might not have been standing now outside the Golden Rose in the rain if Colonel Brandt, the famous horseman of the 1936 Olympics, hadn't reached down and moved the briefcase because it was bothering him. He moved it just enough so that when the bomb it contained exploded, it killed several men, but not the one it was supposed to kill: Adolf Hitler.

So, on the twenty-first of July, 1944, Captain Heinrich von Staden had left the German Embassy in Madrid, carrying with him as many documents as he thought both pertinent and useful, and presented himself at the office of his counterpart at the British Embassy.

His counterpart had not been especially surprised to see him. "Pity about the bomb, wasn't it?" he had said.

Von Staden had nodded. "Yes, a pity."

"They won't try again, will they?"

"No, they'll all be dead shortly."

"Canaris too?"

"Yes, Canaris too."

"Mmm. Well, what do you think we should do with you?"

"I have no idea."

"Why don't we just send you back to London and let them sort it out?"

"Very well."

So they had flown him back to London and they had sorted it out. First there had been the solitary confinement and then the interrogation, followed by a long stretch in a POW camp. Then there had been more interrogation, and finally, there had been the one long, especially grueling session which had lasted sixteen hours until, against all rules, Major Baker-Bates had said, "How'd you like to go to work for us?"

"Do I have a choice?"

"No, not very much of one, I'm afraid. The POW camp, of course. You could always opt to go back there."

"I think not," ex-Captain von Staden had said, which was why he was now standing outside the Golden Rose in the rain.

The streets had been crooked in that old section of the city where, before the war, Frankfurt had done its drinking and whoring. Those streets which had been cleared were still crooked, with narrow winding paths that led off into the rubble and ended, sometimes, apparently nowhere.

Von Staden watched as the woman came out of the Golden Rose, opened her umbrella, and hurried off down the narrow, crooked street. He moved after her, keeping close to the edge of the uneven rubble. The woman turned off the street into one of the twisting paths. Von Staden followed, not hurrying, but keeping the woman within twenty meters, not letting her get farther ahead than that. Another path led off the one that they were on. The woman stopped, hesitating, as if she were not sure of her directions. Then she turned right. Von Staden gave her a few moments and followed.

The path that she had taken was no more than a meter wide. It went right, left, and right again almost at ninety-degree angles. Von Staden had lost sight of the woman now, so he picked up his pace. He made the final turn and stopped, because the path ended abruptly at a small shrine that marked the site of someone for whom the rubble was both grave and crypt. The shrine was nothing more than a small, painted wooden figure of Christ. Some soggy, faded flowers lay before it. The woman was nowhere in sight.

Von Staden swore and quickly retraced his steps. At the second turning he stopped. Coming from this direction, he could see it—a space no larger than a large crate. It was somebody's hovel, fashioned out of the rubble and a piece of old sheet iron that shielded its entrance from view unless approached from this angle. He realized that she could have closed her umbrella, ducked into the hovel, waited for him to pass, and then doubled back. It would have taken no more than a few seconds.

Walking slowly back along the path to the street, making sure that there were no other holes in which she could be hiding, Von Staden admired her cleverness. This little rabbit knows her warren well, he thought. Now he would have to go back to the Golden Rose. The other one, the man, would be gone by now, of course. But a little chat with the proprietor might be useful to find out how much he knows about his patrons. He will know nothing, but if pressed hard enough, he might produce the bottle of *Schnapps*—the good stuff that he keeps under the counter. With luck, even some Steinhäger. And with the *Schnapps* perhaps will also come some inspiration, which Von Staden knew was going to have to serve as the principal ingredient of his essentially negative report to Major Baker-Bates.

From 1917 until 1935, Brigadier General Frank "Knocker" Grubbs had been a first lieutenant in the United States Army. In 1935, despite the fact that everyone regarded Knocker Grubbs as just a trifle dim-witted, he had been promoted to captain, the rank he had held until Pearl Harbor. Only a national emergency, or, some said, a disaster, could have created the confusion that permitted General Grubbs to rise to his present rank; but rise to it he did, pinning on his single silver star in late 1944.

Some said that Knocker got to be a general because he knew all the right people. But others, and these were his detractors, and there were a legion or two of them, claimed that it was not only because he knew all the right people, but also because he knew all their dirty little secrets. And perhaps that was the real reason that Knocker, although not really very bright, had wound up in intelligence.

Whatever the reason, Knocker Grubbs was determined to retire as a general. He had only one year to go until his thirty were up, and after that, as he often told his wife, "Fuck 'em. We'll go back to Santone and drink Pearl beer at the Gunther and raise quarter horses." Knocker Grubbs, like all men, had his dreams—and his nightmares. His recurring nightmare was that he would be recalled to Washington and reduced to his permanent rank of major. The difference between the retirement pay of a major and that of a one-star general was considerable, and when Knocker had nothing better to do, which was often, he would calculate the difference on the back of an envelope with a kind of morbid fascination. He always burned those envelopes, of course. Knocker Grubbs wasn't a total fool.

Now fifty-three and in what, as he always told his disbelieving wife, was his prime, Knocker, from his pleasant sixth-story office in the Farben building, directed half of the Army counterintelligence efforts in the U.S. Zone of Occupation. The other half was directed down in Munich by some pantywaist colonel with fancy notions who, before the war, had done postgraduate work at Heidelberg—at the fucking Army's fucking expense, Knocker often told his cronies.

The Colonel in Munich might be a pantywaist, but he was also smart, and this had worried Knocker until he remembered that generals could chew out colonels. And one thing Knocker Grubbs had learned and learned well during his twenty-nine years in the Army, and that was how to chew ass.

He had once spent two hours upbraiding the Munich Colonel with vivid epithets culled from Cavalry days, and the results had been delightful. So now that was what Knocker did most of the time. He chewed ass. He was good at it, he enjoyed it, and he dimly perceived that it was the one perfect disguise for his own shortcomings, of which, he was just smart enough to realize, there might be a few.

The ass that Knocker was chewing that afternoon wasn't a colonel's, but it was almost as good because it belonged to a Limey major. To add to the Major's discomfort, an American lieutenant was serving as witness—a Yid lieutenant at that.

149

"Now, let me just get this straight, Major," General Grubbs said as he rubbed his bald head—a gesture that for some reason he thought might make him look harmlessly puzzled. "You were at the bar at the Casino, having a drink, minding your own business, and this guy comes up, this American major, just promoted, he said—except that he wasn't no American major, he was this shit Oppenheimer, and you mean to sit there and tell me *you actually bought the cocksucker a drink?*"

Baker-Bates sighed. "In point of fact, General, he bought me one."

"He bought *you* one," the General said, packing his tone with incredulity.

"A Scotch and soda."

Knocker Grubbs nodded slowly several times. He had a big chunk of a head, still vaguely handsome, with small, very pale blue eyes that looked stupid, the way some very pale blue eyes do. His best features were his strong nose and chin, which rescued his profile from not enough forehead and a wet, weak mouth. What was left of his hair was a smoky gray.

Grubbs stopped nodding, but kept his voice full of amazement. "And so you just stood there, bellied up to the bar with this Kraut killer that half the Army is looking for, and you and him just bullshitted each other: have I got it right, Major?"

"Yes, sir, I'm afraid that you do."

"And you couldn't tell from his accent that he wasn't American?"

"He had no German accent."

"None at all?"

"None that I could detect, General. But he had two American accents. One was what I suppose could be called American standard, and the other was Texan."

"How the fuck would you know what a Texan talks like?"

"Are you from Texas, General?"

"Amarillo."

"Actually, sir, he spoke very much the way you do."

"Like I do?"

"Yes, sir."

"You're not trying to be cute, are you, Major?"

"Only accurate, General."

"I'd hate to think that you were trying to be cute. I don't know what they do with majors with funny little cocksucker mustaches who turn cute in your army, mister, but I know what they do with them in mine. And I'll tell you one more thing, fella: you're goddamned lucky you're not under my command."

"Yes, sir, I would think that I am. Lucky, that is," Baker-Bates said, and decided that Knocker Grubbs wasn't quite real.

"So you two, you and this Kraut killer, parted the best of pals, right? And then you sat down all by yourself in the American officers' club and had a nice, hot American meal, and maybe smoked a couple of American cigarettes, and then when all that was done, you wandered over to see Lieutenant Meyer here, maybe an hour later, and that's when you found out you'd been boozing it up with the Kraut killer that everybody's looking for. And that's when you told the Lieutenant here that maybe it might be a good idea to seal off the complex on account of this crazy Kraut killer you'd just had a friendly drink with might still be killing an hour or two hanging around the PX or the Class Six Store, right? Except that he'd long skipped, and we've got fuck-all ideas about where he skipped to. Are those the facts, Major? I wanta be good and goddamned sure I got the facts right for the report I'm gonna have to send your CO."

"Your facts, sir, are essentially correct."

"How 'bout you, Lieutenant: you think I've got the facts right?"

"Yes, sir; except that we're having copies made of Oppenheimer's photograph, and we'll distribute them throughout the Zone."

"You know what they call that down in Texas?"

151

"No, sir, I don't," Lieutenant Meyer said, wondering how long this dimwit was going to continue with his reaming out of Baker-Bates—who, in Lieutenant Meyer's estimation, had slyly got in a few licks of his own, especially that one about the Texas accent.

"Well, I'll tell you what we call it down in Texas," Knocker Grubbs said. "We call it locking the barn after the horse is gone."

"Gosh, sir, that's vivid," Lieutenant Meyer said.

"They don't say that in England, do they, Major?"

"Not recently, General," Baker-Bates said.

"Well, I'm gonna tell you one final thing, sonny. You're down here because Berlin wants you down here. But you fuck up one more time, and Berlin or no Berlin, I'm gonna have your sweet ass for Sunday breakfast. Do I make myself clear?"

"Quite clear, General," Baker-Bates said. "In fact, extremely so."

"Dismissed," the General snapped.

Baker-Bates and Lieutenant Meyer rose.

"Not you, Lieutenant," Knocker Grubbs said with a mean smile. "Hell, I haven't even half started with you yet."

16 After the plane landed at Frankfurt's Rhine-Main airport, Jackson and Bill Swanton, the INS man, watched as the Army wives filed out of the aircraft first. While the two men waited, Swanton took out a notebook and a pen.

"You ever see one of these?" Swanton said.

"What?"

"The pen. They call 'em ball-points. I bought it for twenty-nine ninety-five on sale in New York." He wrote his name and his Berlin address in his notebook, tore out the sheet, and handed it to Jackson. "Maybe if you get up to Berlin, I could be of some help on your book."

"Thanks very much," Jackson said.

Swanton gave his pen one more admiring glance before

returning it to his shirt pocket. "You know what they say these things will do?"

"What?"

"Write underwater. Now, just what in hell would you want to write underwater?"

Jackson thought about it. "Maybe a suicide note if you were drowning yourself."

Swanton brightened. "Yeah, that's a possibility, isn't it?"

He followed Jackson off the plane. When they reached the terminal, he held out his hand. Jackson took it. "Thanks for the booze, Brother Jackson," Swanton said. "And in Berlin. If you get up there, look me up."

"I'll do that."

When they entered the terminal, a loudspeaker was calling Jackson's name. "Will Mr. Minor Jackson report to the information desk. Mr. Minor Jackson."

The information desk was manned by a harassed Air Corps staff sergeant.

"I'm Jackson."

"Okay, Mr. Jackson," the Sergeant said, opening a drawer and taking out an envelope. "This is for you, and so is the Lieutenant over there." He nodded at Lieutenant Meyer, who was standing nearby and trying not to stare at Jackson.

"What's in the envelope?" Jackson said.

The Sergeant sighed. "I don't know, sir. I didn't open it. I don't usually open other people's envelopes, but if you'd like me to, sir, I will. All I know is that an Air Corps captain gave it to me about three hours ago and made me swear that I'd get it to you. And that's what I've just done, haven't I, sir?"

"You've been swell," Jackson said.

"Can I be of any assistance, Mr. Jackson? I'm Lieutenant Meyer."

"From Milwaukee."

"Yes, sir."

"My nursemaid."

154

"Liaison, Mr. Jackson, but if you want to call me a nursemaid, or anything else that might come to mind, even something a little vulgar, well, that's just fine, because I'm used to it on account of this very afternoon I spent one hour and fifteen minutes having my ass chewed out by a one-star general who's not very bright, but who does know how to chew ass, and who called me names that are a lot worse than nursemaid. So if you want to call me that or, as I said, anything else that comes to mind, that's just fine, Mr. Jackson, sir."

Jackson stared at him. "You're in shock, pal."

"Probably. It's been a very long, very rough day."

"What kind of orders did you get from Washington about me?"

"Very explicit ones. I'm to be at your beck and call and worm my way into your confidence."

"We're off to a good start."

"Yes, sir. I was hoping you'd think so."

"Think you could beckon or call up a drink around here?"

"Yes, sir. There's a VIP lounge. With only a little skillful lying I can probably get us into that."

"Let me see what this is all about first," Jackson said, and ripped open the envelope. Inside were a key and a plain white card. On the card were written an address and the message "Try to make it by nine." The message was unsigned.

Jackson handed the card to Lieutenant Meyer. "You know where this address is?"

Lieutenant Meyer glanced at it. "Yes, sir. It's a rather nice address not too far from the zoo. I mean it will be a rather nice address if it's still standing."

"Can we have a drink and still make it by nine?"

Lieutenant Meyer glanced at his watch. "Easily."

"Well, let's go do that and you can worm your way into my confidence some more."

It took Lieutenant Meyer, talking steadily, a little more

than fifteen minutes to relate virtually all that he knew about Kurt Oppenheimer. When he was finished, so were the drinks. Lieutenant Meyer tipped his up, let an ice cube bounce against his teeth, swallowed the last drop, put the glass down, and stared at Jackson.

"Tell me something," he said with the air of a man ready to receive a confidence.

"Sure."

"Why 're you looking for him?"

He really expects an answer, Jackson thought. Not only that, but he also expects a truthful answer. Jackson smiled and said, "I don't think I said I was looking for him."

"Washington says you are."

Jackson kept his smile in place. "Washington hopes that I am."

It was a long, bleak stare that Lieutenant Meyer gave Jackson. "Well, shit, mister."

"Disappointed?"

"Oh, hell, no," Lieutenant Meyer said. "I don't feel silly, either."

"You'll get over it."

"You used to be with the OSS, didn't you?"

"Is that what Washington says?"

"That's what it says."

"Then it must be true."

"How good were you?"

"Average," Jackson said. "Maybe C-plus."

Lieutenant Meyer shook his head. "They wouldn't let you run like this if you were just C-plus."

"I wouldn't put too much faith in Washington if I were you."

Lieutenant Meyer's mouth tucked itself down at the corners as he again shook his head. "Jesus, that's all I need, a mystery man." He reached into the pocket of his blouse and brought out several cards. "Well, here you go, mystery man," he said, and slid the cards over to Jackson.

"One of them will get you into the PX so you can buy cigarettes and toothpaste. Another one's for the Class Six Store where you can buy your booze. That one you've got your finger on will let you eat at the officers' club. The food there's not so hot, but it's cheap, and if you don't eat there, then you're going to have to depend on black-market restaurants. They're as expensive as hell, but since you're a mystery man, and probably rich with it, maybe you can afford them. And the last one's for gasoline, if you should get hold of a car—which I hope to hell you will, since I don't much like playing chauffeur. As for where you're going to sleep, Washington said that's going to be up to you, so I don't really give much of a shit."

"I'll manage," Jackson said, smiled, and pocketed the cards.

Lieutenant Meyer studied Jackson for several seconds. He took in the gray hair and the lean face with its almost too regular features. Had it not been for the not-quite-gray eyes, the face would have been a toss-up between pleasant and handsome. The eyes made it too alert for either, Lieutenant Meyer decided. Much too alert. His brains leak out through his eyes. Otherwise he'd be Fraternity Row, maybe rush captain at Phi Delta Theta—if you took away ten years and all that gray hair.

"Let me guess," Lieutenant Meyer said.

"Sure."

"Dartmouth."

Jackson shook his head and smiled slightly. "The University of Virginia."

Lieutenant Meyer didn't bother to keep the sneer out of his voice. "The gentleman factory."

"I suppose."

"You know something, Mr. Jackson, sir?"

"What?"

"I've been a little slow, maybe even a little dense, but I think I'm beginning to figure out why you're in on this thing."

"Why?"

"Money. There's money in it somewhere, isn't there?"

Jackson smiled again—a cool, remote, totally cynical smile. "You're getting warm, Lieutenant. Very warm."

At five minutes until nine the jeep, with Lieutenant Meyer at the wheel, drew up at the address near the Frankfurt zoo. Jackson used his lighter to examine the card the Air Corps Sergeant had given him.

"You're sure this is the right address?"

"I'm sure," Lieutenant Meyer said. "Some house, isn't it?"

"Some house," Jackson agreed, got out of the jeep, and reached for his bag.

Still staring at what he could see of the house, which was illuminated only by the lights that came from two of its windows and the jeep's headlights, Lieutenant Meyer said, "Fifteen rooms. At least fifteen rooms. You sure you don't know who owns it?"

"I have no idea."

"Somebody rich."

"Apparently."

"Not even touched," Lieutenant Meyer said, shaking his head. "You notice that? Both houses on either side wiped out by the bombs and this one's not even touched."

"I noticed."

"You sure you don't want me to wait?"

"For what?"

"To make sure it's the right address."

Jackson shook his head. "It's the right address."

"But you don't even know who lives here."

"I didn't say that, " Jackson said. "I said I didn't know who owns it."

Lieutenant Meyer sighed. "More mystery-man shit."

"Sorry."

"Sure you are." Lieutenant Meyer started the jeep. "Well, if you want to beckon and call some more, you know where I am."

"I know. Thanks, Lieutenant, for everything. You've been most helpful."

"I've been a stupid jerk is what I've been," Lieutenant Meyer said, and drove off.

Jackson watched him go and then walked up to the iron gate set in the chest-high brick wall that seemed to surround the house. The gate was unlocked. Jackson went through it and up the stone path to the door. He tried the door, but it was locked. He took out the key that had been in the envelope along with the card and inserted it into the lock. It turned easily.

Jackson pushed open the door and went through it into an entry hall that was illuminated by a kerosene lamp. He put his bag down on the parquet floor and looked around. The lamp rested on a table. Farther back, a flight of stairs curved up to the second floor. To Jackson's left were a pair of sliding doors. They were closed, but some light leaked out from underneath their lower edges.

Jackson went over to the doors and tried them. They were unlocked. He shoved them apart and went into a room that was lit by another kerosene lamp and the glow that came from the grate of a coal-burning fireplace. Two large, high-backed chairs were drawn up on either side of the fireplace. Next to one of the chairs was a small table. On it were two glasses and a bottle of whiskey.

Still looking around, Jackson noticed some dark oil paintings on two walls and in a far corner a baby-grand piano with its lid up.

"Where are you?" he said.

"Over here," the dwarf said. "By the fire."

17   Jackson moved over to the two large chairs, glanced briefly down at the dwarf, warmed his hands before the coal grate, and, without turning, said, "Where're the women, Nick?"

Ploscaru wriggled with pleasure. It was exactly the cool and laconic greeting that he had hoped for. The American was so absolutely predictable.

"I've failed you, my boy," Ploscaru said with mock despair. Then he brightened. "But there is a little parlor-maid that we could scare up for you if . . ." He let the trail off and finished it with a small gesture.

"Never mind," Jackson said, and turned from the blazing fire. "There's no coal in Germany, Nick. I've been reading *Time* magazine. There's no coal in the American Zone, anyway. When they divided Germany up, Russia got the wheat, Britain got the coal, and America got the scenery."

"There's a ton of coal in the cellar, I believe."

The dwarf was wearing his green silk dressing gown and his red slippers. His green eyes seemed to dance with anticipation over the questions that he knew would come.

"Okay, Nick. Whose house?"

"A cousin's. A distant cousin—thrice removed, as I believe you say in the States. He's actually a Swede and he's with the United Nations. Something called UNRRA. What ever does UNRRA stand for?"

"It's the UN Relief and Rehabilitation Agency."

"Yes, well, my cousin runs the DP camp at a place called Badenhausen. It used to be a concentration camp, I understand, but now they keep DP's there. I wonder if any of those who are now its guests were once its inmates. Well, no matter. In any event, my cousin is on leave for a month, and so we have his house until then. It's rather a nice place. Fourteen rooms, I think, with a staff of five. So much better than a hotel, don't you agree?"

"Sure."

"We'll need a car, of course. The butler gave me a tip on one that we can look into tomorrow."

"The butler."

"Didn't I mention the household staff? I thought I did. There's the butler; the cook, of course; a gardener; and two maids. Rather decadently colonial, don't you think? I mean, all the servants. Shall we have a drink? No bourbon, I'm afraid, but there is some rather decent Scotch."

"I'll fix them," Jackson said, and stepped over to the glasses and the Scotch bottle. "Have a nice trip over?"

"Very pleasant."

"Let me guess. The Air Corps again."

"How very perceptive of you, Minor. There was this young captain that I'd known in Ploesti. Shot down, you know. He was only a second lieutenant then, but he still believes that I somehow saved his life. Well, I bumped into

161

him in Washington and he mentioned that he was making what he called a 'goodie run.'"

"A goodie run?"

"Yes, it seems that they sometimes do that—fly bombers full of luxury goods over to what the young Captain called the top brass. Rank has its privileges, Minor. So when I happened to mention that I was interested in getting to Germany, he wanted to know how I got along with animals. It turned out that part of his cargo was six Pekingese that belonged to some general's wife. I get along famously with animals, as you know; even Pekingese, which are, quite frankly, terrible little beasts. So my young Captain and I struck a bargain. He agreed to give me a ride over if I would look after the dogs. It was a quite pleasant trip, as I said. Very quick. We didn't even stop once, although we did land at Wiesbaden instead of Frankfurt, which was a bit inconvenient. A huge plane —one of these B-29 things. But there was miles of room so I had no trouble in bringing along a few cigarettes. How many did you bring?"

"A carton," Jackson said.

"Well, I brought a few more than that. As a matter of fact, it was the young Captain who suggested that they would come in quite handy."

"How many's a few more, Nick?"

"Let me think. About forty-eight thousand, actually."

"Jesus."

"That's four big cases. There was a fifth case, but when we landed at Wiesbaden, I was inside of that, of course."

"So they smuggled you in along with your cigarettes."
Naturally."

"I wonder."

"You wonder what?"

"When they catch you, whether you'll be shot or hanged."

Ploscaru chuckled, reached into a pocket of his dressing gown, and took out the Swiss passport. He handed it to Jackson. "Page three, I think. A most official-looking

162

entry visa properly stamped by the U.S. Constabulary, which is handling the borders, you know. It cost me two cartons of cigarettes at the DP camp that I spoke of. My cousin, before he left, put me onto a most expert forger there, a Czech. My cousin, I'm sorry to say, dabbles a bit in the black market himself."

Jackson examined the stamp. "It looks all right." He handed back the passport. "So you've been here awhile?"

"Almost twenty-four hours."

"Then you must have left Washington just after you saw me off at the station."

"Baltimore, actually. We flew out of Baltimore. Now tell me, how was your trip?"

"Rotten," Jackson said. "I was met at the airport by a Lieutenant Meyer. Lieutenant LaFollette Meyer, who's with the CIC here."

"The counterintelligence people."

"Right. Lieutenant Meyer seemed to think that I was going to help him find Kurt Oppenheimer."

"You disabused him of that notion, I trust."

"Not completely. Lieutenant Meyer will probably come in handy. I turned mysterious instead."

Ploscaru nodded judiciously. "Yes, that's often effective. He's young, I take it?"

"Twenty-six or so. He gave me a rundown on Oppenheimer. It seems that he's just killed somebody else."

"Who?"

"Somebody called Damm. From what Meyer tells me, Damm may have needed killing, but the Army's getting awfully upset with Oppenheimer. It's not only the killing that bothers them. It's also the fact that he's going around posing as a U.S. Army major."

"What a wonderful disguise!"

"It fooled Baker-Bates."

"Dear me. Is he here?"

"Uh-huh. Your old pal. Apparently Oppenheimer braced him at the American officers' club. They had quite a chat. Oppenheimer even bought him a drink."

Ploscaru chuckled. "Poor Gilbert must be absolutely livid."

"They also think that Oppenheimer has a list."

"A list of what?"

"Of the people that he's going to kill next."

Jackson watched as the dwarf slowly lit one of his Old Gold cigarettes. When the cigarette was burning satisfactorily, Ploscaru reached for the drink that Jackson had poured him and took a long swallow. Then he sighed.

"You'll have to interpret that for me," Jackson said.

"What?"

"The sigh."

"It means, I suppose, that instead of the brief respite that I'd hoped for, we must instead be up and doing."

"Doing what?"

"Why, finding young Oppenheimer, of course."

"When?"

"We start tomorrow morning."

"Not tonight?"

Ploscaru frowned, but the wrinkles in his forehead quickly smoothed themselves out. "Oh, I see. You're joking just a little, aren't you? You must be terribly tired."

"You're right; I am."

"We'll get a good sleep tonight, have a nice breakfast tomorrow, and then be off to our appointments."

"Appointments?"

"Yes, you have one for ten o'clock tomorrow with Leah Oppenheimer. She arrived late yesterday from Paris. A terribly complicated trip, I understand, by train."

Jackson nodded slowly. "You're not coming with me?"

"No, I think not. I have my own appointment to keep."

"What appointment?"

"Why, my appointment at the zoo, naturally."

It had stopped raining an hour before. From his seat on the bench near the zoo's pond, Ploscaru watched as the neatly dressed old man took the small cloth bundle from his briefcase. The old man, limping slightly, had

164

arrived some five minutes before. He walked with the aid of a heavy cane. For a while, for nearly the full five minutes, he had stood at the edge of the pond, leaning on his cane and gazing out at the ducks.

Now he took the bundle from his briefcase and started calling to them softly. The ducks ignored him until one of them, more curious or hungrier than the rest, left the pond and, quacking loudly, waddled up to the old man, who opened the cloth bundle and fed the duck some bits of bread. The duck ate them hungrily and quacked for more.

The old man raised his heavy walking stick and quickly beat the duck to death. Then he stuffed it into his brief-case, snapped that shut, and looked around furtively. When he saw Ploscaru, he stiffened; looked as if he were about to explain, or at least try to; apparently thought better of it; turned; and limped quickly away.

Enjoy your duck dinner, old man, Ploscaru thought, and looked at his watch. For once he was early, or nearly so. Had he not been early, he would have missed the duck's execution. He wondered how long the old man had gone without eating anything but bread before hunger had driven him to do what he had just done. A day? Two days? Three? Ploscaru settled on three, because the old man had looked very neat and respectable. He wondered what he had been before he had turned duck killer. A teacher? A minor bureaucrat, perhaps? Something stiff and proper, anyway. Something with a handle to it, a title of sorts, so that the old man could be called Herr This or Herr That. Now he can be called Herr Duck Killer.

The dwarf grinned a little and took out an Old Gold. Just as he was lighting it, a hoarse voice from behind him whispered, "Nicolae, is that you?"

Without turning, Ploscaru said, "Who else would it be, Mircea?"

"I had to be sure," the hoarse voice said.

"For God's sake, man, come out from behind the bushes."

The big, shambling figure that emerged from behind the clump of evergreens belonged to Mircea Ulescu, not quite a giant, but well over six feet tall, who swooped down on the dwarf, lifted him by his armpits, stood him on the bench, bent down, and kissed him wetly on both cheeks.

"Nicolae, Nicolae, Nicolae! It's really you."

"Of course it's I, you lummox," the dwarf snapped, but grinned as he wiped the wet from his cheeks.

"Yesterday at the camp, I knew it was you, but I said nothing. One never knows, these days. But then when I got the note and it said to be here at the zoo—"

"I know all that, Mircea," the dwarf said, interrupting.

"Still as crazy for zoos as ever," the big man said, gazing fondly down at Ploscaru, who still stood on the bench. "Little Nicolae." Two tears formed in the inside corners of the big man's eyes and rolled down his cheeks. The eyes were an impossibly soft gray, a romantic's eyes, and they didn't at all seem to go with the thrusting nose or the wide slash of mouth that could have belonged to someone who, early in life, had been taught never to smile. Except for the eyes it could have been a soldier's face. Or an unhappy policeman's.

"Little Nicolae," Mircea Ulescu said again, and patted the dwarf on the head. "My oldest friend."

"Stop it, you fool," Ploscaru said gruffly, although unable to disguise his pleasure. "Can we sit down now like two adults?"

"Sit," Ulescu said, quickly producing a dirty handkerchief, which he used to dust off the bench. "Sit, Nicolae; sit, and we shall talk in our own language of the old days. How weary I grow of speaking German. It's a barbarian's language."

"You were speaking it eagerly enough when I last saw you."

The big man nodded gloomily. "Once again I picked the wrong horse. First the Iron Guards, then the Germans."

"You didn't wait for the Russians, I see."

"They would have hanged me. The Germans made me promises, none of which they kept. I came back with them. What else could I do? Oh, Gód, Nicolae, how I miss Bucharest and the old days." Two more tears rolled down the big man's cheeks. He used the dirty handkerchief to mop them up.

"So now you're a DP?"

"I'm not even that legally. Romania was a belligerent nation. A citizen of a belligerent nation can't be a DP— not legally. Now I'm an Estonian."

"You can't speak Estonian."

"But I speak French like a native. So I claim that I was born in Estonia, but reared in Paris. I have the authorities very confused."

Ploscaru brought out his Old Golds and offered them to Ulescu, who smiled, shook his head, and produced a package of Camels. "I prefer these, Nicolae," he said, and lit both cigarettes with an American Zippo.

The dwarf eyed the big man more carefully. "Even as a DP, Mircea, you don't appear to have been missing many meals."

The big man shrugged. "Because of the terrible suffering that we DP's have undergone, the authorities feed us two thousand calories a day. It's mostly stew, but still quite nourishing." He changed the subject abruptly. "Did you see that old fellow kill the duck, Nicolae? Wasn't that something? I don't think it was his first time, do you? No, I think he comes here regularly, perhaps once a week, and goes home with a nice duck dinner."

"You're prospering, Mircea." The dwarf made it a flat accusation.

The big man bridled a bit. "And look at you with your nice little suit." He fingered its material. "Tailored, of course, but then your clothes were always tailored. It couldn't be that you're still with British intelligence, could it, Nicolae? No, of course not. The British would never pay enough for you to be able to afford such a nice little gray suit. Possibly the Americans, eh? Someone told me that there at the end, just before the Russians came, you and the American fliers became very thick. Where have you come from, Nicolae—America?"

"California."

"Really?"

The dwarf nodded.

"Hollywood? Have you seen Hollywood?"

"I lived there for a while."

"And the women, Nicolae. Tell me about the women. You would know them all. You always did have luck with women."

"Beautiful."

"Ahh."

"But not as beautiful as in Bucharest in the old days."

"No, of course not."

There was a silence as the two men seemed to lapse into reverie. Mircea Ulescu stole a look at the dwarf.

"Nicolae," he said.

"Yes."

"I have become a thief." The confession came out as a hoarse whisper.

"So."

"Can you imagine it? I, Mircea Ulescu, have turned common thief."

"Not so common, I'm sure."

"But still a thief, even though a good one."

"Well, one must do what one must these days. Tell me, are there many thieves at the camp?"

"It's a den of them."

"And what do you steal, Mircea?"

The big man shrugged. "We're organized into gangs." He brightened a bit. "I'm the leader of mine, of course."

"Of course."

"We steal only from the Americans. Cigarettes, gasoline, coffee, Tootsie Rolls." He frowned. "Can you imagine a conquering nation with a sweet called Tootsie Rolls?"

"The Americans are a strange but wonderful people, Mircea."

"Yes, I know. Others in the camp steal from the Germans. The Poles especially. The Poles like to beat the Germans up, steal their pigs, and rape their women. But Poles are like that. They think they are justified. We, naturally—my bunch—we steal only from the Americans. And sometimes we do business with them, too."

"Do you do business mostly with officers or with other ranks?"

"Mostly with officers."

"I am looking for a certain officer, Mircea. At one time you were a very good policeman. Tell me, are you still?"

"I have not forgotten the old techniques. One does not forget those so easily, Nicolae."

The dwarf nodded. "You mean the judicious bribe, the suborned witness."

The big man shrugged again. "Those and others."

"I was in Frankfurt for only an hour or so before I learned that any documentation that I might need for my stay here could be most readily obtained at the DP camp."

"Ah, so that's what you were doing there. You must have been to see Kubista the Czech. He is our best forger."

"I believe that was his name. Are there a number of forgers in the DP camp?"

"Several, but Kubista is the best."

"This American officer whom I spoke of. He might have use for the services of a forger. Do you think you might look into that for me, old friend? Find out whether an American officer, possibly a major, has bought himself some documents recently? There would be a little something in it for you, of course."

"I hesitate because of friendship to ask how much is a little, Nicolae."

"Shall we say a hundred dollars?"

"Greenbacks?"

"Of course."

"In advance?"

"Naturally," the dwarf said, and took out his wallet.

18   The butler wasn't a very good driver. Or perhaps it was just that he wasn't too familiar with his employer's official UNRRA car, an Army-surplus 1941 Ford sedan with a lot of hard miles on it. He stalled frequently, grated the gears, and drove in second most of the time as though unaware of or indifferent to the third gear.

"This afternoon, Herr Doktor," the butler said over his shoulder to Jackson, "we'll go to inspect a proper car."

"Fine," Jackson said from the back seat of the Ford into which he had been ushered by an imperious gesture from the butler. Jackson wasn't at all sure why he was being addressed as Herr Doktor, but assumed that it was some fairy tale that the dwarf had spun for the butler's benefit. He wondered idly whether he was supposed to be a doctor of medicine or of philosophy.

"I described the car yesterday to Herr Direktor."

"Herr Direktor?"

"The little gentleman."

"Ah, yes," Jackson said. "Herr Direktor Ploscaru."

"It is a rare name for a Swiss."

"Very rare."

"But I think it is wonderful for a person with such a handicap as the Herr Direktor's to achieve so important a position."

"The best things sometimes come in small packages," Jackson said, wincing at his own banality.

"How true," the butler said gravely. "How very, very true."

There was no more conversation for several blocks. Then the butler said, "I was not always a butler, you understand, Herr Doktor."

"No?"

"No. Before the war and even during it I was a caterer in Berlin. I had my own firm. We specialized in weddings and—and certain civic affairs." He sped over the last a bit hastily, Jackson thought.

"Then after the war, when the Americans arrived, I went to work for them in a position that entailed many grave responsibilities."

"I'm sure."

"It did not last."

"What happened?"

"My brother-in-law, whom I had taken into my catering firm and taught the business, denounced me to the Americans for having been a member of the Party. I was discharged and the Americans gave my brother-in-law my job, which was what he had in mind all along."

"Were you?"

"Please?"

"A member of the Party."

171

The butler shrugged. "Naturally. As I said, my firm catered many civic affairs—receptions, mostly. To be awarded such affairs, one had to be a member of the Party. It was simply a business proposition. I did not, of course, participate in its activities. I am without politics, and I thought the Party mostly foolishness. But my brother-in-law, on the other hand . . ." The butler's voice trailed off.

"What about him?"

'He was very much interested in politics. He tried to join the Party six separate times and was rejected each time—on the ground of emotional instability." The butler took one hand off the wheel and tapped his right temple significantly. "*Ein sonderbarer Kanz.*" A queer customer.

"Not quite right, was he?" Jackson said.

"Not quite. I told the Americans this, naturally. It was my duty."

"Just as it was your brother-in-law's duty to inform them about you."

"Exactly. Regulations must be observed, or where would any of us be?"

"Where indeed?"

"Unfortunately, two months later my brother-in-law went berserk and killed the American who had hired him. Strangled him to death. A captain and a very fine fellow, I thought, even though he did dismiss me."

"You bore the captain no grudge?"

"Certainly not. He was only abiding by the regulations."

"Maybe if he hadn't, he'd still be alive."

The butler turned the idea over in his mind, then shook his head negatively. "It is probably better not to think about such things."

"Probably," Jackson said.

Ten minutes later they were at the address that Leah Oppenheimer had given him in Ensenada at a time that now seemed months ago. The butler hastily got out from behind the wheel and hurried around to Jackson's door as fast as he could, which wasn't very fast because he was at least sixty and seemed to suffer from an arthritic right leg.

"What are you called?" Jackson said as he climbed out.

"Heinrich, Herr Doktor."

"That's a pretty bad limp you've got, Heinrich."

"I know. It is arthritis. I was hoping that the Herr Doktor perhaps could give me some advice."

"Take two aspirin twice a day and keep it warm and dry."

"Thank you very much, Herr Doktor."

"You're welcome," Jackson said, and started for the building in which Leah Oppenheimer was staying. He noticed that the address was in a block of apartment houses that had suffered only minor damage from the bombing. The stone used to construct them was the dull red Rhenish sandstone that had been used to build much of Frankfurt. Across the street the same stone composed a heap of rubble, which might at one time have formed the twin of the building that he was now entering. Jackson found it strange that bombs could have leveled one block and left the one directly across the street virtually unscathed. He wondered what percentage of Frankfurt had been destroyed: sixty percent, seventy? The ruined sections all looked depressingly the same. Before the war Frankfurt had not been a handsome town. Now it was ugly. Curiously enough, it still looked old, though. Old and ruined and ugly.

The address said that the apartment number was 8. According to the directory in the small foyer, number 8 was occupied by E. Scheel. Jackson started up the stairs and found number 8 on the third floor. He knocked, and the door was opened by a young woman wearing a fur coat. Jackson thought the coat looked expensive.

"Fräulein Scheel?"

"Yes. You must be Mr. Jackson. Please come in."

"Thank you."

After entering the apartment, Jackson found himself in a small reception area. Three doors led off it. There was no furniture in the reception area other than a small, very thin Oriental rug. Jackson thought that the rug looked expensive too.

"You will excuse me if I do not offer to take your coat," Eva Scheel said. "There is no heat today, and I think you will be more comfortable with it on. Leah is just through here."

She opened a door, and Jackson followed her into a sitting room. By the window facing the street sat Leah Oppenheimer. She wore a belted camel's-hair coat turned up around her throat. When she saw Jackson, she smiled and held out her hand. Jackson took it, bowing slightly just the way they had taught him to bow all those years ago at that school in Switzerland. You may be almost broke, he told himself, but your manners are still expensive.

With her smile still in place, Leah Oppenheimer said, "So we meet again in yet another country, Mr. Jackson."

"So it would seem," he said, wondering whether she had planned the slightly stagey remark beforehand or whether it had just come naturally. He couldn't quite decide which he preferred. Either way it reminded him of her wretched prose style.

"You have already met my friend, Fräulein Scheel."

"Yes."

"Do sit down, Mr. Jackson. Once more, you are just in time for tea."

Jackson chose a spindly-looking chair upholstered in maroon velvet whose legs ended in serpent's heads. Each serpent's mouth was wide open and in it was clutched a glass ball. He noticed that the rest of the furniture in the room was just as awful. Eva Scheel chose a similar chair closer to the tea table.

The Oppenheimer woman made her usual ritual out of serving the tea. "Although we have no heat," she said, "the electricity was on for two hours just before you came, so we managed to boil some water for tea."

Because he couldn't think of anything else to say, Jackson said that that was nice.

"Remember those delicious little cakes that we had in the hotel in Mexico, Mr. Jackson?"

Jackson said he remembered.

"Well, I'm afraid we'll have none of those or anything like them this time because of my own stupidity. It would have been so easy for me to bring some things from Mexico City. But fortunately, Fräulein Scheel has come up with a solution."

Jackson couldn't bring himself to ask what the solution was, so he merely smiled in what he hoped was a polite and interested way.

"The solution," Eva Scheel said in a dry tone, "consists of some delicately sliced sweets called Milky Ways, courtesy of the American Army."

"Eva has an American friend, a young officer," Leah said, handing Jackson his cup of tea. "He seems like a very nice young man. I met him last night. His name is Meyer. Lieutenant Meyer."

Over the rim of his cup, Jackson eyed Eva Scheel with new interest. Well, what have we here? he wondered. A nice little German girl dying to get to America, or something else? Something else, he decided after trying to visualize Eva Scheel in bed with Lieutenant Meyer, which was a game he often played. For some reason, the Scheel-Meyer combination just didn't work. He also had to decide quickly whether to mention that he had already met Lieutenant Meyer. If you don't, it'll be a silent lie that could complicate things. One of Jackson's few personal rules was never to lie if the truth would do.

"Would that be Lieutenant LaFollette Meyer from Milwaukee?" he said, and hoped that the smile on his face was a winning one.

"Do you know him?" Leah said.

"We met yesterday at the airport. Lieutenant Meyer is very much interested in your brother—in an official sort of way."

Leah Oppenheimer nodded sadly. "Yes, I know. He had many questions for me last night, most of which I could not answer. Isn't it terrible—all those people?"

"You mean the dead ones?"

"Yes."

"That your brother's killed?"

"I did not know. During the war I knew that he had to do awful things. But now . . ." She shook her head. "He must be terribly ill. That's why we must find him, Mr. Jackson: so that we can get him proper medical treatment."

She was lying, Jackson realized, about not having known that her brother was something more than a harmless scamp, but he decided to let it pass because, again, it was simpler that way.

"You think they'll let you do that?" he said.

"What do you mean?"

"There are three governments looking for your brother —the Americans, the British, and the Russians—or so I've been told: about the Russians, I mean. What I'm saying is do you think that they'll simply let you spirit your brother away to some nice quiet sanitarium and then forget about all those people he's killed?"

Eva Scheel rose, picked up a plate, and offered it to Jackson. "Have some Milky Ways, Mr. Jackson; they really go quite nicely with tea."

The candy bars had been sliced into quarter-inch-thick pieces and arranged with a great deal of care on the plate. Although Jackson wasn't overly fond of candy, he took one, smiled his thanks, and popped it into his mouth. She's giving her friend time to think, he thought as he watched Eva Scheel put the plate back on the table, resume her seat, and start stroking the collar of her fur coat as though she found it comforting.

176

"The Russians," Leah said in almost a whisper. "I did not know about the Russians." She looked at Jackson and then at Eva Scheel. "Why would the Russians . . . ?" She didn't finish her question.

Eva Scheel shrugged and looked at Jackson. "Perhaps Mr. Jackson would know."

"I can only guess," he said.

Leah nodded. "Please."

"Oil."

"Oil?"

"And politics. In the Middle East or Near East or whatever you want to call it, they're all mixed up. The United States doesn't have any Middle East policy—at least, none that's discernible. The Russian policy is quite obvious. They want to move the British out so they can move in. Right now they're tilting toward the Arabs, because they're smart enough to realize that you can't be at odds with the Arabs in Palestine without its reverberating throughout the rest of the Moslem world— and that means Saudi Arabia and Bengal and Malaya and North Africa and the Dardanelles; not to mention those sections of Russia which are also Islamic. Your brother, ill or not, is a very good killer. The Russians could drop him in almost any place where things are in a state of flux—Iran, for example, or Iraq—and if your brother took out just the right person or persons, then the resulting mess could be all the excuse that the Russians would need to move in."

"What an interesting theory," Eva Scheel said with a smile that was almost polite. "A bit farfetched, but interesting."

"Then there's Palestine," Jackson said.

"What about Palestine?" Eva Scheel said.

Jackson looked at Leah Oppenheimer. "Your brother's politics are a bit strange. Do you think he's still a Communist?"

She shook her head. "I have no way of knowing."

"Let's say that he is. Let's even say, for the sake of argument, that he's the fervent kind. Now suppose the Russians were able to hand the Palestinians a top-notch killer who was also a renegade Jew who could pass as an American or an Englishman—or a German refugee. Don't you think the Palestinians might make good use of him—perhaps even infiltrate him into the Irgun or the Stern Group?"

Leah Oppenheimer shook her head vigorously. "That's ridiculous."

"Is it?"

"My brother could never be anyone's paid assassin."

"Nobody really knows what your brother is—or what he could be, given sufficient incentive. Right now he's killing bad Germans, or thinks he is. I don't really think that bothers the Americans or the British or the Russians too much, not as long as he just keeps on killing those who're really rotten. But there's no percentage in it—at least, not for the Russians or the Americans or the British. Right now his talents, such as they are, are being wasted. Any one of the three could use him somewhere else—and right now the Middle East seems the most likely spot."

"I'm surprised that you included the Americans, Mr. Jackson," Eva Scheel said.

"Why?"

"I thought they would be too—well, pure."

"We lost our purity during the war. Like virginity, once you lose it, you never get it back."

"Do many people find your flippancy as offensive as I do?"

Jackson stared at Eva Scheel for several moments. Finally he said, "I wasn't trying to be flippant; I was just trying to state the problem, and believe me, there are problems. For example, you. You might be just one hell of a problem."

"I beg your pardon."

"You're a friend of Lieutenant Meyer's. Lieutenant

178

Meyer is looking for Kurt Oppenheimer. He wants to find him and lock him up someplace. Kurt Oppenheimer's sister and I are engaged in a conspiracy to prevent this. So the problem is to prevent what we conspire about here today from getting back to Lieutenant Meyer. I don't think I can make it any clearer than that."

"I have known Leah and Kurt Oppenheimer far longer than I have known Lieutenant Meyer, Mr. Jackson."

"Sure."

"You sound unconvinced."

"I'm sorry."

She gazed at him steadily for a long time without blinking. "I assure you," she said in a low, almost passionate voice, "I would never betray two of my oldest friends to someone like Lieutenant Meyer."

Jackson wanted to ask what was so wrong with Lieutenant Meyer, but before he could, Leah Oppenheimer said, "We can trust Eva, Mr. Jackson. We must."

Jackson shrugged. "It's up to you, of course. I'm sorry, but whenever anyone says, 'Trust me,' I tend to run very fast in the opposite direction."

"You are very cynical for an American, Mr. Jackson," Eva Scheel said.

"I'm very cynical for anyone, Fräulein Scheel. It keeps me from being disappointed."

"How terribly amusing," Eva Scheel said with a little smile. "It makes you sound so very, very young."

"Please," Leah said before Jackson could fire back. "Somehow I don't think this is a time for bickering." She looked at Jackson solemnly. "Can I take it from what you've said thus far that you are still going to help us, Mr. Jackson—you and Mr. Ploscaru?"

"We've still got a deal."

"I understand that these new complications—my brother's being so terribly ill—might make it more difficult for you than we had thought. My father and I discussed such a contingency before I left, and he had authorized me to increase your fee from fifteen to twenty-five thousand dollars. Is that satisfactory?"

Jackson nodded. "How is your father? I apologize for not asking sooner."

Leah gave her head a small shake. "The operation was not a success. I'm afraid that he is permanently blind."

"I'm sorry."

"Thank you. It would appear that things are not going too well for the Oppenheimer family just now." She paused and then said, "We must find my brother, Mr. Jackson. I can't bring myself to agree with your terrible theories about the Americans and the British and the Russians. Frankly, I don't think that any of them are interested in taking Kurt alive. They would be just as happy if he were dead. I don't know if you remember, but when we first met I spoke of getting help for my brother. There is such a place in Switzerland, a sanitarium, a very fine one. Of course, it will be expensive. Extremely expensive."

"I imagine."

"Then when he is better, perhaps he could . . ." She stopped. "I don't know. I don't want to think about that just yet."

"Don't, dear," Eva Scheel said, leaning over and placing a hand on Leah's arm. "There's no need to think about it now."

"Okay," Jackson said, and rose. "When we find him we'll get him to Switzerland. That's not as easy as it sounds, of course."

"Of course not," Leah said.

"I'll talk to Ploscaru. He'll probably have some ideas. He usually does."

"How is Mr. Ploscaru?" Leah said. "I'm so sorry that we still haven't been able to meet."

"Ploscaru," Eva Scheel said. "Is that a Balkan name?"

"Romanian," Leah said. "We have talked on the phone and corresponded, but we still have not met. I do look forward to it."

"I'll tell him that," Jackson said.

"I don't mean to be overly inquisitive," Leah said, "but could you tell me what he was doing that was so important that it would have kept him from our meeting today?"

"Sure," Jackson said. "He was out looking for your brother."

Eva Scheel accompanied Jackson to the foyer, opened the door for him, and held out her hand. When he took it, she said, "I really hesitate to say this again, Mr. Jackson but you can rest assured that nothing that was said here today will get back to Lieutenant Meyer."

Jackson nodded thoughtfully. "There's not really just a hell of a lot to tell him, is there?"

"No," she said slowly, the half smile back on her face. "As you say. not a hell of a lot."

They said goodbye then, and Eva Scheel watched as Jackson made his way down the dimly lit stairs. So there goes the opposition, she thought. Very quick, very intelligent, and doubtless very competent, but lacking, perhaps, in a certain amount of animal cunning. It could be that the dwarf supplies that. Well, printer, she thought as she turned and closed the door, we must meet again, and soon, because now I have something to tell you. She found herself quite surprised at how much she was looking forward to it.

19   In the dream, Heinrich Himmler was only a meter away. And in the dream it was always raining as Kurt Oppenheimer slowly drew the pistol from the pocket of his SS greatcoat, the belted leather kind; aimed; and squeezed the trigger. Then, in the dream, there was always the business of deciding whether to shout it in Latin or German. Sometimes it was one and sometimes the other, but most of the time it came out in Latin—"*Sic semper tyrannis*"—just before he squeezed the trigger of the pistol: which he knew would never fire. And it was always about then that Himmler smiled and became someone else. He became Kurt Oppenheimer's father, who frowned and demanded to know why his son was standing there on the street with no clothes on. After that Kurt Oppenheimer would look down at himself and discover that he was cold and wet and naked. Then he would wake up.

In reality, it had been raining that day in Berlin, and he had been wearing the stolen belted leather SS great-coat, plus the rest of the uniform of an SS captain, and there had been a pistol in his pocket. A Lüger. He had been standing there in a group of SS officers when Himmler got out of the car.

He and the Reichsführer had looked at each other from less than a meter away. But there had been no shout, and the pistol had remained in the greatcoat's pocket, because Kurt Oppenheimer had suddenly realized what he had long suspected: that he was afraid to die.

Sometimes when he awoke from the dream, as he did now, lying on the cot in the cellar of the ruined castle near Höchst, Oppenheimer would compare the dream with what had actually happened. In the dream he felt shame. But the shame came from standing naked in front of his father. Had it been shame he felt when he turned away from Himmler, the pistol still unfired in his pocket? No, not shame. The shame happened only in the dream. In reality, there had been that great surge of relief when he realized that he would do no dying that day.

After that January 19 of 1945, the day he had turned away from Himmler, he had also turned away from killing. He had gone back to living in the bombed-out ruins and scrounging food wherever he could. Then there was that air raid in early May. Had it been the last one of the war? He wasn't sure, because there had been the explosion, he remembered that, and then he remembered very little until he heard the voices debating whether it was worth the effort to dig him out because he was probably already dead.

He had shouted something then, or tried to, and they had dug him out. He was unhurt except for a few scratches. He learned then that the Russians had taken Berlin and that the war was over. He told the men who had dug him out that he was very hungry and thirsty. They gave him some water, but they couldn't give him any food, because they had none. Nobody has any food, they told him. Nobody but the Russians. If you want food, go see the Russians. Then they had laughed.

But he didn't seek out the Russians. They were after him, the Russians. Because of the Himmler thing. They had learned about it. How? Well, the Russians had their ways. Now they were combing the city for him. When they found him, they would arrest him and try him for cowardice. He would be found guilty and then they would shoot him. He would suffer a long time before he died.

A part of him always knew that his fears were groundless. This part of him, the mocking part, would stand aside as he cowered in some bombed-out ruin and with biting logic explain all about the irrationality of his fears. Finally, the fears began to go away and depression set in. The mocking part of him was not nearly so adept at dealing with depression. About all that this mocking self could tell him was that he was slightly mad. But then, he already knew that.

Sometimes, however, the depression would immobilize him for days at a time. He would sit, virtually motionless, in whatever ruins he happened to find himself in, with his knees drawn up and his arms wrapped tightly around them. During these times he would neither sleep nor drink nor eat.

It got better in early June after he killed the rat. He killed it with a stone, skinned it, cooked it, and ate it. For nearly a week after that he lived on rats. They gave him enough strength to go poking about in the destroyed building in which he found himself. In a heap of rubble that once had been a bathroom he discovered a piece of broken mirror and looked at his reflection for the first time in more than a month. He started laughing. It went on for a long time, the laughter, and although at the end it may have turned into a kind of hysteria, when it was all over he felt better. Much better.

In fact, he felt so much better that he dug around in the rubble of what had been the bathroom and found a straight razor, a brush, and a cracked, gilt-embossed shaving mug with just a bit of soap left in its bottom. He walked three blocks to the nearest water, brought back a large tin of it, and shaved off his beard, cutting himself only twice in the process.

He didn't eat rats after that. Instead, he stole food when he could, and when he wasn't doing that he wandered aimlessly about Berlin. After a week or so of this he no longer even trembled at the sight of a Russian soldier, although somewhere far deep inside he remained totally convinced that each Russian soldier had orders to arrest him on sight. When his mocking self told him, for at least the hundredth time, that this was madness, he would reply, sometimes aloud, "Well, it just possibly could be true."

On July 2, 1945, he noticed a group of gawkers standing at a corner, so he joined them, as he nearly always did. The object of the gawkers' curiosity was a jeep. In it were two American soldiers, obviously lost. They were the first American soldiers that the gawkers had seen, and they belonged to the Second Armored Division, which had finally entered Berlin that morning.

One of the soldiers was a big man of about thirty with flaming red hair. He wore a carefully trimmed pirate's beard and the stripes of a master sergeant. Next to him, behind the wheel, was another sergeant, a three-striper with smart, bitter eyes and a mouth that snapped open and shut like a purse.

The red-haired Master Sergeant was examining a map. The other Sergeant was smoking a cigarette. He flicked the butt away and watched idly as the gawkers scrambled for it.

"I told you that was the wrong fuckin' turn," he said to the Master Sergeant.

"Ask them," the Master Sergeant said.

"Ask 'em what?"

"Ask if any of these good burghers speak English."

The three-striper stood up in the jeep. "Any of you fuckers speak English?"

It could have been because he was bored, or because he was curious, or simply that he had never spoken to an American soldier, but Kurt Oppenheimer found himself saying, "I speak English."

"Git over here, boy," the three-striper said.

Oppenheimer moved over to the jeep. The man with the red beard examined him with greenish-blue eyes that seemed to be filled with a private kind of laughter.

"We are, I'm afraid, a trifle lost."

"Perhaps I can help."

"Do you know Berlin?"

"Fairly well."

"We are trying to get to Dahlem."

"You're going in the opposite direction."

"I told you we took the wrong fuckin' turn," the three-striper said.

"You speak very good English," the red-bearded Sergeant said.

"Thank you."

"Doesn't he speak good English?" the red-bearded man said to the Sergeant behind the wheel.

"Like a fuckin' Limey."

"We're going to need someone."

The three-striper nodded glumly. "Might as well be him." He stared at Oppenheimer. "Whadda they call you, boy—Hans or Fritz?"

"Hans, I think," Kurt Oppenheimer said.

"Git in the jeep, Hans; you're hired."

"I beg your pardon?"

"My name is Sergeant Sherrod," the red-bearded man said. "My associate here, Pecos Bill—"

"My name ain't Pecos Bill. I wish to fuck you'd quit

186

callin' me Pecos Bill. My name is James Robert Packer from Abilene, Texas, and my friends, which you're gittin' to be not one of, call me either Jim or J.R.—I don't give a shit which, as long as it's not Jim Bob or Jimmy Bobby; but you can even call me that, long as you quit callin' me Pecos Bill."

"You through?"

"I'm through."

"Good." Sergeant Sherrod turned back to Oppenheimer. "Pecos Bill here and I are in need of a guide, interpreter, and dog robber. Are you familiar with the expression dog robber?"

"No."

"It means factotum."

"Servant."

"Not quite," Sergeant Sherrod said, "but close. Americans don't have servants. They have hired hands, the girl who lives in, mother's helpers, and maids, but seldom servants. The British have servants; the Americans have help. A subtle distinction which I think we need explore no further, at least for the moment."

"Oh, Lordy, how long's this shit gonna go on?" Sergeant Packer asked nobody in particular.

"You were never a Nazi, were you, Hans?" Before Oppenheimer could reply, Sergeant Sherrod continued. "An idle question, I realize, but in recent months Pecos Bill here and I have inquired of perhaps three hundred citizens of the Reich whether they were ever members of the Nazi Party, and to a man, they have declared that they were not. This leads one to the interesting question of who's been minding the store these past few years."

"I am a Jew," Oppenheimer said.

Sergeant Sherrod grinned. "Another rare species. If you agree to work for us, Hans, you'll be paid in cigarettes. You can fatten yourself up on U.S. Army rations, and we can probably scrounge you some different clothes, which although not stylish, will be somewhat better than the

187

rags and tatters that you're now wearing. Well, sir, what do you say?"

"You're quite serious, aren't you?" Oppenheimer said.

"Totally."

"I accept."

"Git in, boy," Sergeant Packer said.

The gawkers watched glumly as Oppenheimer climbed into the back of the jeep. As they drove off, the red-bearded Master Sergeant turned and offered Oppenheimer a Pall Mall. It was with a luxurious sense of well-being that Oppenheimer accepted a light and drew the smoke down into his lungs.

"How much are American cigarettes bringing on the black market, Hans?" Sergeant Sherrod asked.

"I have no idea."

"That, I think, will be your first assignment," the red-bearded man said with a smile. "To find out."

During the next few weeks Oppenheimer learned that the two American Sergeants had one simple objective: to make $50,000 each on the Berlin black market. He also learned that they both knew exactly what they would do with the money.

Sergeant Packer was going to buy a certain ranch with his, just outside of Abilene. The Sergeant, who had taken a liking to Oppenheimer and occasionally referred to him as "a pretty good little old Jew boy," often described the ranch in loving detail. The descriptions were so graphic that it became almost as real to Oppenheimer as his own former home in Frankfurt. Sometimes, in his dreams, the two places became blurred.

But Oppenheimer took more than a dream from Sergeant Packer. He also took from him his accent and his detailed knowledge of the city of Abilene, Texas. Both, Oppenheimer felt, might prove useful someday, although he wasn't at all sure how.

The red-bearded Master Sergeant's dreams were of a

somewhat different nature. Before enlisting in the Army, Sergeant Sherrod had been an assistant professor of economics at the University of California at Los Angeles. Twice he had turned down a battlefield commission. His postwar dreams were clearly mapped out—provided he reached his $50,000 black-market goal.

"With half of it, I intend to buy oceanfront lots," he sometimes told Oppenheimer. "I don't care much which ocean, as long as it's warm—Spain, Southern California, Florida, Hawaii, and maybe even the Caribbean will do. The remaining twenty-five thousand I intend to plunk into something called IBM, which is a stock I am convinced will make spectacular gains during the next few years. Then, after a few more years of penury in Academe, I will be able to tell the world to go fuck itself—to use one of Pecos Bill's more graphic expressions."

"You know what he is, don'tcha, Hans?" Sergeant Packer said.

Oppenheimer shook his head. "No. What?"

"He's a fuckin' Communist, that's what."

"Are you, Sergeant?"

The red-bearded man smiled. "A renegade Marxist perhaps, but scarcely a Communist. There's a difference, you know."

"Yes," Oppenheimer said. "I know."

By the time the Russians were given the plates, the two Sergeants had made perhaps $5,000 each, mostly from cigarettes whose sales Oppenheimer had negotiated in the thriving black market that had sprung up in the Tiergarten.

"I don't understand," Sergeant Packer had said. "You mean to say we just gave those fuckers the plates to print up their own money?"

"Exactly. Our Secretary of the Treasury, Mr. Morgenthau, seems to believe that nothing is too good for our gallant Russian allies, including the privilege of printing their own money, which we, of course, eventually will have to redeem. From what I understand, the Russians intend to pay off their troops with it."

"You mean it's gonna be good money?"

"Just as sound as the occupation marks that we print. Naturally, the Russians are wise enough to issue one proviso. Their troops will have to spend the money in Germany, not in Russia."

"You know something?" Sergeant Packer said thoughtfully. "Some of those old Russian boys ain't been paid in two-three years."

"More, in some instances," said Oppenheimer.

"Now, just what item would they like to spend all that lovely money on, Hans?" Sergeant Sherrod said.

"Watches," Oppenheimer said promptly. "In Russian villages there is often only one man who is rich enough to own a watch. A watch is a symbol of considerable substance."

"You mean to say everybody has to go see this one old boy just to find out what time it is?" Sergeant Packer said, obviously shocked.

"Well, there are clocks, I suppose."

"How much are they paying for watches, Hans?" the red-bearded Sergeant asked.

"It varies. But it's somewhere between five hundred and a thousand dollars."

"But if all these old Russian boys're gonna be paid all at once," Sergeant Packer said, "then the price for watches is gonna go up, right?"

"The inexorable law of supply and demand, which I've been scoffing at for years," Sergeant Sherrod said, "will again go into operation. Our problem is supply. Where are watches plentiful?"

"Switzerland," Oppenheimer said.

"Ah, but how does one get into and out of Switzerland undetected with a suitcase full of watches?"

"It can be done."

190

Sergeant Sherrod stared at Oppenheimer carefully. "Could you do it?"

"Yes."

"For some reason," Sergeant Sherrod said, "I thought that you might."

Carrying $5,000 in U.S. currency taped to his stomach, Oppenheimer used the same routes and the same crossing into Switzerland near Singen that he had used during the war. Nothing was changed now, except that it was easier.

In Zurich, he bought one hundred wristwatches a few at a time from different dealers. Most of the watches had black faces with sweep second hands, and all of them had easily removable backs. The Russians liked to open their watches up and examine their insides. They also liked to count the jewels. A few dabs of fingernail polish would increase the number of jewels in each watch that Oppenheimer bought from seventeen to twenty-one.

Back in Berlin, the three men fed the black-faced watches slowly to the Russians. They became such highly prized items that the last five sold for $1500 each. The two Americans' total profit, less expenses, amounted to $97,500. They sent the money back to the States in the form of postal money orders, never more than $1,000 at a time. Less than a week after they sent the final $1,000, the Army woke up to what was going on and clamped down. But by then, Sergeant Packer had bought his 640-acre ranch, and Master-Sergeant Sherrod had bought his first 100 shares of stock in International Business Machines and was negotiating by mail for three beachfront lots in Malibu.

Kurt Oppenheimer's share amounted to $10,000, which he took in the form of cigarettes. In Berlin in 1945 he discovered that he was a very rich man. He also discovered something else while occasionally answering Sergeant Sherrod's Headquarters Company telephone. He discovered that he was usually mistaken for an American.

It was while pondering this information one evening in a café on the Kurfürstendamm that he spotted the Gauleiter from Bavaria. The Gauleiter's name was Jaschke, and during the war he had ranked high on the death list of Oppenheimer's long-destroyed organization. The Gauleiter had made it a point to cleanse his district of Jews. By 1943, not one was left. All 1,329 of them—men, women, and children—were either dead or in concentration camps. The Gauleiter, Oppenheimer remembered, had been given some sort of commendation.

Oppenheimer followed Jaschke from the café. On a dark street, he accosted the Gauleiter with "Your name is Jaschke."

"No, it is not. You are mistaken. My name is Richter."

As in the dream about Himmler, Oppenheimer slowly drew the Lüger from a pocket of his raincoat and aimed it at Jaschke. "Your name is Jaschke," he repeated, wondering what would happen next.

"No, no, you are wrong. See, I have proof." Jaschke reached for his inside coat pocket, and Kurt Oppenheimer squeezed the trigger of the Lüger. He was slightly surprised when the pistol fired, and even more so when most of the top of Jaschke's head seemed to explode.

Oppenheimer turned and walked away. He had been wondering what to do with his newly acquired black-market wealth and now he knew. It was very much like having an avocation and the leisure to pursue it. He would again seek out those who needed killing and kill them. You are quite mad, you know, he was promptly informed by the old, familiar mocking self whom he had not heard from in several months.

"Yes, I know," Kurt Oppenheimer replied, and after a few more steps realized that he had said it aloud.

20

An American Army deserter with whom Kurt Oppenheimer had once done a little business in Munich was the one who finally gave the authorities their first clue. It happened six weeks after Oppenheimer left Berlin. The deserter had sold Oppenheimer a Walther pistol—the same pistol, in fact, which later he would use to kill the man who sold identities, Karl-Heinz Damm.

The second in what was to be the long series of deaths had been that of an ex–Waffen SS lieutenant colonel, and for a time the Army investigators entertained the notion that the American deserter might have been the one who had shot him three times. The deserter finally convinced them that he hadn't and in doing so gave them an extremely accurate description of the man to whom he had sold the Walther. The only thing misleading about his description was his claim that the man who had bought the pistol spoke English with a heavy German accent. It was an accent, of course, which Oppenheimer sometimes employed.

But everything else about the deserter's description tallied almost exactly with the extensive dossiers that both Bureau IV and Bureau V of the SS *Reichssicherheitshauptampf,* or National Central Security Office, had once maintained on Kurt Oppenheimer. The pattern of operating was the same, as were the height, weight, and coloring. The only item missing from the SS files was a photograph. There was none.

The Americans shared their discovery with the Russians and the British. They also offered the information to the French, but the French that week were miffed about something and rejected the offer. The Russians and the British, however, were very much interested, and as the killings went on they became even more so.

Sitting now on the edge of his cot in the cellar of the ruined castle near Höchst and waiting for the water to boil for his tea, Kurt Oppenheimer tried to remember the faces of all the men he had killed. For some reason, the faces of those he had killed before the war ended were clearer than those he had killed afterward. These latter faces tended to blur and sometimes even took on the features of Sergeants Packer and Sherrod. He often thought of the two Americans, who had been shipped home months before, and wondered what they were doing. Packer he always pictured on a horse, dressed like a cowboy, and Sherrod, red beard bristling, was always lying near the surf on some warm beach.

He had no trouble remembering Karl-Heinz Damm's face, however, because Damm he had known quite well. Damm, in fact, had been the only one he had really despised. The rest had been merely symbols that he had

194

destroyed. He had decided that you didn't need to hate a symbol in order to destroy it. All you had to do was squeeze the trigger. It was really quite simple.

He rose and poured the boiling water into the teapot. Then he took the list that he had torn from Damm's ledgerlike book and studied it. The first name on the list was in the American Zone, in Russelsheim, only 19 miles from Frankfurt. The second name on the list was in the British Zone, in Bonn—or was it Bad Godesberg? No matter. He would do the one at Russelsheim first. Today he would demote himself to lieutenant. It would be the last time that the American officer uniforms would be of any use. Yesterday in the Casino he knew he had pushed his luck by approaching the British Major. But it had been amusing. He realized that the British were probably looking for him. And there was even the possibility that the Major had been one of those who were doing the looking. He had that hunter's look about him, and besides, British majors weren't all that common in the American Zone. It would be even more amusing if the British Major somehow discovered that the American who had bought him a drink was actually the very man that he was looking for.

You want them to catch you, fool, his mocking self told him. "Well, yes, naturally," Oppenheimer said aloud. "I've always known that."

The Opel Motor Works at Russelsheim, about halfway between Frankfurt and Mainz, covered five hundred acres and at one time had been the largest automobile-manufacturing plant in Europe. At its peak it had turned out nearly 5,000 cars and trucks a month and had employed some 24,000 workers.

Both the RAF and the U.S. Army Air Corps had bombed it by day and by night, but despite their combined efforts the Opel plant was still operating at 40 percent of capacity at the war's end. Now it was back in operation, after a fashion, and supervising the entire plant and its 4,137 German workers was Lt. Jack Fallon, who before the war had been a shop steward for a United Auto Workers (CIO) local at the Ford plant in Dearborn, Michigan. To help him run his new empire, the Military Government had allotted him two enlisted men, a three-quarter-ton truck with a trailer, and an interpreter.

It was the interpreter whom the CID Lieutenant wanted to see.

"Jesus, you don't think he's a Nazi or something, do you?" Fallon said. "I've already lost two interpreters because somebody claimed they were Nazis. Hell, this guy couldn't be a Nazi. He was in a concentration camp."

"It's just routine," Kurt Oppenheimer said.

"Okay, I'll see if I can find him for you."

Fallon turned in his swivel chair and yelled through the open door, "Hey, Little, where the hell's Wiese got off to?"

"Beats the shit out of me, Lieutenant," Cpl. Virgil Little yelled back.

"Well, go find the fucker and get his ass in here."

"Yes, sir."

Fallon leaned back in his chair. "It might take a while," he said. "This is one hell of a big plant."

"That's all right," Oppenheimer said.

"They keeping you guys busy?"

"Fairly so. How about you?"

Fallon sighed. "It's a mess. You know who I get orders from? I get orders from G-Five in Frankfurt. Except that sometimes their orders are just the opposite of the ones I get from G-Four—that's production control. And before I can turn around, here comes a new set of orders in—this time from OMGUS up in Berlin. And if that wasn't enough, those G-Five fuckers down at Seventh Army in Heidelberg think they've got to put their two cents' worth in. I don't know what the hell I'm doing half the time."

"Sounds rough," Oppenheimer said, producing a pack of Camels, and offered them to Fallon.

Fallon shook his head. "Let me give you an example of what I mean." He looked hopefully at Oppenheimer and was encouraged by the sympathetic nod that he got.

"What we're trying to do here is turn out trucks—small ones, you know, three-quarter-ton jobs. But in the meantime we're also supposed to be turning out radiators and carburetors, and these we ship off to the D-B plant at Mannheim."

"D-B?" Oppenheimer said.

"Daimler-Benz."

"Oh."

"Okay, swell, we turn out four hundred and sixteen radiators and six hundred and two carburetors, right?"

"Right."

"Then they shut down the fucking gas on us. Well, we get our gas from Darmstadt, and Darmstadt has to have coal before it can turn out gas. But Darmstadt depends on getting its coal from somewhere up in the Ruhr, in the British Zone. Well, they're not mining any coal up in the Ruhr, or if they are, those British fuckers are keeping it for themselves. So D-B is screaming for its radiators and its carbs and I'm screaming back that I can't turn 'em out without gas and I can't get the gas unless Darmstadt gets the coal. So you know what they tell me to do?"

"What?"

"Improvise."

"Jesus."

"So here's what I do. I take one of those trucks that we turned out and I write it off. I mean the records on it just disappear. It was never produced, if you know what I mean? Then I start nosing around the black market and I find some guy who's got coal. You can find it if you know where to look. So I say to this guy, 'How'd you like a brand-new truck?' Of course, he wants to know what the catch is. Well, the catch is that he's gotta use the truck to haul enough coal over to Darmstadt to provide me with gas for three weeks."

"That's goddamned ingenious," Oppenheimer said.

Fallon ran his hand through his short brown hair. He was a wiry man, not too tall, a little past thirty, who wore a look of perpetual exasperation on a face that was too young to have so many lines in it.

"Well, hell, I don't know if it's ingenious or not. All I know is that I'm going home next month—if they don't court-martial me first. I tell you one thing, though. I've learned some tricks here that're gonna set those Ford fuckers back on their ass if they don't watch out." He smiled happily at the pleasing prospect, and most of the exasperated look went away.

Cpl. Virgil Little came into the office a few minutes later without knocking, followed by a German civilian dressed in a brown suit and black shoes. Corporal Little was about twenty, with a thinker's face and a scholar's stoop. The German civilian was more than twice his age, with a round face, small blue eyes, and a thin-lipped, unforgiving mouth that separated a tiny chin from a rather large nose. What remained of his hair was a dull taupe shade.

"Here he is, Lieutenant," Corporal Little said. "Anything else?"

Before Fallon could reply, Oppenheimer said, "I'd like the Corporal to remain, Lieutenant. All right?"

Fallon shrugged. "Okay."

"And the other enlisted man. Would you have him come in too?"

"Tell Baxter to come in," Fallon said.

"Hey, Baxter," Corporal Little called through the door. "The Lieutenant wants you."

A big, sleepy-looking youth of about nineteen shambled in and looked around. He was Private Louis Baxter, whose one passion in life was automobiles. Working in a plant where they were actually manufactured was for him an experience of unending joy.

"Would you close the door, please?" Oppenheimer said.

Baxter turned and closed the door, then turned back.

"Private, I think you should sit over there," Oppenheimer said, indicating a chair, "and you, Corporal, over there."

Baxter sat where he was told, but Corporal Little looked first at Lieutenant Fallon, who frowned slightly, then nodded. Corporal Little sat down.

That left only the German standing in the center of the large office. He looked calmly at Oppenheimer, smiled slightly, then looked back at Fallon.

"May I ask the purpose of this meeting, Lieutenant?"

Fallon nodded at Oppenheimer. "The Lieutenant here will tell you."

The German nodded, looked back at Oppenheimer, nodded again almost enough for it to be a slight bow, and said, "Please?"

"Your name?" Oppenheimer said in a bored voice.

"Wiese. Joachim Wiese."

"Your age?"

"Forty-three."

"Place of birth?"

"Leipzig."

"Occupation?"

"Interpreter."

"Occupation before the war?"

"Teacher."

"What subjects did you teach?"

"English, French, and Latin."

Oppenheimer stared at Wiese for a long moment, smiled, took out the pack of Camels, rose, and offered the German one. Wiese relaxed visibly and accepted the cigarette. Using his Zippo lighter, Oppenheimer lit the German's cigarette, smiled again charmingly, and said, "You're lying."

"I do not lie," the German said stiffly as his face turned bright pink.

"What the hell's this all about?" Lieutenant Fallon said.

Oppenheimer went back to his chair and sat down. He

reached into his back pocket as if for a handkerchief and brought out the Walther instead.

"For Christ's sake," Fallon said.

The Walther was aimed at the German who said his name was Joachim Wiese. "We're going to have a court-martial, Lieutenant," Oppenheimer said. "It won't take long. I will be the prosecution; you will be the judge; Corporal Little, I think, will be the defense counsel; and Private Baxter—let's see—Private Baxter, yes, will be sergeant at arms."

"What the fuck are you talking about?" Fallon said, and started to rise. Oppenheimer waved the gun at him, and he sat back down.

"I'm talking about friend Wiese here. You see, Lieutenant, his name is really not Wiese at all." He smiled up at the German. "Tell them your real name."

The German's face was beginning to sweat. "I don't understand," he said. "My name is Wiese. I was a teacher. Then they sent me to Dachau. I almost died there. My wife, she—she did die." He spread his hands imploringly. "I have proof—documents."

"And very good documents, too. You bought them from a man called Damm—Karl-Heinz Damm—in Munich on June 2, 1945. You paid the equivalent of ten thousand dollars for them in Swiss francs. It was an excellent bargain."

The German was afraid to move his body, so he only turned his head to look at Fallon. "I—I don't understand any of this, Lieutenant. Can't you do something? It is all some terrible mistake. You have seen my documents. Tell him that you have seen them."

"I've seen them," Fallon said in a flat voice.

"Good," Oppenheimer said. "The judge has seen the documents, so we will stipulate that they have been entered as evidence. Now to get on with the prosecution. You see, Your Honor, the accused was not always an interpreter and was never, never a teacher of English or

200

French or Latin. No, he was in a quite different business during the war—the slave-labor business. Would you care to tell us about the labor business?"

The German shook his head vigorously. The pink had gone from his face. It was now a chalkish white. "I don't understand," he said. "I don't understand any of this."

"No? You have never heard the name Oskar Gerwinat?"

Again the German shook his head. "No. Never."

"Strange. Well, Oskar Gerwinat was in the slave-labor business. He was a contractor. By that I mean he was given contracts to feed and house the slave laborers. Well, Herr Gerwinat was an excellent businessman. He soon discovered that the less he fed his charges, the more profitable his business. If they died, from exposure or overwork or hunger, well, no matter. There were always many more where they came from: Poland, France, Holland—places like that. Herr Gerwinat was not the largest contractor in his particular field, but he had a very nice little business going, mainly in the Ruhr area. The most reliable figures estimate that two thousand three hundred fifty-four of Herr Gerwinat's charges died from hunger or exposure or overwork—or sometimes, I would assume, all three. Now are you quite sure you have never heard of Oskar Gerwinat?"

The man charged with being Oskar Gerwinat was trembling now. "Never," he said, and sounded as though he were choking on something. "It's all a mistake—a terrible mistake."

"The prosecution will now introduce new evidence," Oppenheimer said. He took from his pocket one of the sheets that he had torn from Damm's ledgerlike book and, without taking his eyes from the German, handed it to Fallon.

Fallon looked at it. "Hell, this is in German. I can't read this."

"The photograph that's pasted on the page."

"There're two photos."

"The top one."

"Yeah, that one's Wiese, all right."

"Taken through a window, wouldn't you say? But still, quite a fair likeness."

"Yeah, it's him, all right."

"Now we will have the interpreter translate the evidence into English for you, Your Honor. If you'd be so kind as to hand it to him."

The German accepted the sheet of paper and looked at it. As he read, his face crumpled up so that with his nearly bald head he looked very much like a wizened infant about to cry. Then the tears did start. He sniffed, shook his head, and silently handed the sheet back to Oppenheimer.

"No? Well, there is really nothing much more here, Your Honor, than what I've already told you. These are the notes that a very meticulous blackmailer made for future use. But if you think that it would serve the course of justice, I will—"

"No," the German said, and sank to his knees. The tears were still running down his face. In German he said, "Yes, yes, it's true. It's all true. I am Oskar Gerwinat. I—"

"What's he saying?" Fallon said.

"He just confessed that he is Oskar Gerwinat."

"Is that what you said, Wiese?"

Wiese-Gerwinat, his head bowed, muttered, "Yes."

"Jesus," Fallon said.

"The accused has admitted his guilt," Oppenheimer said with a cheerful smile, "but I do think we should still hear from defense counsel. Corporal Little?"

"Gosh, Lieutenant," Little said to Fallon. "What am I supposed to say?"

"Nothing. You're supposed to say nothing."

"Well, I could say that he's always been a pretty nice old guy around here."

"Shut the fuck up, will you, Little?"

"Yes, sir."

"Now, look," Fallon said to Oppenheimer. "I don't know who the hell you are, buddy, but—"

The German lunged for the Walther before Fallon could finish. Oppenheimer stepped back quickly and shot him twice in the chest. The German fell back down to his knees, whimpered something, then sprawled heavily on the floor. He twitched several times before dying.

"Jesus Christ," Fallon whispered.

"He shot him, Lieutenant," Private Baxter said in a shocked voice. "He just hauled off and shot him."

"It's—it's like a play," said Corporal Little, who had spent a year at the University of Nebraska and was already at work on a novel about his experiences in postwar Germany. He immediately resolved to scrap what he had written and start afresh. Staring at Oppenheimer, he began to make careful mental notes.

Oppenheimer gazed down at the dead Oskar Gerwinat for a moment and looked up at Fallon. "He really deserved it, you know."

Fallon shook his head. "You're crazy, fella."

Oppenheimer nodded. "Probably. Now, one of you will have to come with me for a while. Which one shall it be?"

Fallon's quick mind immediately sensed what Oppenheimer needed. "You're taking a hostage, right?"

"Only for a while."

"I'll go."

"No, Lieutenant, I think not. You're a bit too quick for me, I'm afraid."

"Let *me* go, Lieutenant," Corporal Little said, anxious not to miss anything that might prove useful to his literary career.

Oppenheimer nodded again. "Can you drive a jeep, Corporal?"

"Sure."

"Good. You'll be back within two hours—provided that the Lieutenant doesn't make any calls for an hour."

"No calls," Fallon said.

"Good."

Fallon frowned. "Let me ask you something."

"Of course."

"Are you really an American?"

"Would it make any difference?"

Fallon shook his head slowly. "No, not a hell of a lot, I guess. You're not going to hurt the kid, though, are you, if I don't make any calls for an hour?"

"No, I won't hurt him," Oppenheimer said. He turned to Little. "Are you ready, Corporal?"

"You bet," Corporal Little said.

21 They were expecting the jeep at
the rear entrance to the Displaced Persons camp at Badenhausen. Within three hours after Oppenheimer drove
it in, the jeep would be completely disassembled and its
parts sold on the black market.

The rear entrance to the DP camp wasn't really a rear
entrance. Even a fairly close inspection would not have
revealed the cleverly cut high steel-mesh fence that was
rolled back to let Oppenheimer drive the jeep through.
The DP's were not prisoners at the Badenhausen camp,
and the jeep could just as easily have been driven through
the main entrance. But then some of the UNRRA officials
might have seen it and started asking questions. Whether
other DP's saw it didn't matter. Nearly everyone had his

own fiddle going, in most cases it was common knowledge, and informers were dealt with by being informed on. If that didn't work, there were always the three Poles who, for a fair price, would administer a sound beating.

After the Greek and the Latvian rolled the fence back into place, Oppenheimer got out of the jeep without a word and headed for the small shed that housed the operations of Kubista the Czech. Although Oppenheimer heard the jeep when they started the engine and drove it off, he gave it no farewell glance. For Oppenheimer, that part of his life was over. Now he would become someone else, and already he was ridding himself of the Americanisms he had so carefully acquired.

Oppenheimer smiled slightly as he remembered the young American Corporal's almost interminable, sometimes sympathetic, and always naive questions as they had driven away from the Opel plant. Oppenheimer had answered most of them with questions of his own.

Are you really an American, sir? Could an American have done what I did? Sir, do you mind if I ask you how you felt when you did it? Is it always necessary to feel something, Corporal? Was that the first time you ever did anything like that, sir? Shouldn't your question really be whether it will be the last time? You mean you're going to do it again, sir? I don't know, Corporal; should I? Do you mind if I ask you this, Lieutenant? Do you sort of think of yourself as a kind of avenging angel? I'm not sure that I believe in angels anymore, Corporal. Do you?

And then there had been the final question when, six miles away from the Opel plant, Oppenheimer had stopped the jeep to let Corporal Little out.

"I don't know how to ask this one, sir," Corporal Little had said as he got out from behind the wheel and Oppenheimer slid over under it.

"You mean am I crazy?"

"Well, yes, sir, that's kind of what I had in mind."

"As a bedbug," Oppenheimer had said, remembering one of Sergeant Packer's expressions.

Little had nodded thoughtfully as if that were just the answer he had wanted.

"Well, hell, sir, good luck, I guess."

"Why, thank you, Corporal. Thank you very much."

Oppenheimer knocked on the door of the shed and went in after the voice in German said, "Enter." Inside, the room seemed to be half jumble sale and half printing plant. Several metal bins lined one wall. They were filled with civilian clothing—suit coats, pants, vests, and shoes —none of which seemed to match. One bin was filled with nothing but men's hats. Near the bins on a wooden pole hung an assortment of U.S. Army uniforms—Eisenhower jackets, officer's pinks, trench coats, field jackets, leather flying jackets, fatigues, OD's, and even two WAC uniforms.

The wooden pole hung with Army garments more or less divided the jumble sale from the printing operation, which was composed of a small hand press, paper of various weights and qualities, and a wide assortment of rubber stamps. Samples of some of the hand press's legitimate efforts were tacked up on the walls: mostly official camp regulations and proclamations.

Next to the engraving bench sat Kubista the Czech, the camp printer, clothing merchant, and master forger. He was a gaunt man of average height who just escaped being emaciated. He looked up when Oppenheimer came in; nodded his long, narrow head; and said, "I see we have demoted ourselves to lieutenant."

"It makes a change," Oppenheimer said. "I shall miss being an American officer. It was a rather carefree life."

"I have your new life here for you," Kubista said, reached into a drawer, and brought out a small stack of wallet-size documents. He dealt them off one by one. "Your basic identification card, of course; your interzonal pass; your British Zone ration books; rent receipts; some wartime odds and ends that could be useful for verisimilitude; and three letters from your lover, who lives in Berlin and misses you rather desperately."

Oppenheimer went through the documents one by one. He smiled at his new name. "Ekkehard Fink. The finch. Did you know that Fink has a rather unpleasant connotation in English?"

"No."

"It means informer, I think."

"I must remember that. There are many around here to whom it could be applied."

"Probably."

"Even I have been tempted."

"Oh?"

"Twice recently. Here," he said, rising and taking a dark blue suit from a nail. "Try this on. Over there on the chair are a shirt, tie, shoes, and the rest of it. We'll pick you out a hat and overcoat later."

Oppenheimer started removing his uniform. "Tell me about your temptation."

Kubista reached into his pocket and brought out a pack of Chesterfields. He lit one, inhaled deeply, blew the smoke out, and looked at his cigarette with pleasure. He had deep-set, moist brown eyes that stared out from behind thick, wire-framed spectacles. What was left of his hair was white. His nose was long and thin and wandered a bit where it had been broken by a camp guard in 1942. He had an old man's sunken mouth which caved in on itself because most of his teeth were missing. He looked sixty. He was thirty-eight.

"What an indescribable luxury is American tobacco."

"One of the few currencies that can be either consumed or spent with equal pleasure," Oppenheimer said. "Tell me about your temptation."

"Yes, that. The first occurred yesterday morning. A German. He came to buy a bicycle, and after he found one that suited him he made very discreet inquiries about obtaining documents and was directed to me. It turned out that he was a printer—and a good one, if I'm any judge. We had quite a nice little chat. He claimed to be looking for a long-lost brother. Younger brother. It seemed that he had heard that this young brother, a bad sort, was posing as an American officer. My new printer friend wanted to find him and put him on the path to righteousness and redemption. I didn't believe him for a second, and he didn't expect me to. He did mention a sum of money. Quite a nice sum. He seemed rather well off, did my printer friend."

Oppenheimer finished knotting his tie. "What did you reply?"

"I told him I would have to ask around. He said he would be back tomorrow."

"And the second tempter?"

"Ach, that one. Well, he's one of us. A thief. Quite a good one, as a matter of fact. He's a Romanian who pretends to be an Estonian. He made no bones about whom he was looking for—an American officer who recently might have bought himself some new identification. He also mentioned a sum of money, although he was not nearly so generous as the printer. I told him the same thing. That I would make inquiries."

Oppenheimer nodded and slipped on the suit coat. "Too bad you don't have a mirror."

"You look very nice," Kubista said. "Poor but respectable."

"I turned the jeep over to your associates."

"Excellent."

"And then there is this." He opened the palm of his hand. In it lay a diamond, slightly more than a carat in weight.

"Well," Kubista said, picking up the stone and holding it up to the light. "I was not expecting this."

"I am hoping that it will buy silence," Oppenheimer said. "Not total silence, only partial silence."

Kubista nodded. "You are wise. Too many are already making inquiries. Soon the American authorities will be making them."

"And you will have something to tell them."

"Good."

"But first you can sell what you know to your printer friend and to the Romanian."

"Even better. But how much can I sell them?"

"You can sell them where I've been, but not where I'm going."

Kubista smiled. "The cellar in the old castle."

Oppenheimer nodded.

"Is your immense store of cigarettes included?"

"Unfortunately, yes."

Kubista smiled again. "Then I will adjust my price accordingly."

By the time Lieutenant Meyer and Major Baker-Bates got there, the U.S. Constabulary, with their lacquered blue-and-yellow helmet liners, were swarming over the Opel plant at Russelsheim like so many potato bugs.

The Constabulary was what the Army had come up with when it suddenly discovered that it had not many more than 150,000 troops to keep order in its zone of occupation and menace the Russians at the same time. What it lacked in numbers it decided to make up for in visibility.

Immediately scrapped was the Eisenhower jacket, which made what troops there were look like so many gas-station attendants—unless they were six feet tall and had a male model's physique. The Ike jacket was replaced with a brass-buttoned blouse on whose left shoulder was a 2½-inch gold disk patch bordered in blue. When they weren't wearing their flashy helmet liners, members of the Constabulary had to wear visored service caps. On their feet were highly polished paratroop boots, and the final touch of what someone had decided was class came in the form of a Sam Browne belt. Hanging from the belt was a .45-caliber automatic.

It was all mostly for show, but since the Germans

admired nothing as much as a snappily turned-out soldier, a jeepful of Constabulary troops zipping through a village could keep the American presence very much in the German mind. They were called the Constabulary because someone had remembered that that was what the Army had called its troops when it had occupied the Philippines after the war with Spain. It also had a nice semi–police-state ring.

The body of the dead Oskar Gerwinat had been removed from Lieutenant Fallon's office by the time a Constabulary captain ushered in Meyer and Baker-Bates. Lieutenant Fallon had already told his story to some CID types, who were still hanging around waiting for him to get his breath so he could tell it twice and probably three times. Reluctantly they agreed to let Meyer and Baker-Bates have their crack at Fallon, but only after Meyer dropped the names of a couple of USFET generals who, he claimed, were expecting a full report within the hour.

The first thing Meyer did was show Fallon the photograph of Kurt Oppenheimer. Fallon studied it carefully, then looked up and said, "Yeah, that's the guy. He's German, huh?"

"He's German," Meyer said.

"Well, he sure talks one hell of a good brand of American."

"Tell us about it, Lieutenant," Baker-Bates said. "Start at the beginning and tell it just as you remember it."

So Fallon told it again, and after he got to the point where Oppenheimer had introduced his "evidence" in the form of one of the pages that he had ripped from the blackmailer Damm's ledgerlike book, Lieutenant Meyer interrupted.

"It was just a page?"

"Yeah, a page with two photographs on it."

"But there was also information on it?"

"Sure, but I couldn't read it because it was in German."

"This information. Was it typed or written?"

211

"It was written."

"In ink?"

"Yeah, sure, ink."

"Okay," Meyer said, "go on."

So Lieutenant Fallon went on, and when he was through, Lieutenant Meyer brought him back again to the page that had been torn from Damm's ledger. In fact, Lieutenant Meyer opened his briefcase and took out the ledger itself.

"Take a look at this, Lieutenant, and see if the page that you saw is like the pages in this ledger."

Lieutenant Fallon flipped through the ledger. "Yeah, I'd say it was. I'd say it was exactly like them, except that the one I saw was torn along one edge like it had been ripped out."

"Let's go back to that page for a moment," Major Baker-Bates said. "You said there were two photographs on it?"

"One was a photograph of Wiese, or Gerwinat, or whatever the hell his name was. It looked like it had been taken through a window when he wasn't looking. What I mean is that Wiese didn't look like he knew his picture was being taken."

"And the other photograph?" Baker-Bates said.

"Same thing, except that it didn't look like it was taken through a window."

"It was of a man?"

"Yeah, a man."

"Can you describe him?"

"Hell, I just glanced at it. I would say he was a guy about forty or forty-five."

"Was he fat-faced, thin-faced, did he wear glasses, what?"

Lieutenant Fallon shook his head. "Honestly, I don't remember. I don't think he wore glasses, but I couldn't swear to it."

"No, that would be too much to hope for," Baker-Bates said.

Lieutenant Meyer sighed. "Okay, let's take it once more step by step."

A pained expression appeared on Fallon's face. "You mean the whole thing?"

"No, just when he handed you the sheet of paper with the photographs on it. What did he say?"

"He just had me look at it, and when I said I couldn't read German, he said he'd have the interpreter translate it. You know, Wiese."

"How long did you look at the page?"

"How long—just a few seconds."

"But you tried to read it?"

"Sure."

"Now think carefully. Was there anything that you can remember not from the section of the page that concerned Wiese, but the other section—the lower one?"

Fallon screwed up his face in honest concentration. Meyer and Baker-Bates waited patiently. Finally, Fallon shook his head. "About the only thing I could read was the numbers."

"What numbers?"

"There were a couple of numbers for some kind of address. Two of them, I think. Either twelve or thirteen or maybe fifteen. I remember that it was a low number."

"How did you know they were for an address?"

"Because they were just before Something-strasse. Well, hell, I know what a *Strasse* is."

"But you don't remember what *Strasse* it was?"

"I sure don't."

"What a pity," Baker-Bates said.

"But I remember what came right after the address."

"What?"

"The name of the city. That I could read. Would that be any help?"

Meyer and Baker-Bates looked at each other. Then Meyer, in a very careful voice, said, "That might help just a little, Lieutenant. What city was it?"

"Bonn," Fallon said. "The reason I remembered it was

213

because last month when I took a trip up the Rhine that was as far as we got. It's a pretty little town. You guys ever been there?"

"Not recently," Major Baker-Bates said.

When they went back out to Meyer's jeep after questioning both Corporal Little and Private Baxter, Major Baker-Bates was in a buoyant mood that bordered on ebullience. "Well, it looks as though it's back in my court, doesn't it?"

It was a glum nod that Meyer gave him. "Bonn's in the British Zone, all right."

"You'll be coming to Bonn, of course? "

"I'll have to check."

"I do so hope that you can. It'll give me the opportunity to reciprocate your splendid hospitality."

"Of course, there's a chance that he might not go to Bonn."

"Oppenheimer?"

Meyer nodded.

"Oh, he'll go to Bonn all right."

"What makes you so sure?"

"He has a list, doesn't he? Sort of a things-to-do list—although, in this instance, it's a people-to-kill list."

"Yeah, he's got a list."

"And he's German, isn't he?"

Again, Meyer nodded.

"Did you ever see a German who, given a list of things to do, didn't start at the top and work his way right down to the bottom? They are, Lieutenant, a most methodical people. It's one of their primary virtues, provided that they have any virtues at all."

"Oppenheimer's a Jew."

"But he's also a German, my boy. He has his little list of things to do, people to kill. He's started at the top and he'll work his way down right to the bottom."

"Unless somebody stops him."

"Oh, I'll stop him all right," Major Baker-Bates said. "I'll stop him in Bonn."

214

22 Some twenty kilometers east of the Opel plant, the UNRRA Ford sedan turned in to the dairy farm. At the wheel was Heinrich, the butler-chauffeur and former caterer of Nazi social affairs in Berlin. His two passengers were Jackson and the dwarf. In the trunk of the car were fifty cartons of American cigarettes.

The farmhouse was built of reddish stone with a slate roof, as was the dairy barn, which was attached to it at a right angle. In the middle of the barnyard—and in Jackson's opinion, far too close to the house—was a huge, steaming pile of manure.

"Let me guess," Jackson said, nodding at the manure pile. "He's got it hidden under that."

The dwarf wrinkled his nose. "It's a sign of prosperity, you know."

"He must be a very rich man."

"I will bring him," Heinrich said, and got out of the car. Skirting carefully around the manure pile, he went up to the farmhouse and banged on its door with a fist. The door was opened a suspicious inch or two. Heinrich said something, the door opened wider, and the farmer came out.

He was a stocky, thick-waisted man of about fifty dressed in rubber boots and stained, dirty green coveralls. On his head was a shapeless black felt hat, and under it his face wore the wary, careful expression of a peasant who's convinced that he's about to be cheated. His eyes were small, blue, and cunning, the eyes of a skilled bargainer. Jackson decided that he would let the dwarf do all the dickering. The dwarf was good at it.

Jackson and Ploscaru got out of the car, but no introductions were made. The farmer stared at them a moment, especially at Ploscaru; grunted; and jerked his head in the direction in which he intended to lead them. He moved off, and the three men fell in behind.

"Why all the mystery, Nick?" Jackson said as they followed the farmer around toward the back of the barn.

"It's not a mystery, it's a surprise," Ploscaru said. "Everybody likes surprise."

"I don't."

"You'll like this one."

In back of the barn, the farmer stopped at a crude shed without walls that apparently had been erected to afford some protection to a four-foot-high stack of hay. All there was to the shed was its plank roof and the four poles that supported it.

The farmer picked up a rake and started pulling the hay down and to one side. The hay was only a few inches deep on top. Underneath it was a stained, patched canvas that covered something. When most of the hay was gone, the farmer peeled away the canvas, and Jackson said, "Sweet Jesus!"

It was red, and it had two bullet holes through its

windshield. A leather strap was buckled around its immense hood. The radiator cap was adorned with a three-pointed star.

Jackson looked at the dwarf, who was beaming. "Isn't it beautiful?" Ploscaru said.

"It's a monster," Jackson said.

"Are you familiar with this particular model, Herr Doktor?" asked Heinrich, obviously anxious to serve as docent.

"It's a Mercedes," Jackson said.

"Ach, but what a Mercedes. It's the SSK 38-slash-250, designed, as you know, by Dr. Porsche. It has the 7.069-liter engine and is supercharged, as you can see. Horsepower, I would say, around 200. It's supercharged by the Roots-type double-vane blower, and—"

"Tell me about the bullet holes," Jackson said.

"Ach, those. Well, perhaps we should let its proprietor tell you about those." He turned to the farmer. "He wants to know about the bullet holes in the windshield."

The farmer spat into some hay and shrugged. "What is there to know? It was your planes that did it."

"My planes?" Jackson said.

"Well, your plane, then. There was only one. An American fighter. He came in low and got him through the head."

"Who?"

"The Colonel."

"What kind of colonel?"

"An SS colonel, except that he was no longer in uniform then. It was right after Frankfurt fell to the Americans. The Colonel was trying to get to Switzerland, or so he said before he died. I buried him over there." He pointed with his chin to a grassy mound of earth under a plane tree.

"And kept his car," Jackson said.

The farmer shrugged again. "Who's to say it was his car? He was a deserter. He probably stole it."

"But you want to sell it now?" Ploscaru said.

The farmer looked up at the sky. "I might."

"You have the papers, of course."

The farmer quit looking up at the sky and frowned. "No papers."

"Well, that does present certain kinds of problems."

"What kind of problems?"

"Obviously, for a car with papers there is one price. But for a car with no papers—well, naturally, there must be another price."

"Especially for one owned by an SS colonel who only drove it to the gas chamber on Saturday nights," Jackson said in English.

The farmer glared. "What did he say?"

"I said that it probably uses a lot of gasoline. Probably two kilometers to the liter. Maybe three."

"It has a big tank. Besides," the farmer continued with another shrug, "you're an American. Gasoline is no problem for you."

"So how much are you asking for this twelve-year-old contraption?" Ploscaru said.

"I will not take marks."

"All right, no marks."

"Either cigarettes or dollars."

"How much in dollars, then?"

The farmer couldn't keep the craftiness and greed from spreading across his face. "Five hundred dollars."

Ploscaru nodded several times as though he found the price perfectly reasonable. "That's with the papers, of course."

"I told you. No papers."

"Oh, I see. Then your price *without* papers must be around two hundred dollars, right?"

"Wrong," the farmer said. "It is an unusual car, a rare model. Anyone would pay at least four hundred dollars for it."

"True, true," Ploscaru said. "They might pay that much if there were papers to go with it and if there weren't two

218

bullet holes in its windshield. Think of the questions that will be asked when one goes to get the glass replaced."

"Perhaps three-fifty," the farmer said.

"Three hundred, and we're taking a terrible risk."

"Done," the farmer said, and held out his hand. Ploscaru shook it, then turned to Heinrich. "How much are cigarettes bringing on the black market today, Heinrich?"

"Ten dollars a carton, Herr Direktor," he said automatically.

"Thirty cartons?" Ploscaru said to the farmer.

He nodded. "Thirty cartons."

"You forgot to ask him one thing," Jackson said.

Ploscaru looked up. "What?"

"Does it run?"

"It runs," the farmer said. "It runs very fast."

The narrow road was long, straight, and free of traffic. When the speedometer reached 70 kilometers per hour, Jackson jammed the accelerator to the floor, the supercharger cut in with a howl, and the big open roadster leaped forward as though shot from some immense rubber band.

The dwarf knelt on the passenger seat, his lips peeled back by both the wind and a grin that was almost manic. "Faster!" he yelled above the supercharger's howl. "Faster!"

Jackson kept his foot down, and the speedometer quickly reached 160 kilometers per hour. He kept it there for a few moments, then took his foot from the accelerator, and the big car slowed. He let its speed drop back down to a sensible 60 kilometers per hour.

"How fast did we go?" Ploscaru asked.

"About a hundred miles per hour."

"I like to go fast. It's something to do with sex, I think. I get quite aroused."

"This is some car you found, Nick."

"How does it handle?"

"Better than I would've thought. Very smooth, very

219

quick. Even a kid could handle it. I'm not sure that they remembered to put the springs in, though. Run over a marble and you feel it clear up your spine. Not to be picky, but don't you think maybe it's just a bit flashy for our line of work?"

"Flashy?"

"Yeah, flashy. We're supposed to be a trifle clandestine, aren't we? You know, sly and sneaky. This thing's about as sneaky as a parade."

"But fast."

"Very fast."

"We might need it, then."

"For what?"

"To get from here to there very quickly."

When they got back to the big house near the Frankfurt zoo, one of the young maids was waiting for them with an envelope and the important air of someone who gets to deliver the bad news.

"He said to give it to either of you," she said after making her curtsy.

"Who?"

"The man who brought it. He came on a bicycle. He said it was of the gravest importance. A matter of life or death, he said."

Ploscaru's eyebrows went up. "He said that?"

"I am almost positive, Herr Direktor."

Jackson took the envelope and followed Ploscaru into the sitting room, where a coal fire burned in the grate.

"Open it while I make us a drink," Ploscaru said.

Jackson examined the envelope, which was made of thick, cream-colored paper. There was nothing written on its front or back, so he smelled it. There was a slight scent that he decided was lavender. He opened the envelope with his finger and took out a single sheet of paper.

He recognized the handwriting immediately. But even

if it had been typed, he felt that he would automatically have identified its sender from the florid prose. There was no salutation, and the note began abruptly: "A terrible thing has happened. I am in despair and must see you at once. Please do not fail me in this hour of grave need." It was signed with Leah Oppenheimer's initials, L.O.

He traded the letter to Ploscaru for a drink. "A maiden in distress," Jackson said.

Ploscaru read the note quickly, looked up, and said, "She does like a bit of melodrama, doesn't she? I suppose you'd better go see her."

"Aren't you coming?"

The dwarf shook his head. "I think not. You seem to be handling her quite well, and there is the chance that I may have an important appointment tonight."

"She keeps asking about you."

"Make my excuses."

"I think she's getting tired of excuses."

"Then take her to dinner. There's quite a good black-market restaurant that I've heard about. Here, I'll give you the address." He wrote the address with a gold pencil on the back of the letter and handed it to Jackson. "You can even give her a ride in the car. She might like that."

"I think I'll run her past the gas station just to see what the fellas think."

"Sorry?"

"Nothing."

When Leah Oppenheimer opened the door of the apartment on the third floor, Jackson lied and said, "I came as soon as I got your note." Actually, he'd had another drink first.

"You are so very kind," she said in a voice that was almost a whisper. "Do come in."

As she led him into the room where she had served tea and sliced Milky Ways, Jackson had the feeling that he was being led into a funeral parlor by the most bereaved relative of the deceased. It was still cold in the room, and Leah Oppenheimer had her camel's-hair coat on.

"I am sorry, but there is no electricity," she said, indicating two candles that burned near the table where tea had been served. "No heat either, I'm afraid, but do sit down."

"What's happened?" Jackson said, choosing the same chair that he had sat in before.

"It's horrible. It's so horrible that I can't believe it." Her voice almost broke, and now that she was under the candle light Jackson could see that she had been crying.

"Tell me."

"My brother, he . . . he . . ." Then the tears started, as did the sobs. Jackson rose and patted her on the shoulder. He felt clumsy. She reached for his hand and held it pressed against her cheek. She cries the same way she writes, Jackson thought, found his handkerchief with his other hand, and gave it to her.

"Here," he said, "blow your nose."

"Thank you." She blew her nose, wiped away the tears, and looked up at him. "You're always so very kind. I feel I can trust you. I—I've always felt that from the first moment we met."

Jackson tried not to grimace. She's reading it, he decided. She has this mental script that some idiot has written for her and she reads from it.

"Better?" he said, freeing his hand and using it to give her shoulder another pat.

She nodded.

Jackson resumed his seat and said, "Tell me about it. Tell me about what's so horrible."

She folded her hands in her lap and looked away, as though it would make the telling easier. "My brother."

Jackson waited. When she said nothing after several moments, he said, "What about him?"

Still looking away, she said, "They say he has killed somebody else."

Jackson sighed. "Who're they?"

"Lieutenant Meyer. He was here earlier. He said my brother shot and killed a man at the Opel plant. What could he have been doing at the Opel plant? It's at Russelsheim, you know."

"Who did he kill?"

"A man. He held a trial, found him guilty, and then killed him."

Jackson took out his cigarettes, thought about offering Leah Oppenheimer one, decided against it, lit one for himself, and said, "I want you to do something for me."

She looked at him then. "Of course. Anything."

"Tell me exactly what Lieutenant Meyer said."

It took her a while, nearly half an hour, what with her asides, rhetorical questions, and the several long periods during which she said absolutely nothing, but instead gazed silently down at her hands.

When Jackson felt that she was through, he said, "That's it? You've told me everything he said?"

"Yes. Everything."

"Where is your friend?"

"Eva? She and Lieutenant Meyer went out. It will be their last night together for perhaps some time. They will probably be out quite late. She wanted to stay with me, but I told her no, that it wasn't necessary, that it might be better if I were alone with my thoughts."

She's reading again, Jackson thought.

"So I was alone for a time, and when I could no longer bear it, I sent you that silly note. You were so very kind to come."

"Why isn't Lieutenant Meyer going to be around for a while?" Jackson said.

"Why? Because he feels he has to go to Bonn, of course."

"Of course. But why Bonn exactly?"

"Because that's where my brother's going. Didn't I mention that?"

"No. You didn't.

223

"It's important, isn't it?"

"Yes," Jackson said. "It's important."

It took Jackson a while to convince her that she should accept his invitation to dinner. Several times he almost gave up, but instead persisted, and when at long last she accepted, she suddenly found she couldn't go the way she was dressed.

"It will only take a minute to change," she said.

It took her twenty minutes, but when she came out of the bedroom she looked far different from the way she had looked when she went in. She looked, in fact, Jackson thought, almost beautiful.

She had done something to her hair, although he was not quite sure what except that it was no longer worn in her usual maiden-lady fashion. Instead, it fell in soft waves almost to her shoulders. She also had done something to erase the evidence of her tears—perhaps a skillful application of makeup, Jackson thought, but wasn't sure, because there was no evidence of makeup except for the faint touch of lipstick that she had added.

The dress helped, too. It was a plain black dress. Your simple, basic black, Jackson decided, which probably cost a hundred dollars. It was cut low and close enough to show off her breasts to good advantage, and for the first time he wondered how it would be to go to bed with her. He was faintly surprised that he hadn't wondered about that before, because, like most men, he usually speculated about it shortly after meeting a woman. Any woman.

She stood there in the center of the room, almost shyly, as if she were not at all sure that he still wanted her to go.

"You look very nice," he said. "Very pretty."

"Do you really think so?"

"Yes."

"What do they call this in the States?"

"Call what?"

"What we are doing."

"I think they call it going to dinner."

She shook her head. "No there is another word that I've read. They call it a—a date, don't they?"

"Sometimes."

"Is this like a real date?"

"Absolutely," Jackson said, praying that she wouldn't simper.

Instead, she smiled shyly and said, "It will be my first one, you know."

"Your first one ever?" Somehow, he managed to keep the shock out of his voice, if not the surprise.

She nodded gravely. "My first one ever. Do you still want me to go?"

"Sure," Jackson said, and smiled as though he really meant it and was rather amazed to realize that he did.

23 Although the beer was no better than usual, the Golden Rose was crowded that night. It was so crowded, in fact, that the printer had to share a table with two other people, a man and a woman, who had almost nothing to say to each other. Bodden decided that they were married.

He had been waiting nearly thirty minutes when Eva Scheel came in. She stood at the entrance just past the heavy curtain, one hand clasping her fur coat to her neck as she tried to spot Bodden in the crowded, smoky room. He waved. She nodded and started toward him.

She sat down at the table after first giving the silent couple an automatic "Good evening," which they muttered back, their first words in nearly twenty minutes.

"You have eaten?" she said.

Bodden nodded and smiled. "Earlier. A fat chicken. Very tasty. The sour one down in the cellar cooks well. And you?"

"At the American officers' club. A steak. They recently decided to let Germans in. Proper Germans, of course." She looked around the room and frowned. "We must talk. But not here. Is your room far?"

"Not far."

"We'd best go there."

Bodden smiled. "It's a cold place; no heat, you know. But I managed to locate a bottle of brandy."

"We'll warm ourselves with that, then," Eva Scheel said.

There was only one chair in Bodden's room. One chair, a bed, a pine table, a wardrobe, a window, and a bicycle that he carried up and down three flights of stairs to keep it from being stolen.

"Home," he said as he ushered her into the room.

Eva Scheel looked around. "I've seen worse."

"And better, too, no doubt. You have a choice—the bed or the chair."

"The bed, I think." She walked over and sat down on it. "I see you found yourself a bicycle."

"At the DP camp in Badenhausen," Bodden said as he opened the wardrobe and took down a bottle of *Branntwein* and two mismatched glasses. "There was a man there. A Czech called Kubista. Apparently he's the resident forger. We talked. For a price, he might sell me some useful information. I would have bought it on the spot had I had the funds."

"How much?"

"A hundred American dollars."

"This Czech. He has done business with Oppenheimer?"

Bodden nodded as he handed her a glass of brandy. "He hinted as much."

She took from her coat pocket a small purse, opened it,

and counted out ten $20 bills. "Buy it," she said. "After that, you will be going to Bonn."

"And what will I find in Bonn?"

"Oppenheimer, if you're lucky. He has killed another."

"A busy man."

"He has a list. The next one on the list is in Bonn."

Bodden smiled. "Your young American officer must have been in one of his talkative moods."

"Very. I heard it all for the first time when he came to see Oppenheimer's sister this afternoon. I heard it for the second time, plus his theories, over my steak. Now when I tell it to you I'll be hearing it for the third time."

She told him then, everything that Lt. LaFollette Meyer had told her, including his disappointment over the fact that the search for Kurt Oppenheimer would now be centered in Bonn and under the jurisdiction of the British and Major Baker-Bates.

When she was through, Bodden refilled their glasses. "It will be a miracle if I find him first."

"Berlin doesn't expect miracles."

Bodden nodded thoughtfully. "You have heard from them?"

"This morning. A courier. She brought instructions plus an enormous amount of money."

"How large is enormous?"

"Twenty-seven thousand dollars."

"You're right; that is enormous."

"Two thousand is for our expenses."

"And the other twenty-five?"

"With that you will buy Oppenheimer from the dwarf, should the dwarf find him first."

"But I am still to try to find him myself, since Berlin, no doubt, is as economical as always."

"You are to try very hard."

"You have met the dwarf?"

Eva Scheel shook her head. "No, but I have met his colleague. The American called Jackson."

"What did you think?"

228

She took a sip of her brandy and frowned. "I'm not sure. He is not your typical Americăn. He lacks ambition, I think. An American without ambition is rather rare, you know. If he had it, or a purpose that he believed important, I feel he could be very hard, very ruthless."

"How old is he?"

"In his early thirties."

"Intelligent?"

"He is no fool. He also has some interesting theories."

"Such as?"

"Such as the theory that Berlin—or I suppose I should say, Moscow—wants Oppenheimer in Palestine. Jackson came up with the unusual suggestion that a renegade Jew could be quite useful to the Palestinians. And to Moscow."

"Your Mr. Jackson has a complicated mind."

Eva Scheel nodded. "Yes, I thought you'd think so."

Bodden clasped his hands behind his head, leaned back in his chair, and gazed up at the ceiling. "The dwarf is playing a double game, of course. That's to be expected. He's a Romanian, and they must learn it in their cradles. But what about this Jackson? You say he is without ambition. Deception requires a certain amount of that."

"A good point. The dwarf, I suppose, could simply be using him. My young American tells me that Jackson has some unofficial but very influential connections with American intelligence in Washington. I would say that the Americans are letting Jackson run to see where he goes. My young American had a very unusual description for Jackson. How good is your English?"

"Try me."

"He called Jackson an 'ex–OSS hotshot.' "

"Hotshot I know from the Pole."

"What Pole?"

"The one who taught me American English. A very funny fellow." He was silent for a moment. Then he said, "What would happen, do you think, should this Jackson learn that the dwarf was playing a double game?"

"Nothing perhaps. He might only shrug—unless it

turned out badly for him. In that case, I would hate to be the dwarf."

Bodden was again silent for several long moments as he examined all that he had been told. "Then," he said finally, "there are the British."

She sighed. "I was wondering when you would get to them. I was almost hoping that you wouldn't."

"Why?"

"Because if the British find Oppenheimer first, then Berlin has additional instructions for you."

"What?"

She dropped her gaze to her drink. "You are to kill him—somehow."

"Well, now."

There was yet another silence until, looking at him this time, she said, "Have you ever done anything like that before?"

He nodded. "I have killed, but I have never murdered. There is a difference. At least, I like to think there is. It makes my sleep more restful."

She went back to the inspection of her drink. "Could you do it?"

This time the silence was longer than ever. Bodden at last decided that there was nothing to lose by being honest. "I don't know," he said. "It would depend on—on many things."

She looked up at him. "Opportunity?"

"Yes, there is that. If the British had him locked up, there might not be any opportunity."

She nodded. "That's why I will also be going to Bonn. As I said, Berlin doesn't expect miracles. But it would be no miracle if the British were to let his sister and her oldest friend in to see Oppenheimer, would it?"

Bodden frowned with his forehead. Distaste was written across the rest of his face. "They don't expect *you* to kill him, surely?"

"No, but I could easily slip him the means to kill himself.

It is really only a very small pill."

"Which he would choose over a hanging."

She smiled slightly, although there was no trace of humor in it. "If Berlin can't have Oppenheimer for themselves, they would be quite happy for the British to hang him—or the Americans. But they won't hang him—either of them."

Bodden was beginning to understand. He nodded slowly. "Yes, I see. If Berlin is willing to pay twenty-five thousand dollars for an assassin, think what he must be worth to the British—not to mention the Americans."

"They are very rare, I suppose," she said. "Assassins. Good ones, anyway. Tell me, printer, do you ever think of yourself that way—as an assassin?"

"No," he said. "Never."

"I thought not." She patted the bed by her side. "Sit over here—beside me. That way you won't have to keep hopping up to fill my glass. We are going to finish it, aren't we—your bottle—just to keep warm?"

Bodden rose. "I thought we might." He kicked the chair over near the bed, placed the bottle on it, and sat down next to her.

"You know what they say about Berlin in the winter, don't you?" he said.

"What?"

"That there're only two places to keep warm—in bed or the bath."

"You have no bath, of course."

"Only a bed."

"Then that will have to do."

He kissed her then. She was quite ready for it, both her mouth and her tongue eager and exploring. When it was over, she leaned back on the bed, supporting herself on her elbows.

"There is no hurry, is there, printer?"

"None."

"We will finish the bottle first and you can tell me

231

about yourself and then we will go to bed. It has been a long time since I have been to bed with a man."

"What about your young American?"

"He is a very nice boy and, like most boys, very eager, very impatient. Were you ever like that, printer—young and impatient and eager?"

"A long time ago."

"Tell me about it. Tell me about you and what you did before the war in Berlin."

He leaned back and put an arm around her. She shifted slightly so that her head rested on his chest. "I had my own shop," he said, "not far from the Adlon Hotel; do you know it?"

"A very fashionable district."

"I was a very fashionable printer. The rich liked me—the rich and the poor poets. I printed their invitations and calling cards—the rich, I mean. No one was anyone unless they had them done by me. I did the best work in Berlin, and I was very expensive. By being expensive I could afford to print the poor poets. You know the kind of thing—slim volumes on thick paper. I also did commercial work—fancy brochures, things like that; more bread-and-butter stuff. And, of course, there was the political material. I printed that too, and kept on printing it even after I was warned not to. I was what your young American friend would call a very 'hotshot' Social Democrat at the time. They came for me eventually, the Gestapo. They wrecked the plant. I got to watch that. Then they took me away, and finally I wound up in Belsen. And there I broadened my political horizons."

"So you could eat."

"So I could eat."

"You sound as though you like to live well, printer."

"It is a weakness."

"I suffer from it too. Do you think you ever will again?"

"Not unless a miracle happens—one of those kinds that you say Berlin doesn't believe in."

She was silent for a moment. Then she turned onto her stomach and looked at him. "Twenty-five thousand dollars can buy a great many miracles, printer. Twenty-seven, actually."

He grinned and wrapped a strand of her hair around his finger. "You have dangerous thoughts, little one."

"So do you"

"I'm surprised."

"At my thoughts?"

"That you didn't mention them sooner."

"It could be done."

"It would also be dangerous."

"No more dangerous than killing a man whom you really don't want to kill."

He gave the strand of hair a gentle tug. "I bet you even have a plan."

She kissed him—a quick, friendly, warm, wet kiss. "You're right, I do. Make love to me, printer. Make love to me and then I will tell you about my plan."

"To abscond with twenty-five thousand dollars."

"Twenty-seven, actually."

He grinned again. "With that much money I could afford you, couldn't I?"

She kissed him quickly again. "That's right, printer. You could."

24 On the way to the black-market restaurant, Leah Oppenheimer didn't even seem to notice the huge old roadster or the stares that it attracted. She sat silently in the passenger's seat, a silk scarf around her head and a small, polite, shy smile on her lips: the kind of smile, Jackson decided, that a proper young woman would wear on her very first date.

After parking the car near the restaurant, he gave a shabbily dressed middle-aged man five cigarettes to watch it. For another two cigarettes the man offered to dust the car off with a dirty rag that he produced from underneath his hat. Jackson shrugged and paid him his price.

The restaurant was called the Blue Fox Cellar, and it was located in the bowels of a building that had been erected sometime in the late eighteenth century. There was nothing left of the building now except for a pile of rubble and a new, jerry-built entrance that was about as inviting as the entrance to a New York subway.

To get to the restaurant itself they had to go down a steep flight of stairs, then along a corridor, and through another door. But before they were allowed through that, they were inspected by an eye that peered out at them from a speakeasylike peephole. Jackson thought that the eye looked beady, but he didn't say anything.

Past the door, they found themselves in an immense, round room with stone walls and a wide stone staircase that hugged the curving wall as it descended into the dining area thirty feet below. The place was lighted by a number of kerosene lamps and what Jackson estimated to be hundreds of thick, squat candles.

At the bottom of the stairs they were met by a bowing, properly obsequious headwaiter dressed in white tie and tailcoat, who showed them to a table, took their coats, and handed them their menus. Before examining the bill of fare, Jackson looked around at the other diners.

Most of them were Germans: prosperous, flush-faced men in their forties and fifties. Nearly all of them were accompanied by much younger women who seemed to be eating hungrily. There were also a number of middle-ranking American Army officers: majors and lieutenant colonels mostly, with a sprinkling of captains. The Americans' women, for the most part, seemed better looking, better dressed, and not quite so hungry. On a small raised platform a four-piece string ensemble played moody waltzes. A few couples danced.

The shock that Jackson got when he examined the menu almost cost him his appetite. The prices were higher than New York's highest, higher even than the astronomical black-market prices he had paid in Paris during the week's leave he had had there in '45 just before they had flown him out to Burma. He guessed that it was going to cost him 10,000 marks to get out of the Blue Fox Cellar. Ten thousand marks was about fifty American dollars.

Leah Oppenheimer smiled shyly and asked if he would mind ordering for her. Since the menu was written in bad French and boasted caviar and champagne, he ordered both plus coq au vin, a salad, and a Moselle, which the menu claimed to be prewar. He ordered in French, and the German waiter replied in English.

Although the caviar was a bit suspicious and the champagne equally so, the chicken was good, as was the Moselle. Leah Oppenheimer ate and drank everything that was set before her. Afterward, she said that she really didn't care for a dessert, but wouldn't mind the coffee and brandy that Jackson proposed instead.

The brandy made her bold, or perhaps just less reserved. With her elbow on the table and her chin cupped in her hand, she gazed at Jackson and said, "You have done this many times, haven't you?"

"Well, not exactly like this," he said, thinking of the bill that was yet to come. "This is rather special."

"I think you have had much experience with many women."

Jackson could think of nohing to say to that, so he smiled and hoped that it was a noncommittal smile and not a leer.

"But you have never married."

"No."

"Do you think you will one day?"

"I'm beginning to wonder."

"I think you will marry a nice American girl and settle down and live in—in Tulsa, Oklahoma."

Jackson realized that for her Tulsa was as remote as Timbuktu. Perhaps even more so. "I think you're a lousy fortune-teller," he said.

"When I was young, I thought that I would like to get married someday," she said. "But now, of course, I'm too old."

"You are pretty old, all right—at least twenty-seven or twenty-eight," he said, slicing at least a year from her age because he thought it might make her feel better.

"That is old for a European," she said, and sighed—somewhat dramatically, Jackson thought. He also wondered if she had gone back to reading from her awful script again.

"My friend, Fräulein Scheel," she said, and paused.

"What about her?"

"She is both very fortunate and very foolish, I think."

"Why?"

"There is this very nice young American—but you know him, don't you: Lieutenant Meyer?"

"We've met."

"That's right; of course. Well, she has allowed him to think that she will marry him, but she has no intention of doing so."

"What's the matter—doesn't she care for Milwaukee?"

"She says he is far too callow a youth."

She's reading from the script again, Jackson decided. "Did she say callow?"

They had been speaking English, and Leah Oppenheimer blushed slightly as though embarrassed. "Is that not the correct word—callow? In German it is *ungefiedert*."

"It's the correct word all right. It's just that Lieutenant Meyer didn't seem all that *ungefiedert* to me."

"Eva has always liked older men," she said, turning almost confidential. "Even when we were young girls together, she was a terrible flirt. The Scheel family was quite well-to-do before the war, you know, and they had many visitors, and Eva was always flirting with the men, even the ones who were old enough to be her father. I think she misses it."

"What? The men?"

"No, being well-to-do. I think that finding herself in reduced circumstances is very difficult for Eva." Jackson by now was almost beginning to believe that there really was a script and that it had been written for her by a Victorian novelist. A lady novelist.

"Didn't you do any flirting when you and Fräulein Scheel were younger?"

She seemed almost shocked by the suggestion. "Oh, no. I was far too shy."

"What about later, when you were in Switzerland? There must have been some boys around."

"But not many Jewish boys, Mr. Jackson. By then, I suppose, there were not too many Jewish boys around anyplace in Europe."

That was a topic that Jackson had no desire to pursue, so instead he asked her to dance.

That idea also seemed to shock her. "I have not danced since school in Switzerland, and then it was only with other girls."

"It's like swimming or riding a bicycle. Once you learn, you never forget." He wasn't at all sure that this was true, but he felt that it was probably encouraging.

"I would be awkward."

"I'm a strong leader."

"Well," she said hesitantly, "if you don't think I—"

"You'll do fine," he said.

The string ensemble was playing "As Time Goes By" with a rather methodical Teutonic beat, and at first she was a little stiff. But then she gained confidence, and when she did she allowed herself to relax and move in closer. Jackson decided to find out how she would enjoy dancing cheek to cheek. When she made no move to draw away and even pressed in closer to him, he gave serious consideration for the first time to the possibility of taking her to bed. A little later, when her thigh began to move between his legs, he knew that he would.

She was, Jackson had discovered, remarkable in bed. He lay there in the twisted down comforter, spent and still panting slightly, waiting for his breathing to return to normal so that he could light a cigarette. While he waited, he reviewed the three-quarters of an hour of grappling, probing, tasting, touching, and other rather complicated acrobatics that had gone into their lovemaking.

Leah Oppenheimer sat up in the bed, bent over, and found his shirt on the floor where it had been hastily discarded in a puddle of clothing. She took cigarettes and matches from its pocket, lit one, and handed it to him. He noticed that her face and eyes seemed to be glowing.

"Thanks," he said.

She watched him smoke for a moment and then said, "So that is lovemaking?"

"That's it. I can't think of anything we left out."

"That was my first time. I'm very glad that it was with you."

"Uh-huh."

"Was I adequate?"

"You weren't adequate, you were fantastic."

"Really?" She seemed pleased.

"Really."

"I was worried that—well, you understand."

"Sure."

"You know when I decided that I would do this if you asked me?"

"When?"

"In Mexico. In the hotel. When we were sitting there with my father. Couldn't you tell?"

"No."

"I thought you could. I thought I was very obvious. If my father's eyes had been all right, I'm sure he would have been able to tell. At least, he would have suspected."

"I couldn't tell."

"Was I too clumsy?"

"You weren't clumsy at all. You were very—inventive."

That also pleased her. "You're sure? You're not just saying so?"

"I'm sure. That thing you did with the ribbon."

"You didn't like it."

"No, it was fine. Quite a sensation. Somebody once told me it was the specialty of a Mexican whorehouse he'd once spent a little time in."

"Was I like a whore? I tried so hard to be."

239

"You were fine. I just wondered how you happened to think it up—the ribbon thing."

"Oh, that. Well, that came out of the books too. Was it interesting?"

"Extremely. What books?"

"In the villa in Switzerland. My father rented this villa from a man, and it had a library. There was one glass case that was kept locked. I found the key. The books were all written in English, but they had been written a long time ago—in the 1890's, I think, because everybody went about in hansom cabs. They were mostly stories about what men and women do to each other. I read them aloud to myself sometimes because I thought it would be good for my English. Some of them were very exciting. Occasionally, when they would do something really interesting to each other, I would make a note about it in my diary."

"For future reference."

She nodded solemnly. "I thought if I were ever to get married, it would please my husband. Of course, we did not do all that I read about."

"We didn't?"

"No, there are many other things. Some of them, I think, are very strange. Do you like strange things?"

"Sometimes."

"Do you want to do this with me again?"

"Very much."

"I was not sure. You will be going to Bonn, of course—you and Mr. Ploscaru."

"Tomorrow."

She frowned—a puzzled, earnest sort of frown. "Do you think they have little whips in Bonn?"

"I have no idea," Jackson said.

When he let himself into the big house near the zoo, Jackson could hear Ploscaru banging away at the piano as he sang "Deep Purple" in his rich, true baritone. Jackson went through the sliding doors into the large sitting room where the coal fire burned in the grate. The little parlor-maid was standing near the piano. She tried to curtsy, but couldn't very well because she had only her underwear on. Instead, she snatched up the rest of her clothing and ran wordlessly from the room, her face and much of the rest of her a deep crimson. The dwarf finished singing about sleepy garden walls and breathing names with sighs and grinned at Jackson.

"Let's have a drink," he said.

"Did I interrupt something or were you already finished?"

"Quite finished, thank you. How was your dinner?"

"Expensive. We'll be going to Bonn tomorrow."

"Oh? Why?"

After Jackson finished telling him why, Ploscaru nodded and took a swallow of the drink that Jackson had mixed. "Interesting. The poor man sounds quite mad. Do you think he is?"

"Probably."

"But still in all, rather cunning. It will be interesting to see where he lived."

"Where who lived?"

"Why, Oppenheimer. But I didn't tell you, did I? Of course not. There hasn't been time. It cost a pretty penny, but I purchased some information from a DP earlier this evening that could be useful. It's Oppenheimer's address. It seems that he's been living in a ruined castle not far from Höchst. We'll go there tomorrow first thing and then on up the Rhine to Bonn. It should be quite pretty this time of year. We'll go along the west bank, don't you think?"

"Sure," Jackson said. "The west bank."

"I'm glad you agree. You get a much better view of them from the west bank."

"View of what?"

"Why, of the castles, of course."

"Of course," Jackson said.

25 Bodden had just opened the footlocker that contained the Thompson submachine guns, the .45 automatics, and the M-1 carbines when he heard the car drive up. It sounded as though it were a big car, possibly even a truck. The engine was cut off, and then a door was slammed shut with a thunk. A moment later there was another thunk. That means two of them, he thought. At least two.

He examined the footlocker full of weapons in the cellar of the old castle and decided on a carbine. He picked one up, slapped a magazine into place, jacked a cartridge into the chamber, and swore mildly and silently at Kubista the Czech. Bodden had paid the Czech one hundred dollars that morning for the information about the old castle that had once been Kurt Oppenheimer's home or lair or hideout, and he was upset with himself for not having suspected that Kubista would sell the information to someone else. You knew he'd do that, he thought. You just didn't think he'd do it quite so soon.

After making sure that the safety catch was off, Bodden turned toward the stone steps that led down into the cellar. He held the rifle across his chest, the way a hunter might hold it. He heard the voices then and was a bit pleased to realize that he could understand them because they were speaking English. They were talking about the padlocks that he had smashed open with the big rock. He had really had to batter the locks before they popped open.

"What if he's still there?" he heard one of the voices say. It was a man's voice, an American's.

"He won't be," the other voice said, not quite so deep, but almost. It was a man's voice too, but it spoke English with an accent of some kind that Bodden couldn't identify.

"But if he is?" the American said.

"Then we'll talk."

"Let's hope that's all he'll do."

Bodden could now hear the footsteps as they descended the stone staircase. He turned slightly so that the carbine pointed in the general direction of the steps. His finger was on the trigger, but when he saw the dwarf, he took his finger from the trigger and held the rifle down at his side.

When the dwarf caught sight of Bodden, his eyebrows went up slightly. Then he nodded and said, "Good morning." He seemed to ignore the rifle.

"Good morning," Bodden said. So that's the dwarf, he told himself. And the one behind him with the gray hair is the one called Jackson—the one without ambition.

"Are you the landlord?" Ploscaru said.

"You interested in a nice, dry cellar?"

The dwarf started brushing his hands off. "I noticed that the locks were broken. Vandals?"

243

"There's a lot of them about. DP's mostly."

Jackson, after looking around the cellar, nodded toward the cases of cigarettes. "Your former tenant apparently liked a cigarette now and then."

Bodden nodded. "It would seem that way, wouldn't it?"

"The broken locks. Does that mean he was behind in his rent?"

"Something like that," Bodden said.

The dwarf walked over and fingered the sleeve of one of the American officer uniforms that were hung as though awaiting inspection. "Very neat, your tenant. Pity that he got behind in his rent."

"Yes," Bodden said, "a pity."

"Any idea where he might have gone?" Jackson said, nudging one of the jerry cans of gasoline to see whether it was full.

"No idea. He owe you money?"

"Something like that," the dwarf said.

They heard the engine then. This time there was no doubt that it was a truck—a diesel-powered one by the sound of it. A door slammed, then another, and voices began jabbering at each other—Polish voices.

"Well, little man," Bodden said to Ploscaru. "Do you wish to lose your wallet?"

"Not particularly."

Bodden knelt quickly by the footlocker and opened its lid. He took out one of the .45 automatics, checked to make sure it was loaded, studied the dwarf carefully for a moment, and then tossed him the pistol. Ploscaru caught it deftly, with a smile.

"And you, my friend," Bodden said to Jackson. "You have a preference?"

"Anything that's handy."

"Here," he said, lifting out one of the Thompson submachine guns. "The gangster's weapon."

He tossed it to Jackson, who caught it easily and checked it over with sure, quick movements. The voices

244

were still jabbering away at each other in Polish, but closer now, and all three men turned toward the stone steps.

There were six of them, all shabbily dressed, except for the very tall one who seemed to be their leader. When he caught sight of the dwarf, he looked as if he were about to smile, but thought better of it—possibly because of the three guns that were aimed in his direction.

"Well," the tall man said in German, "what have we here?"

"A reception committee," Bodden said.

"But why so unfriendly?" the tall man said. "Surely we can do business?"

"No, I think not," Bodden said. "I think it would be far better if you and your friends were to leave." He waved the carbine a little as though to emphasize his point.

The tall man's eyes roved over the cases of cigarettes and candy. "We are prepared to pay a fair price. No one in Frankfurt pays a . . ."

The tall man never finished his commercial, if that was what it was, because the dwarf took two quick steps backward and jammed the muzzle of his automatic into the small of Bodden's back. Ploscaru held the automatic there with both hands, but had to raise his arms to do it.

"I think, landlord, the wisest thing for you to do would be to put your rifle down on the floor very carefully."

The surprise came and went quickly from Bodden's face. He frowned, and then the frown was replaced by a smile—almost a merry one. "No," he said.

"No?"

Bodden nodded, still smiling. "You see, little man, I made a decision long ago. And the decision I made was simply this: if anyone ever pointed a gun at me again to make me do something I had no wish to do, then the one who pointed the gun would have to use it."

Ploscaru cocked his head to one side as though studying the philosophical soundness of Bodden's resolution.

"A brave decision," he said, taking a quick step to one side, "but a foolish one."

He brought the automatic around with both hands and slammed it into Bodden's right kneecap. Bodden didn't scream, although he sucked in what seemed to be an enormous gulp of air. His right leg started to crumple. As he fell, he let go of the carbine. Ploscaru caught it before it hit the ground, put it down carefully, and then nudged it away with his foot. Bodden was now on the stone floor, his lips bitten, clutching his kneecap with both hands.

"For Christ's sake, Nick," Jackson said.

"He'll walk in an hour or two. Over the years, through necessity, I've become quite an expert on kneecaps." Ploscaru turned to the tall man. "Now, Mircea," he said in Romanian, "you can load your truck."

Mircea Ulescu, the ex-policeman turned thief, grinned broadly, and his soft gray eyes shone. "Ah, Nicolae, it is like old times, no?" He turned quickly and snapped orders at the other five men in Polish. They hurried over to the cases of cigarettes and started carrying them up the cellar steps.

"So, Mircea, you are speaking Polish now," Ploscaru said.

The big man shrugged. "What could I do, Nicolae? They would not learn German. They are such a stubborn race, the Poles."

Jackson looked at the submachine gun that he was still holding in his hands, frowned at it with something like mild distaste, put it down on the stone floor, and moved over to Bodden. Jackson stared down for a moment at the man, whose lips were still stretched back in a grimace of pain. Then he knelt down beside him and brought out a package of cigarettes and some matches.

"Do you smoke?" he asked.

"I—also—drink," Bodden said with an effort. He managed to accept a cigarette and a light.

"Let's see if the tenant left anything behind." Jackson

rose, opened the footlocker in which Oppenheimer had kept his tea things, found a bottle of bourbon and two teacups. He moved back over to Bodden and poured both teacups nearly full.

"Here," he said, "some American painkiller."

Bodden took a swallow. "An acquired taste, I'd say."

"Quickly acquired," Jackson said, raising his own cup. "Who are you, friend?"

Bodden turned his grimace into a smile of sorts. "Nobody."

Jackson nodded, almost sympathetically. "But not the landlord."

"No. Not the landlord."

"A friend of the tenant's—or rather, the former tenant?"

"Maybe."

"And maybe not."

"And maybe not," Bodden agreed. He took another swallow of the bourbon, sighed, and said, "Your little friend—he's a bit treacherous, isn't he?"

"A bit."

"The next time—well, the next time I'll not be quite so trusting."

"When's this next time going to happen?"

Bodden studied Jackson for a moment. "Soon. I'd say quite soon, wouldn't you, Mr. Jackson?"

Jackson didn't bother to try to hide his surprise at the mention of his name. "You've got me at a disadvantage there, friend."

"A small one, but still the only one I seem to have. However, if you need a name to go with my face, I'll be happy to oblige."

"Don't bother."

"Good. I won't."

"Let me guess something," Jackson said.

"Of course—but first, perhaps, another drop of your American *Schnapps*. As you say, it's a taste quickly acquired."

Jackson filled Bodden's teacup again. "If you happen to

find the former tenant, where will you encourage him to go—East?"

"Why East?"

"As I said, it's only a guess."

"We'll let it remain that. But I'll give you some advice, Mr. Jackson. Not free advice, which is usually worthless, but advice in exchange for the painkiller, which is already beginning to work a little. My advice is this: when you begin to believe that you can trust your little colleague over there—don't."

Jackson grinned. "You hand out good advice, friend."

"I try, Mr. Jackson, I try."

They both looked over at Ploscaru, into whose outstretched palm the big Romanian was counting some bills. There were a lot of them, German marks, and every once in a while the big Romanian would wet his finger to aid the accuracy of his count.

The huge cellar was stripped by now. Nothing remained except for the footlocker of weapons. Even the neatly made cot had been removed by the five Poles. Two of them now came back down into the cellar to make a final check. They seemed to be arguing with each other about something. One of them addressed a question in Polish to the big Romanian.

Ulescu silenced them with a quick frown and went on with his counting. When he was through, he smiled and said, "Well, Nicolae, a profitable morning for us both." Ploscaru nodded and tucked the bills away into a coat pocket. Ulescu turned toward the two Poles and said something to them in their own language. He listened to their reply and then turned back to the dwarf.

"There is a bicycle outside," he said. "Is it yours?"

"No."

"They wish to take it."

Ploscaru shrugged. "Let them."

Jackson rose. "The bicycle stays," he said.

Ulescu looked first at Jackson and then at Ploscaru.

The dwarf examined Jackson for a moment, then smiled slightly, shrugged again, and said, "As he says, the bicycle stays."

Ulescu gave the Poles the news and, before they could argue, waved them away with a big hand.

Jackson turned back to Bodden. He took the cigarettes from his pocket and tossed them down to the injured man, who nodded his thanks.

"Your compassion might get you into trouble someday, Mr. Jackson."

Jackson grinned. "Don't count on it, friend."

"No," Bodden said, "I won't."

Ploscaru walked over to the remaining footlocker, opened its lid again, and looked inside as though studying the contents. Finally, he reached in and brought out the .38 pistol. He checked to see that it was loaded and walked over to where Jackson stood. In his right hand he still held the .45 automatic. The dwarf stared for several moments at Bodden, then handed the .38 pistol to Jackson.

"If we don't kill him," Ploscaru said, "we'll be making a mistake."

"We don't kill him," Jackson said.

"All right," the dwarf said, turned, and walked away.

So, printer, you live a while longer, Bodden thought, and looked up at the American. "*Auf Wiedersehen,* Mr. Jackson."

Jackson nodded. "*Auf Wiedersehen,* friend."

26 The 1946 Ford sedan that was parked in front of the big house near the Frankfurt zoo was olive drab in color and had a white star and U.S. Army markings. It also had wooden bumpers, because there had still been a shortage of chrome steel when it was manufactured in January of that year. Behind the sedan's wheel was a bored Army corporal. Next to him was Lt. LaFollette Meyer.

The Corporal, a car lover, perked up a little when the big Mercedes roadster turned into the driveway. Lieutenant Meyer got out of the sedan and leaned against its front fender. He stared curiously at the dwarf who followed Jackson down the drive.

"We have to talk," Lieutenant Meyer said when Jackson drew near.

Jackson nodded. "I don't think you've met—"

Lieutenant Meyer interrupted. "I talk to you; not to him."

Ploscaru stared up at Meyer for a moment, smiled slightly, shrugged, and turned away, heading for the big house.

"Let's walk," Meyer said.

"All right," Jackson said, and fell in beside him.

"I'm trying to make up my mind about something," Lieutenant Meyer said.

"What?"

"About whether I'm a Zionist or not."

"Which way are you leaning?"

Meyer seemed to think about it for a few moments. "I'm not sure," he said finally. "In a way, if the Zionists have their way it will mean he won."

"Who?"

"Hitler."

"Oh."

"At one time, you know, he was thinking of shipping all the Jews to Madagascar. And at one time the British offered them Kenya. Kenya, from what I hear, wouldn't have been at all bad. Good land, good climate. But it wasn't Palestine. Or Israel. You know what I think Palestine could wind up being?"

"What?"

"The world's largest ghetto."

"The Jews will have to get rid of the British first," Jackson said. "Then they will have to get rid of the Palestinians. If they keep the pressure on, the British will probably pull out. They're broke. They're going to be pulling out of a lot of places in the next few years. But the Palestinians haven't got anyplace to pull out to. The Jews are going to have to fight them."

"And the Syrians and the Egyptians and the Lebanese and probably the Transjordanians."

"Probably," Jackson said.

"I wonder if they could win."

"The Jews?"

"Yeah."

Jackson thought about it. "It probably depends upon which way Russia leans. The Zionist lobby is pretty strong in the States, so Washington will probably tilt that way. Which way Russia will go is anybody's guess."

Lieutenant Meyer nodded, and they walked on in silence for a moment. Then Meyer said, "Remember that buck general I told you about?"

Jackson nodded. "The one you said wasn't very bright?"

"Yeah. General Grubbs. Knocker Grubbs. Well, the Knocker's out and an old friend of yours is in."

"Who?"

"They brought him up from Munich. They say he's brilliant. I don't know, maybe he is. I've only talked to him once, and that was this morning. He speaks German, though, and that's a change. He went to Heidelberg before the war. The Army sent him."

"Has he got a name, this old friend of mine?"

"Sorry, I thought I'd already mentioned it. Bookbinder. Samuel Bookbinder. He's a Jew, like me. Maybe that's why he's still only a colonel."

"He's no old friend of mine."

"You know him, though."

"We met a couple of times in Italy during the war. That doesn't make us old friends."

"Well, maybe he's an old friend of some of your old friends—those ex–OSS wheels in Washington who think you need special handling. Anyway, the cables have been shooting back and forth between them and Bookbinder. You heard the latest about Oppenheimer?"

Jackson nodded. "I heard."

"I thought you would. From his sister. Well, it's a British show now."

"In Bonn."

"That's right, in Bonn. They're sending me up as liaison. You're going, I suppose."

"Yes."

"Okay. First of all, there's this." Lieutenant Meyer took an envelope from his pocket and handed it to Jackson.

"What is it?"

"It's a kind of *laissez-passer*," Lieutenant Meyer said —not doing too badly with the French phrase, Jackson thought. "It's got a four-star general's name signed to it. It should keep the British off your back unless you fuck up all over the place."

"I'll try not to," Jackson said, and put the letter away without reading it.

"Okay, that's one. Now here's two, and two is the one I don't much like, although the Army doesn't care a hell of a lot what its first lieutenants like or don't like. Except I don't think this is the Army so much as it is your ex–OSS buddies in Washington."

"Uh-huh," Jackson said, because Meyer had paused as though expecting some comment.

"Bookbinder pretty much ran his own show down in Munich. He had to, because the Knocker was so fucking stupid. Well, Bookbinder has all sorts of lines out—to Berlin, to here, and even up to Hamburg where the British are. I don't know where he got this; maybe it was from the British. But maybe not. Anyway, he's learned that the Russians have sent someone in."

"After Oppenheimer?"

"That's right. He crossed over up north at a place called Lübeck. The British had a tag on him but it fell off, which didn't make them too happy because they thought he might lead them to Oppenheimer."

"Has he got a name?"

"No name. All that Bookbinder knows about him is that sometimes he's called the Printer."

"When're you going to get to the part that you don't like?"

"Now," Lieutenant Meyer said. "The British don't want Oppenheimer in Palestine. That means somebody else does, but I'm beginning to wonder who." He looked searchingly at Jackson, but Jackson only shrugged.

"You got any ideas?" Meyer said.

"The Irgun is almost a sure bet."

"Besides them?"

"The Russians."

"What about us?"

Jackson stopped walking, turned, and stared at Meyer. After a long moment he said, "If the war were still going on, I'd say yes. It might be something tricky that the OSS would try to pull. Now, I don't know. It's a possibility, I suppose."

"Bookbinder tells me that the Russians want Oppenheimer real bad. If they can't track him down themselves, they're even willing to buy him."

"From whom?"

"From whoever's got him for sale." They had started walking again, but Meyer stopped so that he could stare at Jackson without any liking. "I suppose that means you —and that creepy little pal of yours."

"I'm working for Leah Oppenheimer."

"Sure you are."

"You don't believe it?"

"I don't know what to believe about you, buddy, except that I don't trust you. Or that dwarf. Neither does Bookbinder. Up in Bonn he wants me to ride your ass, and if you start to go sour, I've got orders to stop you— even if it means bringing the British in. You understand?"

"I understand."

"Now we get to the part that I really don't like. It's a personal message to you straight from Washington. It's supposed to be funny, I guess, but I don't think it's very funny at all."

"Get to it."

"Okay. This is it and it's an exact quote: 'Don't sell until you hear our final offer.' You got it?"

"I've got it."

"You understand it?"

"Maybe."

Lieutenant Meyer nodded coldly. "Yeah, I thought you would." Then he turned and walked back to the Ford sedan.

Because of bad roads and worse bridges it took them nearly three hours to reach Remagen. The dwarf had sung most of the way, more loudly than usual in order to make himself heard over the old car's big engine. For the last hour he had been singing German drinking songs. When he hadn't been singing, the dwarf had recounted the histories of the castles they passed. He seemed to know stories about all of them.

They stopped at Remagen for a glass of wine and because Jackson wanted to see what was left of the bridge that the U.S. Army had used to first cross the Rhine.

"You've been along here before, of course," Ploscaru said as they got back into the car and started off again.

"A long time ago. Before the war."

"You remember the stories about this region?"

"Some of them."

"Roland built his castle here in Remagen, you know. He had been courting the fair Hildegunde, who was the daughter of the Count of Drachenfels. But then Roland went off to fight the Moors in Spain, and when he returned he found Hildegunde had become a nun. So he built his castle and sat moping in it until she died and then went off to fight the Moors some more. There it is— over there on your left—the Rolandsbogen. Roland's Arch."

"So it is," Jackson said, not slowing down.

"Now a little farther up we'll catch our first really good view of the Siebengebirge, the seven mountains."

"Where Siegfried hung out."

"Right. After he killed the dragon he bathed in its blood, you remember, which made him immune to any

255

wound—except for a very small spot between his shoulder blades." Ploscaru sighed. "It's not a very original myth— almost a direct steal from Achilles and his heel; but then, the Germans never were the most original of people, not even in their mythmaking."

"As I remember, there were some other folks who're supposed to be running around up there in the Siebenge- birge."

"Really? Who?"

"Snow White and the Seven Dwarfs."

Ploscaru smiled slightly, even a little sadly. "And now there'll be eight, won't there?"

They encountered the British roadblock on highway B 9 just as it reached the Bonn suburb of Bad Godes- berg. A British sergeant accompanied by two privates ap- proached the car and asked Jackson and Ploscaru for their passports.

"You might also want to look at this, Sergeant," Jack- son said, handing over the *laissez-passer*. The Sergeant examined the passports first. He took his time, glancing several times back and forth between the passport photos and the occupants of the Mercedes. He then leisurely opened the envelope and read the letter that it contained. If the four-star General's signature was supposed to im- press him, his face didn't show it. He might have been reading the trolley schedule. He slowly refolded the letter, tucked it carefully back into its envelope, and handed it back along with the passports.

"You'll be staying in Bonn?" he said.

"Bad Godesberg," the dwarf said.

"Where?"

"The Godesberg Hotel."

The Sergeant nodded thoughtfully. "All right, gentle- men. You can go."

The Sergeant watched as the old Mercedes rolled away. Then he turned to one of the privates and said, "Get on the blower to the Major, Charlie, and tell him that the Yank and the midget will be staying at the Godesberg."

The Godesberg Hotel was not the best hotel in either Bonn or Bad Godesberg. The best hotel was probably the Dreesen, where Hitler and Neville Chamberlain had met in 1938 just prior to Munich. However, Bonn had never been known for its hotels, but rather for its university and for being the birthplace of Beethoven, who had left as soon as he could for Vienna and the company of Mozart and Haydn, never to return. The war had nearly bypassed Bonn, although allied bombing and artillery had managed to destroy what some claimed was 30 percent of the city, although others charged that this estimate was far too high.

In its first postwar year Bonn remained what it had always been since the Romans founded it in 12 B.C.— sleepy, which was a guidebook euphemism for dull. And if Bonn was sleepy, Bad Godesberg was unconscious.

The Godesberg Hotel was a three-story building on a side street just off the Ringsdorf. Jackson and Ploscaru had only time enough to check in, unpack, and settle down in the dwarf's room over a drink before someone started knocking at the door.

The dwarf opened it, looked up, and smiled. "Well," he said, "what a delightful surprise. Do come in, Gilbert —and your friend, too."

Maj. Gilbert Baker-Bates, dressed in a tweed jacket and gray trousers, came into the room, followed by the man with yellow hair. Jackson decided that the jacket and trousers were the same that Baker-Bates had worn in Mexico. He tried to remember what the pay of a British major was, but couldn't. He wondered whether it would be worthwhile finding out, but decided not. The dwarf would know. The dwarf always knew things like that.

Once in the room, Baker-Bates didn't look at Ploscaru. Instead, he let his gaze wander around. When it reached

Jackson he nodded, the way one might nod to a dimly remembered acquaintance at a large but dull cocktail party.

Still not looking at Ploscaru, Baker-Bates said, "How are you, Nick?"

"Well. Quite well, in fact. And you?"

Baker-Bates turned to the yellow-haired man. "This one's Ploscaru, of course. And that one over there is Jackson. Minor Jackson."

The yellow-haired man nodded, but only once.

Ploscaru smiled up at him. "I don't believe I've had the pleasure."

"It's not going to be one, Nick. His name's Von Staden. Heinrich von Staden. He's your new nanny. Where you go, he goes."

"Von Staden," Ploscaru murmured. "Von Staden. Yes, I seem to remember now. You were one of Canaris's bright young men, weren't you? In Madrid for quite a while, I believe."

Von Staden said nothing. Instead, he continued to examine the dwarf as if trying to decide whether to add him to some collection.

Rebuffs, however, were Ploscaru's specialty and had been for a long time. He smiled cheerfully and said, "Let's all have a drink, Gilbert, and Minor will show you a letter that you should find most interesting."

"We'll take the drink, but there's no need to wave that letter around. I know what's in it and who signed it, and I'm not impressed. One misstep and we clap you in jail, both of you, and if there's a fuss, well, we'll let Berlin sort it out."

Jackson mixed two drinks. He handed one of them to Von Staden, who accepted it silently. When he handed Baker-Bates his, Jackson nodded toward Von Staden and said, "Doesn't he ever shut up?"

"He's a watcher, not a talker. You should've taken my advice and stayed away from Ploscaru." Baker-Bates looked down at the dwarf. "He's a treacherous little sod —aren't you, Nick?"

"All Romanians are," Ploscaru said with another cheerful smile. "It's in our blood. But let's talk about what we're all interested in. Let's talk about Kurt Oppenheimer. Tell us why you're really interested in him, Gilbert."

"You know why," Baker-Bates said. "Because we bloody well don't want him in Palestine."

"I mean your real reason. No need to be shy; we're all friends here."

"You just heard it."

"But that's the *public* reason, Gilbert. Now tell us the *private* one—the one that scarcely anyone knows."

"There is no private one, as you call it."

"No? How strange. I thought there was. I mean, one can understand why you wouldn't want Oppenheimer in Palestine. But with the Empire crumbling all about you, I thought there would be several spots where you could use a man of his peculiar talents. Greece, for example; Malaya; even India. I mean places where a spot of judicious killing might be in order."

Baker-Bates stared down at the dwarf for several moments and then smiled, but it was a thin, tight-lipped smile without humor or teeth. "I'd almost forgotten how absolutely mad you really are, Nick."

The dwarf shook his head and smiled reasonably. "No, not really. A trifle neurotic perhaps, but then, I have reason to be. Now, we know for a fact that the Russians want poor Oppenheimer. And the Americans, too. And I assume that both would pay a modest sum to whoever might deliver him into their eager hands. But what about *your* people, Gilbert? How much would they bid if he were, so to speak, offered up to them on a silver platter?"

"How much?"

"Yes. How much."

"Nothing," Baker-Bates said, putting his drink down "Not a penny."

"What a shame."

Baker-Bates shook his head slowly. "Don't try it, Nick. Don't try it or we'll step on you the same way that we'd step on a bug." He paused. "A small bug."

He turned and started for the door. Von Staden moved over quickly and opened it. But Baker-Bates turned back to stare for a long moment at Jackson. The Major nodded at the dwarf. "You can't trust him, you know. You really can't."

Jackson smiled. "I know."

27 As soon as Baker-Bates had gone, Ploscaru put his drink down, reached into a pocket, brought out a large wad of German marks, and put them on a table. He then reached into another pocket and brought out another wad. He kept on doing this until the table was almost covered with money. After that he looked up at Jackson and said, "Bait."

"Bait?"

The dwarf nodded. "For our trap."

"Of course. Hell, yes. Why didn't I think of that?"

Ploscaru smiled. "You're not quite with me yet, Minor."

Jackson turned to the bottle and poured some more whiskey into his glass. "I didn't think it showed." He turned back. "Tell me."

"We're going to be quite busy this afternoon and evening."

"Doing what?"

"Why, baiting our trap." Ploscaru used a forefinger to stir the marks around. "This is what we were paid for the contents of the cellar this morning. There are approximately one hundred thousand German marks here—about five hundred American dollars. Provided, of course, that we could change them for dollars, which we can't. Still, one hundred thousand marks is quite a tidy sum, and that's what we'll offer."

"What're we buying?"

"Betrayal."

"From a Judas, I take it."

"Yes, I suppose you could say that."

"Who'll sell out Oppenheimer."

The dwarf looked at Jackson surprised. "Oh, heavens, no. I'm sorry, Minor, but you do have such a logical mind. We really must work on that when we get the chance. But for now, let's start from Square One. What facts do we have?"

"Hardly any."

"No, we have several. The first is that somewhere in either Bonn or Godesberg is young Oppenheimer's next intended victim, right?"

Jackson nodded.

"Good. Now, if I recall what you told me correctly, we have a partial address for that victim."

"You mean what that American officer in the Opel plant remembered?"

"Yes."

"That's no partial address."

"A fragment, then. It was a low number, wasn't it—in the teens?"

Again, Jackson nodded.

"And it was on Something-strasse."

"That's right."

262

"Now, just who do you think young Oppenheimer's next victim will be?"

"I haven't the faintest idea."

Ploscaru shook his head in mild exasperation. "Of course you do."

"Okay. He'd probably have been a Party member with something to hide."

"A reasonably high party member—one who had the necessary funds to buy his new identity. Or hers. It could be a woman. Now, then: before the war, what were Bonn and Godesberg noted for?"

"Not much."

"Exactly. Not much. They were both quiet places with hardly any industry; particularly suitable for what?"

Jackson shrugged. "Okay, what?"

"Why, retirement, my boy. Retirement. Many people, even a number of British, retired here simply because it's such a somnolent place."

"Dull."

"Indeed. Dull. Now, then: what does retirement suggest?"

"Age?"

"Good. But something else, too. Money. You have to have money to retire here comfortably. Quite a bit of money, in fact. Now, we can safely assume, I think, that young Oppenheimer's intended victim has money and that he or she is living comfortably and privately. Privacy, of course, suggests a house, possibly even a villa. So, our search is narrowed to someone who lives quite comfortably and privately in a house or villa with a low number in the teens on Something-strasse."

"Or in one room up in a garret. It could be that way too, Nick. Your theory's fine up to a point. But it could be that whoever bought his new identity from that guy who was selling them—Damm, wasn't it? Well, maybe he or she had only just enough money for that and nothing else. Take that interpreter at the Opel plant, for instance.

He didn't have any money."

Ploscaru shook his head. "Anonymity, Minor. You're forgetting anonymity. Without money, a big city is best for that. With it—well, with it you swim with the other fish: one retired person among many. What could be more anonymous?"

Jackson grinned. "It's all hunch, isn't it, Nick?"

The dwarf thought about it for a moment and then shrugged. "I prefer to call it intuition—with a strong underpinning of facts."

"Or guesses."

"All right. Guesses. But here's something that we don't have to guess about. And that's the sheer joy and delight that the average German finds in assuming the role of informer. They positively dote on it, you know. Children turn in their parents; wives their husbands; brothers their sisters, and so on. They do it for money, for revenge, for personal gain, and probably just because it makes them feel good. During the war, informing was almost a major industry. It still is, except that now they inform to the Americans or the British or what-have-you, because if they do, they might get the job or the room of the person they inform against. So that's what we do this afternoon. We go looking for informers."

"Where?"

"In cafés, bars, Bierstuben—everywhere. We pass the word that we're looking for a former Party bigwig—such a delightful word; is it English or American?"

"Both, I'd say."

"Yes, well, we pass the word along, acting properly mysterious, of course, and mention ever so casually that whoever performs this patriotic service will be suitably rewarded—and at that point we might even flash a little money. And finally, we set a deadline."

"For when?"

"Say, midnight?"

"All right. Midnight."

The dwarf sighed. "I do wish, Minor, that you had a

264

more, well, gregarious personality, like mine. It's such a help in this kind of work. You're so terribly reserved for an American."

"I always thought I was friendly as hell."

"Just a bit more bonhomie wouldn't be at all amiss."

"Golly, Nick, I'll sure try."

"I know you will."

"What about our yellow-haired chaperon? Who gets him?"

"He can't follow us both, can he?"

"Not very well."

Once again, the dwarf sighed. "Leave him to me."

"Okay. And we'll meet back here when—around eleven?"

"No later, I'd think."

"And if this doesn't work, Nick, what then?"

"Why, we try something else, of course."

"What?"

The dwarf grinned. "I really have no idea."

It had cost Kurt Oppenheimer another one of his diamonds to get to Bonn. The diamond had gone to the captain of a Dutch barge that was heading for Cologne with a load of much-needed grain. The barge had been twice searched, once by the Americans and once by the British, but the captain was an experienced smuggler, which was how he had survived the war, and hiding one rather thin man had presented no problem at all.

The barge had anchored for the night on the west bank of the Rhine just opposite the section of Bad Godesberg known as Mehlem. The captain was rowing Oppenheimer to shore in a small skiff. Neither of them spoke. When the skiff reached the shore, Oppenheimer jumped out. He turned to look at the barge captain, who stared at him for several moments, then shrugged and started rowing back out into the Rhine. Oppenheimer scrambled up the riverbank.

A trolley took him into the center of Bonn, and after

that it took him nearly an hour to find exactly what he was looking for.

The whore he decided on wasn't the youngest he had noticed, or the prettiest, or possibly the cleanest. She stood in a dark doorway, a woman not far from forty, and offered her wares in a hoarse, tired, almost disconsolate voice—as though business were bad and she really didn't expect it to get any better.

Oppenheimer had walked past her once, and now he came back. The whore remembered him.

"Change your mind, handsome?"

He smiled. "Perhaps."

"You won't be sorry."

"You have a room?"

"Of course I have a room."

"A quiet room?"

One badly drawn eyebrow went up. "How quiet?"

"Very quiet—the kind that the police never bother."

"It's quiet enough."

"How much?"

"It depends. If you want French tricks, that's extra."

"For all night."

"You have cigarettes?"

"Yes."

"American?"

"Yes."

"Two hundred cigarettes for all night." It was her starting price. She had no idea that it would be paid. It never had been.

"Agreed." He handed her a ten-dollar bill. She looked at it suspiciously. "You said two hundred cigarettes."

"That's for our refreshments. Some wine or *Schnapps*. And some food. Anything. All right?"

"Yes."

"We'll go to your room first. Then you can go back out and buy the wine and other things."

She nodded. "This way."

Like the whore, the room was none too clean, but it had

a bed and a chair and a table. It was on the third floor of an old building. Oppenheimer put his briefcase down on the table and looked around. "It's fine," he said.

"It stinks," the whore said.

The printer had walked most of the way from the Autobahn to the ferry that would take him across the Rhine to Bad Godesberg. In Frankfurt, he had bribed a truck driver to let him ride in the rear with a load of turnips. It had been an uncomfortable trip, but far safer than the train. Once across the river, he could rest his throbbing knee in the Gasthaus where Eva Scheel had instructed him to stay. She had said that the owner of the Gasthaus was a sympathizer. A silent one, hoped Bodden, who was in no mood for a political discussion.

The Gasthaus was a half-timbered affair of eleven rooms with a bar and a sign that said it had been established in 1634. The proprietor's wife showed Bodden to his room, and her only comment was, "There's no heat, but the bed is warm."

Just as the woman was leaving, Bodden asked her the time. She told him that it was a quarter to ten and left, closing the door behind her. Bodden sat down on the bed and started massaging his knee. The long walk had done it no good, although the pain was not nearly so severe as it had been just after the dwarf had smashed it with the pistol.

You have three-quarters of an hour, Bodden told himself as he lay down on the bed. You can use it to rest your leg and think about the dwarf and all the nasty things that you would like to do to him. And the money. You can think about that, too, and how you're going to spend it.

Against all regulations, Lt. LaFollette Meyer had given both Leah Oppenheimer and Eva Scheel a ride to Bonn in the Army's 1946 Ford. He had dropped them off at the Park Hotel in Bad Godesberg and gone in search of

Gilbert Baker-Bates.

The two women had had dinner in the hotel and afterward had gone to their rooms. At ten o'clock that night Eva Scheel went downstairs and inquired at the desk for directions to the Gasthaus that had been established in 1634. It was not a long walk, she was told—not more than thirty minutes. She thanked the desk clerk and started back up the stairs to her room so that she could get her fur coat. If she had brought the coat with her, she might have turned the other way and noticed the dwarf as he moved across the lobby and into the hotel bar.

Outside the Park Hotel the yellow-haired man leaned against a wall and waited for the dwarf to come out. While he waited, Von Staden counted up the number of bars, cafés, and hotels that Ploscaru had ducked into and out of that night. Fifteen so far, he thought. This one would make sixteen. He wondered, as he had wondered all evening, what the dwarf was doing. There had been no opportunity to find out. Tomorrow, he promised himself; tomorrow I will revisit each place and ask. They'll remember him. People always remember a dwarf.

He recognized the fur coat first. She came out and stood on the steps in the hotel's dim light as if trying to decide which way to go. Von Staden got a good look at her profile and then turned quickly away. It was the little rabbit, all right—the one who had lost him in the rubble near the Golden Rose in Frankfurt. The Major had been unhappy about that, Von Staden remembered. Most unhappy. Well, which was it to be tonight, the dwarf or the rabbit?

Because Von Staden had a quick, logical mind, he made his choice almost immediately. He knew where the dwarf had been that night and where he was staying. All the cafés and bars and hotels were carefully written down. They could wait until tomorrow. Tonight he would follow the little rabbit. And this time he would not let her lose him so easily.

At a few minutes past eleven o'clock that night, Bodden and Eva Scheel came out of the Gasthaus and turned right toward the Rhine. They walked slowly, because Bodden's knee had grown stiff. Bodden had to favor the knee, and in doing so he limped slightly.

Across the street, shielded by the dark and the trunks of the old trees, Von Staden felt his excitement mount. Despite the chill in the air, he was sweating slightly. Well, printer, he thought, where did you acquire the limp? And what have you and the little rabbit to talk about? That would be even more interesting.

The sight of Bodden when he came out of the Gasthaus with Eva Scheel had been almost a shock to Von Staden. He had to force himself to hang back. Only when the pair had reached the Rhine and turned right down a path did he allow himself to cross the dark street.

At the thick bushes, he hesitated. Then slowly he edged around them onto the path.

It was a rock that hit Von Staden in the temple, although he never knew it. Nor did he feel himself being dragged down the steep bank and shoved into the water. He drowned two minutes later. He didn't feel that either.

After Bodden climbed back up the riverbank and rejoined Eva Scheel, he said, "A bad business."

"He was the only one who could connect us."

"You're positive?"

"I'm positive."

Eva Scheel was wrong about that, of course. Maj. Gilbert Baker-Bates could also connect her with the printer. But he wouldn't do that for nearly ten hours, and by then it had all fallen apart.

28 When Jackson got back to his room on the third floor of the Bad Godesberg Hotel that night, it was 11:15 and thirteen persons had queued up outside the dwarf's door. Seven were men; six were women. A few of them looked shamefaced. Several others seemed almost arrogant. All studiously ignored one another.

The dwarf's door was unlocked. When he entered the room, Jackson discovered that the furniture had been rearranged. The table that Ploscaru had counted the marks on was now in the center of the room. On it was the money, neatly stacked. Next to the money was a student's lamp, twisted so that its light would shine full into the face of whoever sat down in the single chair drawn up in front of the table. Behind the table were two straight chairs. Ploscaru was in one of them.

"Jesus, Nick, the only thing you've forgotten is the rubber hose."

"Atmosphere, Minor. Atmosphere."

"You've got it looking like the back room at Gestapo headquarters."

"Do you think so? That was just the touch I tried for."

Jackson nodded toward the door. "Are they *all* . . ." He didn't finish his sentence because the dwarf started nodding happily.

"All. Each one has someone to inform against. Isn't it delightful?"

"We're going to be up all night."

"Did you recognize any of them?"

Jackson ran the faces through his mind. "Two or three, I think."

"How many places did you visit?"

"About twenty."

"Good. I went to almost as many. Now, then, I think you should usher them in and out and sit here beside me and look grim and mysterious. I'll do the interrogation —unless, of course, you'd like to."

"No, I'll just look grim and mysterious and frown a lot."

"Shall we begin?"

"Sure."

The first informer was a man of about forty-two. He had a pale, doughy face with eyes like wet raisins. The eyes lit upon the stacked money and never left it. Jackson waved the man into the chair with a silent gesture and then took his own chair behind the table, remembering to frown sternly.

"You have something to tell us, I believe," the dwarf said.

"My name is—"

The dwarf interrupted. "We're not interested in your name."

271

The man blinked, but kept his eyes on the money and started again. "There is this man who should be arrested."

"Why?" the dwarf asked.

"After the war he lied."

"About what?"

"About me."

"What lie did he tell about you?"

"He said I was a member of the Party."

"Were you?"

"No."

"The truth. We will not pay for lies."

"Well, I was a member, but only for a short while."

"How long?"

"Five years. I lost my job. This man informed on me and I lost my job. He got it. The British gave it to him."

"What job was it?"

"It was with the bursar's office at the university. I was an accountant. He got my job by lying."

"He was a member of the Party?"

"No, but he was more of a Nazi than I ever was. He hated the Jews. He used to go to Cologne with his Nazi pals and beat them up. I know. He told me about it."

"And now he has your job?"

"Yes."

"You seem to know him well."

"I should," the man said. "He's my cousin."

The dwarf sighed and turned to Jackson. "One hundred marks."

Jackson counted out one hundred marks and handed them to the man.

"One hundred? I heard it was one hundred thousand."

"Only for the right information."

"Wait—I can tell you some other things about him."

Jackson was around the table now. He took the man by the elbow and steered him to the door. "You're an American, aren't you?" the man said.

"That's right."

"Tell the other Americans about my cousin. The British don't care. Tell the other Americans about him. Maybe they'll put him in jail. That's where he belongs."

"Fine," Jackson said. "I'll tell them."

The next man to sit at the table before the money had a neighbor whom he despised. After that it was a woman whose brother-in-law had bilked her out of some property. Another man claimed that his wife was cheating on him with someone who, he charged, was a war criminal. Further questioning revealed that the wife's lover was actually the husband's boyhood friend. They both were trolley motormen and had been for years.

It went on much like that until the twelfth person entered the room. She was younger than the rest had been, not much more than twenty-two or twenty-three. She was not especially pretty—her protruding teeth kept her from being that—but her body was well fed, almost voluptuous. She loosened her thin black coat and breathed deeply, either out of nervousness or so that the two men could admire her large breasts. Neither Ploscaru nor Jackson recognized her as anyone he had talked to as they made their rounds of cafés and bars earlier that evening.

"Who sent you, Fräulein?" Ploscaru asked.

"A friend," she said. "He told me you would not need to know my name."

"That's right."

"He said you are looking for a man."

Ploscaru nodded.

"A bad man—an evil man."

Again, Ploscaru nodded.

"There is this man I worked for." She dropped her head and stared into her lap.

"What did you do for him?"

"I was a maid."

"He has a house?"

"Yes. It's a large house almost on the Rhine."

"Tell us about him—this man."

273

"He never goes out. Sometimes, though, people will come to see him, but only very late at night. They talk until morning."

"What about?"

She shook her head. "I don't know. He had a cook for a while, but she quit and he made me do the cooking. After the cook left there was only me and the gardener, except the gardener came only three times a week."

"You lived there with him—with the man?"

She nodded. "I had to take care of the whole house. Later, he made me cook and do the other things."

"What things?"

"The bad things."

"What bad things?"

"He gave me money and made me go out and buy him dresses. Then he would make me watch him put them on. He would take off all his clothes and put on the dresses and make me watch. Then he would make me do other awful things. If I didn't, he beat me. He liked to beat me."

"What is his profession?"

She shook her head. "He said he was a teacher before the war—in Düsseldorf. But he said they came and got him and put him away in one of the camps—the one at Dauchau. At first I believed him, but later I didn't."

"Why?"

"When the others came to see him, I could never hear what they talked about. But always when they thought I was not listening they called him Herr Doktor."

"How long did you stay with him?"

"Almost a year."

"Why did you stay with him so long?"

She raised her eyes from her lap then. They stared directly into Ploscaru's. "Because he paid me," she said. "He paid me very well."

"And what made you decide to leave?"

"My mother became ill. I had to go and stay with her."

"How long ago was this?"

"Last week."

"Is your mother still sick?"

"No."

"But you have not gone back to the man who says he was a teacher?"

"No. Not yet."

"What does he call himself?"

"Gloth. Martin Gloth."

"And his address?"

"Are you going to give me money?"

Ploscaru nodded. "We'll give you money. Perhaps a lot of it."

"The address is Fourteen Mirbachstrasse."

The dwarf wrote it down and, after it, Martin Gloth.

"He is crazy," the girl said.

"Yes. What else can you tell us about him?"

"One night when these men came to see him they stayed up all night and talked until dawn. Then the men left and he came to my room and made me do bad things. He had a new bandage on his arm right about here." She indicated where the bandage had been. "He kept it on for almost a week. And then one night when he made me watch him take off his clothes and put on a dress the bandage was gone. There was no scar where the bandage had been. There was something else."

"A tattoo," Jackson said.

The girl looked disappointed. "How did you know?" she said. "He had numbers tattooed on his arm—right about here."

"Pay her the money, Nick," Jackson said.

29

After the girl had gone, her shabby briefcase almost stuffed with marks, Jackson paid off the last would-be informer in the corridor and came back into the room. The dwarf was standing near the table brushing his hands together. The smile on his face made him look almost ecstatic.

"Tell me how brilliant I am, Minor. I must hear it."

"You're brilliant."

"More."

"Shrewd, clever, cunning, smart, crafty, and a credit to your race. How's that?"

"Better. Sometimes I need praise as others need drugs. It's my one failing. Otherwise I'm quite perfect."

"I know."

"Now, then, you understand what we must do."

"I've got a pretty good idea."

"When?"

"They used to lecture us that the wee hours of the morning were best."

"The OSS, you mean."

"Right."

Ploscaru nodded thoughtfully. "Around four, I'd say."

"Let's make it three-thirty. Oppenheimer might have heard the same lecture." Jackson looked at his watch. "It's twelve-thirty now. That'll give me time to wake up his sister and tell her what we're up to."

"I'm not sure that that's terribly wise."

Jackson stared down at the dwarf for several moments. All friendliness had deserted the gray-haired man's face. In its stead was a cold, hard wariness.

"Up until now we've done it your way, Nick," he said. "I've been Tommy Tagalong, not too bright, but loyal, plucky, and loads of fun. Now we're going up against some guy who wears dresses at teatime, but who also just might know how to use a gun. And then there's Oppenheimer, although I don't have to tell you about him. And finally there's you, Nick, and that double-cross you still think you're going to pull off. That worries me too, so I'm going to tell you again just what I told you at the train station in Washington. Think twice."

The dwarf nodded, almost sadly, and started brushing his hands together again. His gaze wandered around the room. "I'm sorry to learn that you still don't trust me, Minor," he murmured. "It comes as quite a blow. It really does."

For a moment, Jackson almost believed him. Then he grinned and shook his head. "You'll recover."

"Yes, of course," Ploscaru said. "But you're quite right about Oppenheimer and the Gloth person. Caution shall be our watchword. Now, just what do you plan to tell Miss Oppenheimer?"

"That she'd better have her bag packed, because her

brother and I might be heading from hither to yon very quickly."

"In the roadster?"

"Uh-huh. In the roadster. That's why we bought it, wasn't it?"

"To be sure. Now, we all know where hither is. But where might yon be?"

Jackson shrugged. "Holland, maybe. It's close. But she must have some safe spot in mind where she can stash him for a while until things calm down. I'll ask her."

The dwarf looked up at the ceiling. "You said, I believe, that you and Oppenheimer will be speeding off. Just what will I be doing in the meantime?"

"You?" Jackson said with a grin. "Why, you'll be sitting on his lap, Nick."

Eva Scheel sat up in bed in the room at the Gasthaus that had been established in 1634 and looked down at Bodden. It was chilly in the room, and she covered her bare breasts with her arms and hugged herself. Bodden watched the smoke rise from his cigarette.

"So, printer," she said softly. "Killing does not excite you."

He sighed and shook his head. "It was a bad business."

"You have a conscience," she said. "I'm glad."

"And you?"

She shrugged. "He's dead. Perhaps he deserved it. Perhaps not. But I feel nothing."

He looked at her. "Are you really quite so hard, little one?"

"No, but I pretend to be. There will be time for remorse later—when we can afford it. It's quite a luxury, you know." She shivered again and wondered whether it was really the cold that made her do so.

Bodden sat up in bed and reached over to a small table for the bottle. "Here," he said, pouring some clear *Schnapps* into a glass. "This will warm you up."

She accepted the glass gratefully, drank, and shivered

278

again as the harsh liquor went down. "We could, of course, just run with the money we have."

He drank from the bottle. "They would find us. You know that. Your plan is better."

"Yes, if it works." She rose and turned. Only the cold made her conscious of her nakedness. He stared at her with interest, if not with desire.

"You still like what you see, printer?"

"Very much."

"We must find something that will excite you."

"Counting a great deal of money might do it."

"Has it before?"

"I don't know," he said, smiling for the first time. "I've never tried it."

She set the glass down and started putting on her clothes. "Leah gave me the name of the hotel where the American said they'd be staying. It will be best to avoid him, so when I get there, I'll send a note up."

"To the dwarf?"

"Yes."

Bodden reached down to rub his still-throbbing knee. "That one I owe a little something to."

"Revenge, like remorse, is another luxury that we can't yet afford."

"Someday."

"Someday," she agreed, and slipped into her fur coat. From its deep pocket she brought out a pistol. She looked down at it curiously for a moment and then handed it to him.

"Well," he said. "A Walther."

"Satisfactory?"

"Perfectly."

Her head tilted to one side a little as she stared down at him. "You may have to use it."

"Yes," he said, "I know."

The whore awoke when Kurt Oppenheimer rose from the chair, causing its legs to scrape slightly.

"You did not sleep," she said.

"A little, here in the chair."

"You could have used the bed."

"I know."

He opened his briefcase and took out a carton of Chesterfields. "Your cigarettes."

"Do you want to—"

He shook his head and smiled. "No, not tonight. Perhaps another time."

She yawned. "What time is it?"

"A little past one."

"You are leaving now?"

"I have a long walk to make."

"At this time of night?"

"Yes."

"Can't it wait till morning?"

"No," he said. "It can't."

Jackson watched as Leah Oppenheimer pulled on her stockings. She wet her finger and ran it along the seams, twisting her head around, looking back and down to make sure that they were straight.

"Why do women always do that?"

"What?"

"Wet their finger and then run it along the seams."

"It keeps them straight."

"The seams?"

"Yes, of course."

"How?"

"I don't know. It just does."

She slipped the dark blue dress over her head, glanced at herself in the mirror, gave the dress a few tugs, and then turned to Jackson.

"All right. Now I am dressed. Where do we go?"

"Nowhere."

"Then why—"

Jackson interrupted. "Sometime within the next few hours we may find your brother."

She didn't seem surprised at the announcement. Instead she nodded solemnly, waiting for Jackson to continue.

"If we do find him, we may have to leave Bonn in a hurry. The question is—where do we go? We need a place that's safe and relatively close."

"Cologne," she said almost automatically.

"That's not much better than Bonn."

"I have certain friends there who are well organized. If you can get my brother to them, then your job will be done." She moved over to her purse and took out pencil and paper. "Here—I will write their name and address."

While she was writing, he said, "There may be complications."

She looked up. "What kind of complications?"

"I don't know. If I did know, they wouldn't be complications—only problems."

She went back to writing the name and address. "And if they do turn into problems, what will solve them?"

"Money, probably," Jackson said, and looked at the slip of paper she handed him, reading the name awkwardly. "Shmuel Ben-Zvi?" His look was questioning. "What kind of name is that—Hebrew?"

The look on Leah Oppenheimer's face was defiant. "Israeli," she said.

"Well, now," Jackson said.

"You have any objections?"

Jackson shrugged. "He's your brother, not mine. You can hand him over to anyone you wish."

"You said that money will solve whatever problems might arise. How much money?"

"As much as you have or can raise from your Israeli friends in the next few hours."

"I will have to go to Cologne. That will take at least two or three hours. Will I have enough time?"

"I should think so," Jackson said.

She nodded thoughtfully as she gazed at Jackson.

"What does Mr. Ploscaru advise?"

"Well, you see," Jackson said, "I haven't really asked, because Mr. Ploscaru may be both the complication and the problem."

When the sleepy fourteen-year-old boy brought the note up to Ploscaru's room, the dwarf read it, gave the boy a tip, and said, "Tell her to meet me at the corner in five minutes."

"Which corner?"

"By the bank."

After the boy had gone, Ploscaru took the big Army .45 from its case and shoved it into the waistband of his trousers. He buttoned his jacked over it and then climbed up on a chair to inspect himself in the mirror. Satisfied that the bulge wasn't too noticeable, he climbed down from the chair and stood for a moment looking thoughtfully about the room. As he thought, he automatically brushed some imaginary crumbs from his palms.

Eva Scheel watched the dwarf approach. When he drew near enough, she said, "I am Eva Scheel, Herr Ploscaru."

The dwarf bowed. "You are, I understand, a friend of Fräulein Oppenheimer's."

"And of her brother's."

"Ah."

"I think we should talk."

"Perhaps a bar would be more comfortable. Someone at my hotel told me that there is one close by that remains open quite late. Shall we go there?"

There was no one in the bar except the proprietor and three solitary drinkers who sat hunched over their glasses. After seating Eva Scheel, Ploscaru moved to the bar, paid extra, and brought back two glasses of what the proprietor had said was his best brandy.

"Now, then," Ploscaru said, wriggling back into his chair, "what shall we talk about?"

"Kurt Oppenheimer."

"An interesting man in many ways. I'm quite looking forward to meeting him."

"You expect that to be soon?"

"Oh, yes, quite soon."

"He needs help, of course."

"Yes, of course."

"I represent certain persons who would like to help him."

"For a man in such tragic circumstances, he seems to suffer from no lack of friends. No lack at all."

"The persons whom I represent would consider it a privilege to help him."

"Yes, I'm sure," the dwarf said, and sipped his drink.

"They would expect to pay for the privilege."

"Did they mention a sum?"

"Fifteen thousand dollars."

Ploscaru turned his mouth down at the corners. "There are almost any number of dear friends who would pay far more for such a rare privilege."

"We could bargain all night, Herr Ploscaru, and still arrive at the same price."

"Which is?"

"Twenty-five thousand."

"Dollars?"

"Yes."

"An interesting price," Ploscaru said. "Not a fair one, but still an interesting one."

"How interesting?"

"Interesting enough for me to consult with my colleague."

"When will you reach a decision?"

"There are still many unknown factors to be resolved, but I would say we would reach our decision by ten o'clock tomorrow morning."

"Where can I reach you—the hotel?"

"No, I think not. I will give you an address. If things work out as I anticipate, we can make our arrangements there. The address is Fourteen Mirbachstrasse here in Bad Godesberg. Would you like to write it down on something?"

"No, I can remember it," she said. "Fourteen Mirbachstrasse, ten o'clock tomorrow."

Ploscaru smiled and eased himself down from the chair. "I'm sorry to rush off like this, but there are still quite a few details to attend to. It's been a most interesting discussion, Fräulein Scheel. I like the way you think. Perhaps another time we might talk about something—well, less commercial."

"Perhaps."

He took her hand, bowed over it, and then looked up at her with an expression that would have been concerned except for the sly look in his eyes. "By the way," he said "do give my best wishes to your friend."

"Which friend might that be, Herr Ploscaru?"

"Why, the one with the sore knee, of course."

She watched him move through the tables to the door. So much cunning in such a small body, she thought. And sex too, of course. Even though he's gone, he left his spoor behind—like an open invitation. If there were time, it might prove interesting—very interesting. A large, capable brain might indicate a large, capable something else. She smiled slightly, looked up, caught the proprietor's eye, and signaled for another brandy. After he nodded his understanding, she took paper and an envelope from her purse and began to write. The sleepy boy at the hotel will take it to the printer, she thought. The printer can keep sleep another time. What happens at Fourteen Mirbachstrasse tonight could be more important than his sleep. Far more important.

When he got back to the hotel, Ploscaru learned that Jackson had not yet returned. He went up to his room and stood in the center of it for a moment, brushing his hands together, quite unaware of the fact that he was doing so,

and wondering which one would do the watching that
night at 14 Mirbachstrasse—the woman in the fur coat
or the man with the damaged knee. He grinned, not quite
aware that he was doing that either. That one will have
her sleep, he decided. She'll have the man go, aching
knee and all. It was the real reason he'd given her the
address—to flush the man out. The man was dangerous
and would have to be dealt with, but at a place of the
dwarf's own choosing.

Whistling "Blue Moon," Ploscaru went to his bag and
from its lining removed a thin British commando knife
and slid it into the silk sheath that was sewn to the inside
of his coat sleeve. After that he poured himself a small
drink from the bottle of bourbon, hopped up into the
room's most comfortable chair, wriggled back, stopped
whistling "Blue Moon," and started singing its lyrics instead.

He was still singing when Minor Jackson knocked at his
door.

30 They drove by the large, dark house at 14 Mirbachstrasse twice and then parked the Mercedes a block away and walked back. A brick wall almost eight feet high surrounded the house. A nearly full moon provided some light—enough, at least, for them to make out the outline of the house through the wrought-iron gate.

It was a stern-looking place, Jackson thought, three stories high and built of some kind of dark stone or brick. It had a mansard roof that seemed to be covered with slate shingles. Jackson tried the high gate without much hope. It was locked.

"Well, up and over, then," Jackson said, and made a stirrup of his hands.

He lifted the dwarf up. He was heavier than Jackson had expected, much heavier.

"Any glass?"

"How thoughtful of you to ask," Ploscaru said. "But no."

"Are you set?"

"Yes."

Jackson felt the dwarf's hand wrap around his wrist. Then he felt himself being smoothly and easily lifted up until he could get his other arm over the top of the wall. The dwarf's strength surprised him.

After he got a leg over the wall and was straddling it, Jackson said, "I'll go first."

He lowered himself carefully and then let go. The drop was less than a foot. The dwarf lowered himself until he was hanging from the top of the wall only by his hands. Jackson wrapped his arms around the dwarf's legs and said, "Okay, I've got you."

They knelt by the wall and peered through some shrubbery. "No dogs, apparently," Jackson said.

"No."

"Now what?"

"What did those lectures advise?"

"Boldness."

"Let's be bold, then."

"I'll knock," Jackson said. "You cover me." He took the .38 pistol from the pocket of his topcoat. Bent nearly double, he scuttled from shrub to shrub as he made his way toward the entrance of the house. The dwarf scuttled after him. Jackson noticed that Ploscaru now had the big Army Colt in his right hand.

"Well, let's see what happens," Jackson said.

He moved up to the door. Next to it, the dwarf flattened himself against the wall. It was a large door, made of heavy oak planking that was bound by decorative iron straps. Jackson knocked again, harder this time. Again they waited, and again nothing happened.

"Nobody home," Jackson said.

"Try the door."

Jackson tried the door handle. It turned easily. He pushed the door open, almost expecting to hear it creak. But it didn't. Instead, it opened smoothly on hinges that might have been oiled. Beyond the door was blackness.

"Let's go back to the hotel and have a drink," Jackson said. "Find some women."

The dwarf moved over to the open door and peered in. "Perhaps there really is nobody home."

"I'll be bold and ask." Jackson stepped carefully through the doorway. The dwarf followed. "Anybody home?" Jackson called.

"You think he speaks English?"

Jackson didn't reply. Instead, he took out his Zippo lighter and flicked its wheel. The lighter flared, providing just enough illumination for him to find a light switch. He pressed it, but no lights came on.

"No power."

"Let's see if we can find some candles."

Jackson's lighter was fading now. But there was still light enough for him to locate a door that led from the entry hall in which they found themselves. He started for the door, the dwarf close behind.

A light came on then. It was the bright, focused yellow of a powerful flashlight. Behind them a man's voice said in German, "A machine pistol is aimed at you, gentlemen. I'm fully prepared to use it."

"Well, shit," Jackson said.

"You will both kneel very slowly," the voice said. "Very, very slowly."

Jackson and Ploscaru did as they were told.

"Now you, little man. You will lower your pistol to the floor and slide it very gently to your left."

Ploscaru slid the Army .45 to his left.

"And you with the gray hair will slide your pistol to the right. Ever so gently."

After Jackson did exactly that, the voice said, "Good. Now you will clasp your hands on the tops of your heads and rise, but very slowly. Don't turn around."

Again they did as they were told. The light stopped dancing around then, as if its source had been laid to rest on a table. Jackson felt something cold press against the nape of his neck. He held his breath and even closed his eyes for a second. But when he felt the hand start moving over his body and patting his pockets, he opened his eyes.

The hand also moved over Ploscaru, but more quickly, almost carelessly, as though the dwarf were too small to conceal anything dangerous.

The flashlight's yellow glow started dancing around again, finally settling on a pair of sliding doors.

"You, little man, will open the doors directly in front of you, but slowly, very slowly."

The dwarf did as instructed. "Good," the voice said. "Your hands back on your head, please." Ploscaru put his hands back on his head.

"Now both of you will walk slowly through the door for exactly five paces and stop. You will not turn around."

Ploscaru and Jackson stepped off the five paces, although the dwarf had to stretch his steps to keep up with the taller man.

There was a click, and lights came on from a pair of floor lamps. They were in a sitting room that contained too much ugly furniture, much of it upholstered in red and brown plush and most of it apparently dating back to the previous century.

"The power wasn't shut off after all, was it?" the voice said. "Only in the entry hall. You see, gentlemen, I was expecting you." The voice laughed then, although it was really more of a giggle than a laugh.

"Now I believe that I'll have you turn around, but ever so slowly, and do keep your hands just where they are."

Jackson and Ploscaru turned. They saw the machine pistol first and the slim, white manicured hands that aimed in unwaveringly at their midsections. The tall man who held the machine pistol was slim, too, almost elegantly so. He was dressed in a black sweater and black trousers, and on his feet he wore black patent-leather slippers. His face was white, the floury, unhealthy white of a face that has been locked away from the sun. On the high cheekbones, however, were two round spots of red that had been either painted or patted into place. Except for the eyebrows, the rest of the face was ordinary enough—a bony chin, thin red lips, a straight nose, and deep-sunk dark eyes. The eyebrows above the eyes were plucked.

"So, what have we here?" the man said. "A dwarf and a gray-haired American. You, little man—you are not American too, are you?"

"No," Ploscaru said.

"Say something else—in German."

"What would you like me to say?"

The man studied Ploscaru for a moment and then smiled. "Of course, Romanian. Am I right?"

"You're right."

"From Bucharest, I'd say. Your vowels give you away. I'm ever so proud of myself. I thought I might have lost the touch." He smiled again with teeth that were too regular and too white. Jackson decided they were false. He tried to guess the man's age and settled on forty, although he felt he could be off ten years either way.

"Do you have names?" the man said, still smiling.

"Mine's Jackson; his is Ploscaru."

"Jackson and Ploscaru. Well. I am Gloth, but you know that, don't you? My little treasure told you, the one who took your money. But then remorse set in—and guilt. She really quite adores me, you know. So she sped back here as quickly as she could and told me all. Naturally, I forgave her, and we wept together and embraced and did other most interesting things and then I waited for you to arrive. Are you always so clumsy?"

"Almost always," Jackson said.

"Really? How interesting. Now I have to decide what to do with you."

"Why not just let us go?" Ploscaru said. "We'll pay you, of course, and then forget we ever met."

"You have money?"

"Some."

"Then I will take it from you after I kill you. You realize that's what I'm going to have to do."

"We didn't," Jackson said.

"Oh, yes. I really have no choice. That's what I told my little treasure just before—but no matter. I would like to continue our chat, gentlemen, but it has been such a long evening. I think we'll go down to the cellar now and do what must be done. If you'll keep your hands on your heads and turn right, you'll see another door. We will go through that. You, Herr Ploscaru, will open the door and switch on the light—it will be just to your left. Then you will put your hands back on your head. Shall we go?"

Gloth waved the machine pistol at them. Jackson and Ploscaru moved over to the door. Ploscaru opened it, found the light, and switched it on.

"Hands back on your head, please," Gloth said.

Ploscaru put them back.

"Now slowly, gentlemen, ever so slowly. I suppose I should tell you that I'm an extremely good shot."

"We believe you," Jackson said.

"Down the stairs now—you first, Herr Jackson."

Jackson started down the concrete stairs. Light came from a single bulb that hung from an insulated wire. Jackson thought about jumping for it and smashing the light with his hands. But it was too high, he decided—almost four feet too high.

When they reached the beginning of the last four steps, Ploscaru stumbled and took his hands from his head to try to catch the banister. He missed and fell headlong down the steps, landing in a crumpled heap. He groaned and twisted around, his hands clutching his stomach.

Jackson started toward him. "No, Mr. Jackson," Gloth

snapped. "Move back and keep your hands just where they were."

"He's hurt," Jackson said, but did as he was told.

"He won't suffer long," Gloth said, and came slowly down the steps.

He nudged Ploscaru with his foot. "Get up. You can get up."

Ploscaru groaned again and got slowly to one knee.

"Now all the way up," Gloth said.

With his hands still clutching his stomach, the dwarf began to rise slowly. He groaned once more, quite horribly this time, then whirled. The commando knife was in his right hand. He plunged it into Gloth just above the groin. Gloth screamed and dropped the machine pistol. He clutched at himself as Ploscaru pulled the knife out. Gloth doubled over, and the knife went back in with a hard, upward thrust. Ploscaru jumped away. Gloth stared down at the knife hilt that poked out of his chest, just below the rib cage. He screamed again—a shrill, frightened scream; tugged at the knife; fell to his knees; screamed yet again; and toppled over. He died then, or shortly thereafter.

Jackson found himself fumbling for his cigarettes. He lit one, dragged the smoke deep down into his lungs, and blew it out. He noticed that his hands were trembling.

"I liked the way you groaned."

"Yes," Ploscaru said. "I thought I sounded quite distressed."

The dwarf reached down, grasped the hilt of the knife, and pulled it out. He stared at it for a moment with distaste, or perhaps revulsion, and then wiped its blade off carefully on the dead man's trouser leg. When satisfied that it was clean, Ploscaru tucked the knife back into the silk sheath that was sewn into his coat sleeve.

"You always keep it there?" Jackson said.

"Not always, Minor. Just upon occasion."

Jackson bent down and picked up the machine pistol.

He examined it carefully and then looked at Ploscaru. "The safety was on."

"Didn't you notice?"

"No."

"What *did* they teach you at OSS?"

"Not enough, I'd say."

Ploscaru found his cigarettes and lit one. Jackson noticed that there was no tremor in the dwarf's hands as he stood smoking calmly and gazing thoughtfully around the cellar.

"I think this will do quite nicely, don't you?" the dwarf said.

"For what?"

"For Oppenheimer."

Ploscaru stepped over to a heavy door and opened it. He glanced inside the room, moved back quickly, and slammed the door. When he turned, his face was pale and stiff.

"What was it?" Jackson asked.

"The girl—his maid. No need to look. She's dead. It's rather nasty."

Jackson shook his head and looked down at the dead Gloth. "I wonder who he really was."

"You can ask Oppenheimer," Ploscaru said, opening another door. "He'll know."

The dwarf inspected another room whose door he had just opened. "This one will do," he said. "Take a look."

Jackson went over to look. It was a small, bare room with no windows. A weak bulb provided what light there was. Ploscaru examined the door, which had a small opening covered by iron mesh. The door was made of heavy, solid wood, with a large steel lock. Ploscaru turned the key back and forth, testing the lock. "This will serve quite nicely."

"What do we do with him?" Jackson said, nodding at Gloth.

"Drag him under the stairs."

"Let's do it, then."

Afterward, they started up the stairs. Halfway up, the dwarf paused and turned. "You know," he said slowly, "it really wasn't such a bad scheme."

"Which one?"

"Gloth's. Perhaps we should see how it works on Oppenheimer."

"You think he's as stupid as we are?"

"Possibly," the dwarf said. "Many people are."

31 Bodden was glad to get off the borrowed bicycle. The ride from the Gasthaus had done his knee no good. He stood across the street from 14 Mirbachstrasse and studied the large, dark house. There was nothing to see—only a big house surrounded by a high wall.

Bodden looked up at the moon and tried to guess the time. It had been about a quarter past three when the boy had brought the note from Eva Scheel. Bodden had then had to rouse the Gasthaus proprietor to borrow the bicycle. The ride had taken another quarter of an hour—possibly twenty minutes. That made it almost four—perhaps a quarter to. The burglar's favorite hour.

The first thing Bodden needed was a place to conceal the bicycle. There was a clump of shrubbery—evergreens of some sort. He wheeled the bicycle over and leaned it against the shrubs. And now you, printer, he thought; some place where you can get off your leg and sit down and watch. There was a large tree not far from the shrubbery. He could lie or sit behind it and still have a view of the gate that led to the house.

Bodden settled himself behind the tree. He wondered if he dared risk a cigarette. He wanted one very much. But no, that would have to wait. Bodden sat, half concealed by the large tree, his throbbing leg stretched straight out in front of him. As he waited and watched, he massaged the knee.

It had been a long walk from the whore's room in the center of Bonn, and Oppenheimer was sweating a little as he drew near the house where the man who called himself Gloth lived. Oppenheimer had not hurried. Whenever possible, he had kept to side streets, but once or twice it had been necessary to use Koblenzerstrasse. Once a British patrol had passed him in a jeep. The patrol had eyed him carefully, slowed, and then driven on.

During the long walk, Oppenheimer had talked to himself—or rather, to his ironic self. Once when he had sat down to rest and smoke a cigarette, his ironic self had commented on the weather. *A nice night for it, no?* For what? *For murder, of course.* An execution will take place, nothing more. *Not too long ago you used fancier words than that—words like justice and duty and obligation to the dead. Tell me, do you still think of yourself as an avenging angel?* I don't believe in angels. *Come, now, that's almost what you told the boy—that American Corporal. You can do better for me. Give me some high-flown sentences with something about the dead not having died in vain.* I only do what needs doing. *You are a fool, aren't you?*

Oppenheimer stopped talking to himself when he reached the high wall. He walked along it until he reached the gate. He paused to study the house. He tried the gate, almost casually, knowing that it would be locked. After studying the house for a few more moments, Oppenheimer walked on.

This is foolish, his ironic self said. *Totally foolish.* It has to be done. *I'll have no part of it.* Then go. *You know what will happen if I do?* "Let it," Oppenheimer replied, surprised to find that he had said it aloud.

He threw his briefcase over the wall, then looked around carefully, marking the other streets and houses in his mind. He turned back to the wall. *I'm not going.* You'll go. *No, not this time.* Too bad, Oppenheimer said, or thought he did, and leaped up, just managing to catch the top of the wall with his hands. He hung there for a moment, gathering his strength. *All you have to do is let go, drop, and walk away.* No, I can't. *Give it up.* No, you don't understand. You never did. There's nothing else I can do.

Oppenheimer pulled himself slowly up until he could grab the top of the wall with an arm. After that it was easier. He got a leg over and lay on the wall for a moment, waiting to catch his breath. Then he lowered himself over the other side of the wall, hung for a second, and dropped. As he crouched by the wall, he asked, Where are you? He asked it silently, but there was no answer. He asked again, and when there was no reply, he realized that he was alone, really alone. And for the first time since they had dug him out of the rubble in Berlin, he also realized that he was terribly and totally afraid.

From across the street Bodden had watched Oppenheimer scale the wall. That one goes up and over like a monkey, he thought. Nothing quite so agile for you, printer. When you go, you'll need a stepladder. The bicycle might do. But there's no hurry. Wait and see what develops. If the one who went over the wall is who you think he is, then it might be better to wait and let him attend to his business first—whatever it may be. Give him a few minutes and then you can go. Smoke a cigarette first and then go crawl over your wall.

Oppenheimer crouched by the wall and checked his Walther pistol. He did it automatically, without thinking. Bent over in a low crouch, he now ran quickly from the wall to some shrubbery, pausing only to give the house a quick look. He would try the door first. It would be locked, but it was always worth a try. Once in—where was it—Stuttgart? No matter. A door had been left open. He tried to remember where it had been, but couldn't.

Still crouched low, he ran to the house. Then, with his back to its brick, he went slowly sideways toward the door. He moved up the steps and stopped breathing so that he could listen. He heard nothing and began breathing again, slowly and silently through his open mouth.

He put his left hand to the door handle and pressed. It moved. He turned it all the way and slowly shoved the door back. He stopped to listen. Again, there was no sound. He pushed the door open just wide enough for him to slip through. But he didn't move. Instead, he stopped breathing again so that he could listen, but there was no sound. None at all. He slowly slipped through the door and stopped. Moving sideways with his hand outstretched, he found a wall. He guided himself along the wall until he found a light switch. He didn't press it, but felt for the door that he knew would be near the switch. Just as he found it, the yellow light came on and the voice said in German, "Don't move or you're dead."

Oppenheimer moved. He whirled and dropped at the same time, firing twice at the yellow light. Then something hard came down on his right wrist, almost smashing it. He could no longer hold the Walther. A hand grabbed his hair and pulled his head back. Something cold and hard pressed up underneath his chin.

"Just one move," the voice said, "just a twitch, and I pull the trigger." Oppenheimer didn't move.

Someone shined the light in his eyes. He closed them. Another voice said, "He's fast, isn't he?"

"I thought he got you."

"No, I moved just after I switched on the flashlight. I moved very quickly."

Oppenheimer dimly realized that the voices were speaking English. That wasn't right. Perhaps he had made a mistake. He wondered if this was the wrong house.

The voice that belonged to whoever was holding the gun underneath his chin said in German, "I want you to get up very slowly."

Oppenheimer rose. "Now turn around." Oppenheimer did so. He heard rather than saw some doors being slid open. "Put your hands on your head," the voice said. After he had done this, the voice told him to walk five paces straight ahead. When he had walked the five paces, the voice told him to turn around. As he turned around, the lights came on. Two men, one of them very little, stood a few feet away from him with pistols aimed at his rib cage. Neither of them was the man who called himself Gloth.

Oppenheimer stared at the little man, the one who was really a dwarf. "You could not be the one who calls himself Gloth, could you?"

"Sorry," Ploscaru said, shaking his head.

Oppenheimer smiled. "No matter," he said, and kept on smiling. It was the last thing he would ever say.

"See what he's got on him," Ploscaru said. "And don't forget to look for a knife."

Jackson moved over to Oppenheimer and went through his pockets. He found some American money, some German marks, a half-smoked package of Lucky Strikes, some matches, a comb, a pencil, and several sheets of ruled paper. There was no knife. Jackson opened the papers and looked at them. They were the sheets that Oppenheimer had torn from Damm's ledger.

"It's his people-who-need-killing list," Jackson said. "You want to know who Gloth really was?"

"Who?"

"Somebody called Dr. Klaus Spalcke—a medical doctor. It says here that his specialty was exploring the pain threshold. He conducted his experiments at several of the camps—there's a list of them here, if you want me to read it."

"Not really," Ploscaru said.

"It says here that his experiments caused the deaths of six thousand four hundred and seventy-one persons. How in hell could they be that exact?"

"I have no idea," Ploscaru said. "Ask him."

"Well?" Jackson said, looking at Oppenheimer.

The man with his hands on his head smiled at Jackson pleasantly, almost curiously, but said nothing.

"I don't think he's in the mood," Jackson said.

"Maybe he doesn't understand English."

"He understands it, all right. He can even talk Texan when he wants to—can't you, Brother Oppenheimer?"

Again, Oppenheimer smiled pleasantly and kept on smiling.

"I think we'd better take him down to the cellar before he decides to do something foolish," Ploscaru said.

Jackson nodded. "I think you're right." He took Oppenheimer by the arm and gestured with his pistol toward the door that led to the cellar. "We've got a nice, warm place all fixed up for you."

Oppenheimer didn't move until Jackson gave his arm a tug. After that he went along docilely, but in a curiously shambling walk, as though he were an old man wearing slippers that he was afraid would come off.

When they reached the stairs, Jackson stopped. "Go on down, Nick," he said. "If our friend here tries something clever like a fake fall, you can shoot him on the way way down."

The dwarf hurried down the stairs and then waited,

with pistol ready, for Jackson and Oppenheimer to descend the steps. There was no trouble. Oppenheimer went quietly but slowly down the stairs, smiling all the way.

Ploscaru hurried to open the door with the steel-mesh window and the heavy lock. Jackson steered the unprotesting Oppenheimer toward the small room. "It's not much," Jackson said, "but you won't be here long." He guided Oppenheimer into the room. As Jackson started to turn, Ploscaru jammed the Army .45 into his back.

"I won't kill you, Minor, but I won't hesitate to shoot you in the leg."

"Well, shit, Nick."

Ploscaru reached around and took Jackson's pistol. "The trouble with you, Minor, is that you mistrust people, but not nearly enough. Now, if you'll just go over and lean against the wall on your hands."

Jackson propped himself against the wall with his hands. Ploscaru backed quickly out of the small room, closed the door, and locked it. Inside the room, Oppenheimer smiled pleasantly at Jackson.

"I'll leave the light on," Ploscaru said, calling up through the iron-mesh window. "Perhaps you can get him to talk."

"Thanks."

"It won't be long."

"You're going to peddle him, Nick, aren't you?"

"To the highest bidder," Ploscaru said, and started up the stairs.

Bodden lay gasping on top of the wall. You're too old for this, printer, he told himself. Much too old. He let his legs go over the side first, then lowered himself until he was hanging only by his hands. Watch the knee he thought. Land wrong and you'll be a cripple. He landed wrong, and his right leg buckled under him. Bodden swore and clasped the knee with both hands, probing it tenderly. The pain was far sharper than before. Gingerly, he tried to rise, but couldn't. The pain was too intense. You need a stick, he thought, something to support yourself with. He dragged himself along the wall, feeling in the grass for a stick or a pole. His hand found something. A hoe, by God! Just the thing.

Using the hoe as a kind of support, he started for the doorway. As he went slowly up the steps, he noticed for the first time that the door was open. Take your gun out, cripple, he told himself. A hoe's a fine thing, but it's not a potato you'll find inside. He was reaching for the Walther pistol when Ploscaru came through the door.

Bodden tried to decide whether to hit the dwarf with the hoe or try for his pistol. The dwarf had no such decision to make. The knife came out of his sleeve in a blurred motion. He ducked low, very low, under the now-raised hoe. He struck once with the knife and then jumped back. The hoe came down, missing him by inches. Then the pain hit Bodden. He dropped the hoe and went down clumsily until he fell sprawling on the steps.

The dwarf approached him cautiously. "You're not dead, are you?"

Bodden stared up at him. "No."

"I knew I should have killed you in Frankfurt. But you'll die quickly enough now."

"You talk too much, little man. Far too much."

Ploscaru nodded. "Probably," he said. He stared down at Bodden, as though trying to decide something. Then he turned and ran lightly toward the iron gate. Bodden watched as the dwarf shinnied up the gate and down the other side. For a moment Ploscaru stared back through the gate at the man who lay sprawled on the steps of the large house. He nodded to himself, smiled a little and then turned and walked quickly down the street. As he walked, he dusted his hands together in either satisfaction or anticipation. It was hard to tell.

302

32 Jackson had been trying for fifteen minutes to get Oppenheimer to talk, but without success. They sat in diagonally opposite corners of the small room as Jackson conducted his one-sided conversation. To everything Jackson said, Oppenheimer smiled in a pleasant but rather loose-lipped way. His greenish-blue eyes were still bright and interested, but they moved constantly, as though everything demanded equal attention.

"I know your sister rather well," Jackson said.

Oppenheimer smiled and inspected a shoe. His right one. He pulled at the shoelace, and when the loop moved a little he smiled even more.

Jackson stared at him with fascination. At first he had

thought that Oppenheimer was simply refusing to speak. This was followed by the suspicion that the silent, smiling man was faking it to throw Jackson off guard. But then came the almost-certain realization that Oppenheimer wasn't faking at all.

"As I said, I know your sister rather well now. She thinks you're crazy."

Oppenheimer gave his shoelace another small tug and smiled delightedly at its movement.

"Or that's what she said at first. She also said she wanted to get you to a sanitarium in Switzerland where they specialize in nuts like you. But it turns out that she was probably lying."

The shoelace received another small, careful tug and another happy smile.

"What she really wants to do is get you to Palestine, where they'll turn you loose on some carefully selected British types and maybe the odd Arab. If you killed enough of them, you might even become a national hero if the Jews ever get independence. You might even become a martyr. That'd be nice, wouldn't it?"

Oppenheimer kept on smiling and playing with his shoelace.

"I fucked your sister, you know," Jackson said.

Oppenheimer laughed, except that it was more of a chuckle than a laugh. It was a deep, throaty, pleased, wise chuckle that sounded full of cosmic secrets. His shoelace had come completely untied.

"You really are gone, aren't you, friend?" Jackson said. "You're out of it."

Oppenheimer took his shoe off and offered it to Jackson. When Jackson took it, Oppenheimer chuckled with delight and began taking off the rest of his clothes. He handed all the items to Jackson, who accepted each one with a small, commiserative shake of his head as he piled them neatly on the floor.

When all of his clothes were off, Oppenheimer discovered the small leather bag that hung around his neck.

He took that off and opened it and ate one of the diamonds before Jackson could get them away from him. Jackson counted the diamonds. There were twenty-one of them, none less than a carat in size.

"If you're real good," Jackson said to the smiling, naked Oppenheimer, "I might give you one later for dessert."

When Ploscaru got back to the hotel, he went immediately up to his room, took four thick sheets of ivory-colored paper with matching envelopes from his suitcase, sat down at the desk, and began to write the invitations. He wrote with an old, broad-nibbed fountain pen and every once in a while would lean back to admire his penmanship. The dwarf had always prided himself on being able to write a beautiful hand.

When the invitations were done, he addressed the four envelopes to Frl. Leah Oppenheimer, Frl. Eva Scheel, Maj. Gilbert Baker-Bates, and Lt. LaFollette Meyer.

Then he went downstairs, shook the sleeping boy awake, and gave him an enormous bribe to deliver the invitations immediately. Once the boy was safely dispatched, Ploscaru roused the desk clerk and reserved a conference room for 8 A.M. When that was done, the dwarf looked at his watch. It was 5:14.

The Sergeant-Major awoke Baker-Bates at 5:33 A.M.

"They found him, sir," the Sergeant-Major announced in the grimly mournful voice of one trained in the art of bearing bad news.

Baker-Bates groggily sat up in bed. "Who? Found who?"

"Von Staden, sir. Old Yellow-Hair. Found him floating in the river over near Beuel. Drowned, he was, with a nasty bump on his head right about here." The Sergeant-Major tapped his right temple.

"Christ," Baker-Bates said.

"Then there's this, too, sir, just in from London patched through Hamburg. It had Top Priority on it, so I thought I'd better rush it right over after Decode got done."

Baker-Bates took the envelope, ripped it open, and took out the single, typed flimsy, which read: "Your last report circulated at highest, repeat, highest level. You are hereby instructed, repeat, instructed to offer up to, but not more than, four thousand pounds for undamaged goods if they become available." It was signed with the last name of the chief of Baker-Bates's organization.

Baker-Bates swore long and bitterly. The Sergeant-Major looked appropriately sympathetic. "Bad news, sir?"

"I told them not to, damn it. I told them not to try to buy him. But they wouldn't listen. So now they're going to try to do it on the cheap. On the bloody, goddamned cheap."

"Yes, sir," the Sergeant-Major said. "Then there's this, too, sir. It's for that young American Lieutenant. It's got Top Priority too, sir, but I thought you'd better have a peek at it first." The Sergeant-Major handed Baker-Bates another typed flimsy.

'You didn't happen to bring a cup of tea along with all this other bumf, did you, Sergeant?"

"Right here, sir, nice and hot."

Baker-Bates accepted the tea, took a sip, and began to read the flimsy: "Lt. LaFollette Meyer, c/o Maj. Gilbert Baker-Bates." After that there was the usual technical gibberish from the sending and receiving units. The message itself read: "R. H. Orr arriving Bonn-Cologne airport from Washington via London 0615 this date ATC flight 359. You will be both briefing and conducting officer." The message was signed by a four-star American general.

Baker-Bates looked up thoughtfully. "So they're sending Nanny. That's interesting."

"A friend of yours, sir?" the Sergeant asked politely.

Baker-Bates shook his head. "When I knew him, during the war, they called him that—Nanny."

"Yes, sir. And this is the last bit, sir; it came by messenger. Caught me on my way up." He handed Baker-

Bates the ivory-colored envelope with the fancy handwriting. Baker-Bates ripped it open and began to read. Then he began to swear. He was still swearing when the Sergeant-Major left to find the young American Lieutenant.

Robert Henry Orr was the first and only passenger off the DC-3 at 6:15 that morning. Swaddled in a huge old raccoon coat, his beard bristling, Orr approched Lieutenant Meyer with both hands outstretched.

"So this is the author of all those absolutely brilliant reports we've been getting," Orr said, grabbing Meyer's right hand in both of his.

"Well, I don't know how brilliant they've been, sir."

"First-rate, my boy; absolutely first-rate. Is this our car?"

"Yes, sir."

Orr climbed into the back seat of the Ford sedan, followed by Meyer. The Corporal closed the door, trotted around to the driver's seat, got in, and drove off.

"From that last report of yours, it seemed that things might be coming to a head," Orr said.

"Something's happening."

"Jackson hasn't been taking you into his confidence, has he?"

"Not exactly, sir."

"Well, we didn't expect that he would. That's one of the reasons I decided to pop over. What about Baker-Bates? Has he been giving you any trouble?"

"None at all, sir. In fact, he's been most cooperative."

"Good. So what's Jackson up to?"

"I'm not sure, sir. But this came this morning." He handed Orr the ivory-colored envelope.

"From Jackson?" Orr said.

"No, sir. From the dwarf."

"Ploscaru?" Orr read the letter enclosed in the envelope and started to chuckle. He looked at Meyer. "Have you read this?"

Meyer nodded. "Yes, sir."

307

"You think he's really going to do it?" he said, still chuckling.

"Nowadays, sir," Lieutenant Meyer said, "I'll believe almost anything."

It was seven o'clock in the morning by the time Leah Oppenheimer returned from her hurried trip to Cologne. The envelope from Ploscaru was waiting for her. After she read it, she immediately went to the hotel room next to hers and knocked. After a few moments the door was opened by Eva Scheel.

"What time is it?"

"A little after seven," Leah said as she went in.

"You're already dressed."

"I have been for hours."

"Is there anything the matter?"

"There's this," Leah said, and gave Eva Scheel the ivory-colored envelope.

Although Eva Scheel already knew what was in the envelope, she pretended to read it. "You don't think it's some kind of terrible joke?"

Leah Oppenheimer shook her head. "No, I don't think it's a joke. Mr. Jackson warned me that something might happen—but I didn't expect anything like this."

"You're going, I suppose."

Leah Oppenheimer nodded. "Will you go with me?"

"Yes, I'll go with you," Eva Scheel said. "Of course I will."

It was still dark when Bodden awoke, surprised to learn that he wasn't yet dead. He lay on the steps of the large house quietly for a moment, trying to remember the last thing he had done. The handkerchief. He had fastened the handkerchief over the place where the dwarf had stabbed him. He gingerly moved his hand inside his shirt and touched the handkerchief. It was soaked. It had not stopped the bleeding, but it had helped.

Well, printer, either you can lie here and die, or you can get up. Maybe you can find something inside the house—some bandages. Even a sheet would do, if you've got the strength to tear it. He pushed himself slowly up to a sitting position. The pain hit, and he had to gasp. If he hadn't gasped, he would have screamed. Then the bleeding started again. He could feel the warm wetness as it trickled and flowed down his side.

He found the hoe where he had dropped it and used it to pull himself up. The pain from his knee combined with the pain from the knife's wound, and he gasped again. It's only pain, he told himself. You can get over it. Printers can get over anything.

With the aid of the hoe, he shuffled slowly through the still-open door and into the house. He turned right and made his way through the sliding doors into the room with the brown and red plush furniture. The kitchen, he thought. What you should do is find the kitchen. As he turned to leave the room, he heard the warm, deep, throaty chuckle. It seemed to come from far away. He looked around and saw the open door that led down into the cellar. He made himself go over to the door. The blood was running down his leg now and into his shoe.

He looked down the stairs. The bottom seemed far away—an impossible distance. Then he heard the chuckle again. It sounded warmer this time. It sounded warm and friendly and uncommonly wise. You need help, printer, he told himself. You'll have to go down those steps. Down there at the bottom of them is someone who can help you.

He started down the stairs, using the hoe, taking one step at a time. The bleeding became worse, and so did the pain. He almost decided to sit down and rest, but then he heard the chuckle again, even warmer and wiser than before, and it helped him continue down the steps, slowly, until he reached the bottom.

There were several doors, and Bodden opened the first one he came to. The sight of the girl's disemboweled body almost made him faint. He knew he was going to be sick. He closed the door and vomited. When it was over, he wiped his mouth with his sleeve. Then he heard the chuckle again.

You always did trust people too readily, he thought. That happy chuckler might be the one who carved up the girl in there. He took the Walther from his pocket and moved toward the door where the chuckle seemed to have come from. Bodden noticed the key in the door's lock. He turned it and swung the door open. The first thing he saw was Minor Jackson sitting in one corner. Then he saw Oppenheimer.

Kurt Oppenheimer smiled at the new visitor and chuckled again.

Bodden nodded at Oppenheimer. "Why doesn't he have his clothes on?"

"I'm not really sure," Jackson said. "You're bleeding, but I suppose you know that."

"Yes."

"What happened?"

"That little dwarf," Bodden said, "he's very good with a knife, isn't he?"

"Very."

Bodden made his way over to one of the walls and leaned against it. The pistol was aimed at nothing in particular. Oppenheimer played with his toes and chuckled again.

"What happened to him?" Bodden said, staring at Oppenheimer.

"I don't know," Jackson said. "I suppose he decided that he just didn't much care for reality."

"Is he completely mad?"

"I don't know about completely, but he's pretty crazy. Harmless, though, I think."

Bodden let the pistol drop to his side. He smiled—a wry, sardonic smile. "We were going to take him from you."

"Who?"

"The woman and I—the Scheel woman. You didn't know that, did you?"

"No."

"That was our plan. We were going to let you and the dwarf catch him and then we were going to take him from you. Some plan."

"And send him East, huh?"

"East? No, we weren't going to send him East. We were supposed to, but that wasn't our plan. Her plan, I mean. No, we were going to take him from you and then sell him to the Americans. Not a bad plan, was it?"

"Better than average."

"You know what I was going to do with the money?"

"What?" Jackson said as he reached over and took the Walther. Bodden seemed neither to notice nor to care.

"I was going to buy a printing shop somewhere. I'm really a damned fine printer."

He started sliding down the wall. His feet slipped out from under him and he sat down hard, although it didn't seem to bother him. "The dwarf—he crossed you, didn't he?"

Jackson nodded.

"I knew he would. Well, things didn't work out too well for either of us, did they?"

"No," Jackson said. "They didn't."

"Tough shit," Bodden said in English, and grinned weakly. "I am told that they say that frequently in Cleveland, Ohio. Is it true?"

"Yeah," Jackson said, "I think they probably say that in Cleveland a lot."

"A Pole told me that they did." Bodden's head dropped until his chin rested on his chest. After a moment, he raised it and looked at Jackson. "The Pole. He was a very funny fellow."

His chin dropped back down to his chest, his eyes closed, and after a moment or two, he stopped breathing.

33 Leah Oppenheimer still didn't want to believe that the dwarf who stood on the chair behind the lectern in the Godesberg Hotel conference room was Nicolae Ploscaru. He's an impostor, she had told herself. Nicolae Ploscaru was no dwarf—he was tall and fair and cruelly handsome. The dwarf had to be an impostor.

She had had to force herself to accept the fact that the dwarf was who he claimed to be. The voice had done it, of course—that low, almost musical baritone with its undercurrent of sexual invitation. It was the same voice that she had heard over the telephone many times. There could be no mistake. It was Nicolae Ploscaru's voice.

"I regret, my dear," the dwarf had said after introducing

himself, "that things did not work out quite as we had planned."

Leah Oppenheimer had been able only to nod dumbly and manage one question. "Where is my brother?"

"With Mr. Jackson," the dwarf had said, smiled, and turned away to nod gravely at Robert Henry Orr and Lieutenant Meyer.

Ten chairs had been set out in the room in two rows of five each. Orr and Meyer sat together, as did Leah Oppenheimer and Eva Scheel. The dwarf, behind the lectern, smiled and looked at his watch.

"We'll begin, ladies and gentlemen, as soon as our last guest arrives."

The last guest was Major Baker-Bates, who entered the conference room two minutes later. He nodded sourly at the dwarf and then spotted Eva Scheel sitting next to Leah Oppenheimer. He smiled for the first time that day. Well, Gilbert, he told himself, the morning's not going to be a total waste after all.

Baker-Bates took the seat next to Eva Scheel's and smiled at her pleasantly. "The printer coming?" he said.

"I'm sorry," she said. "I don't understand your question."

"You understand," Baker-Bates said. "When this charade is done, you and I will have a chat. A long one."

The dwarf rapped for order with a water glass. "I think we'll keep this quite informal, ladies and gentlemen. We are here to auction off a rather interesting item with which all of you are familiar. The terms will be cash, of course, in either American dollars or British pounds. Swiss francs are also quite acceptable. I might add that the item that's being auctioned off is in excellent condition and will be available one hour after the final bid is made. Are there any questions?"

Orr raised his hand. "How can we be sure that you have the item in question?"

"Faith, my dear sir, faith. In all commerce a certain amount of good faith must be exercised by both parties.

313

I have certain goods for sale which you and others wish to buy. I scarcely would have gone to such elaborate arrangements if I did not intend to deliver. Upon delivery, if you are not entirely satisfied, then you have certain methods of recourse, which I would rather not mention."

"I'm relieved that you're aware of them," Orr said.

"Quite aware."

Eva Sheel had not been listening to Orr and the dwarf. Instead, her mind raced furiously as she tried to decide her next move. Something must have happened to the printer, she realized. He might even be dead—killed by either the dwarf or Jackson. So that plan must be abandoned. She had Berlin's $25,000 in her purse. The British Major had somehow connected her with the printer. That meant he knew who and what she was—really was. If she bid on the goods, there was no way that they would let her leave Bonn with them, if hers was the high bid. But still, if she bid, and it was high, then it might be a bargaining chip in her talk with the British Major. She was going to need all the bargaining power that she could muster. She bit her lower lip and decided to bid.

"Now, ladies and gentlemen," the dwarf was saying, "I will entertain the first bid. Do I hear five thousand dollars?"

Ploscaru looked around the room. Orr nodded.

The dwarf smiled. "We have five thousand. Do I hear six?"

"Six," Baker-Bates said.

"Ten thousand dollars," Orr said.

"The gentleman from the United States bids ten thousand dollars. Do I hear eleven?"

"Eleven thousand," Leah Oppenheimer said.

The dwarf smiled knowingly. "Eleven thousand from—shall we say—the soon-to-be state of Israel. Do I hear twelve?"

"Twelve," Baker-Bates said.

"Fourteen," Orr said promptly.

Baker-Bates did his multiplication. With the pound at

$4.03, he decided to bid his limit and get it over with. "Sixteen thousand," he said. To himself he added, And you can bloody well take it or leave it.

"Eighteen," Leah Oppenheimer said.

"Twenty thousand," Orr said.

There was a silence. Ploscaru nodded genially and said, "We have twenty thousand dollars bid, ladies and gentlemen. Do I hear twenty-five?"

The silence continued. "Come, now, ladies and gentlemen, we're not going to let this valuable item go for a mere twenty thousand, are we? Do I hear twenty-five?"

Eva Scheel drew in her breath, held it, let it out, and said in a low, almost defiant tone, "Twenty-five thousand."

Leah Oppenheimer turned and stared at her. Eva Scheel refused to meet her gaze. Four chairs away, Lieutenant Meyer looked ill. "Jesus Christ," he said.

"We have twenty-five thousand from the lady in the fur coat," Ploscaru said. "You're representing whom, my dear?"

Eva Scheel said nothing but instead stared straight ahead.

"My word," the dwarf said, looking with feigned horror at Orr. "Do you think she might be representing our comrades to the east?"

"Thirty thousand," Orr said quickly.

"We have thirty thousand from Uncle Sam," Ploscaru said with a delighted smile. "Do I hear thirty-five?"

"Thirty-five," Leah Oppenheimer said. She was still staring at Eva Scheel. "You could have told me, Eva," she said sadly. "I would have understood. Whatever it is you're doing, I know I would have understood."

Eva Scheel said nothing.

"We have thirty-five thousand bid," Ploscaru said. "Thirty-five. Do I hear forty?"

"Forty," Orr said.

"Forty thousand is bid, ladies and gentlemen. Forty thousand dollars. Do I hear forty-five?"

There was another silence.

"Do I hear forty-five thousand?" Ploscaru said again. There were no bids.

"Forty thousand once," Ploscaru said, and paused. "Forty thousand twice." He paused again, then rapped with the water glass, smiled broadly, and said, "Sold, American," just as Minor Jackson entered the room leading Kurt Oppenheimer by the hand.

Oppenheimer, dressed only in Jackson's topcoat, smiled foolishly, chuckled wisely, and began urinating on the floor.

34 By noon that day in Bonn, the following events had taken place:

The British Army had locked Kurt Oppenheimer away in a quiet, dim room.

Maj. Gilbert Baker-Bates had almost succeeded in persuading Eva Scheel to turn double agent and was confident of turning her all the way around right after the splendid lunch that he had ordered for both of them.

Lt. LaFollette Meyer had decided not to kill himelf after all, but to get drunk instead, up in his room alone, which he was now doing.

Leah Oppenheimer had caught a train for Frankfurt without saying goodbye to anybody, her destination Marseille, where she would board a ship that ultimately would land her in Palestine.

And Nicolae Ploscaru had drunk three glasses of gin alone in the hotel bar and was contemplating a fourth when Robert Henry Orr, still wearing his raccoon coat, dropped heavily into the chair across the table from him.

"Well, Nick, getting quietly drunk, I see."

"Quietly," Ploscaru agreed.

"On what?"

"Some kind of gin. It's all they have."

"Then that's what we'll drink," Orr said cheerfully, and signaled the bartender for another round.

After the drinks came, Orr shrugged out of his raccoon coat. "You know," he said, "the whole thing was really quite clever, almost brilliant. Too bad the poor bastard was mad."

"Yes," Ploscaru said, sipping his gin. "Too bad."

"What're your plans?"

"At this particular moment? None."

"Things are moving in Washington, you know."

"Oh?"

"Yes. Not this year, but next, we should have our own new shop open for business. Interested?"

"In what?"

"Piecework between now and then. We'd pay you a fair price. Afterward, when the new shop opens up, we could arrange something more permanent—and profitable."

"What're they going to call it—your new shop?"

"The National Intelligence Agency, I think—although that's not firm yet. Some don't feel that National's quite right. Makes it sound too much like a bank."

"I'll think about it," Ploscaru said.

"Do that, Nick," Orr said, draining his drink. "I'll be around for a few days."

When Minor Jackson came down from his room with his bag an hour later to check out of the hotel, the dwarf was standing in the lobby. Jackson could see that Ploscaru was rather drunk.

318

The dwarf bowed gravely. "I am here to offer my apologies."

"Get the fuck out of my way, Nick, or I'll step on you."

Ploscaru sighed. "And rightly so, too." He spread his hands. "What more can I say?"

"Nothing."

"You're off, then?"

"That's right."

"May I ask your destination?"

"Amsterdam."

The dwarf looked puzzled. "Amsterdam. Why Amsterdam?"

"It's where they buy diamonds."

The dwarf brightened at the scent of profit, but only for a moment. "I don't suppose—"

"No," Jackson said, turned, and started for the desk. "Minor."

Jackson turned back. The dwarf was standing alone in the center of the lobby. He looked very small. He licked his lips as if trying to think of what he wanted and needed to say. But no words came. Instead, he unconsciously began to brush some imaginary crumbs from his palms. He's begging, Jackson thought. He's standing there alone and as naked as he'll ever be and begging, except that he doesn't really know how to do it.

"Oh, shit," Jackson said. "Get in the car."

The dwarf beamed. "I'll just get my bag." Suddenly, Ploscaru was full of plans "After Amsterdam, you know where we'll go, don't you?"

"Where?"

"Cannes. We'll drive down to Cannes and lie on the beach and drink wine and look at women. Now, doesn't that sound splendid?"

"Sure," Minor Jackson said. "Splendid."